Samuel Wendell Williston

On the Diptera of St. Vincent

West Indies

Samuel Wendell Williston

On the Diptera of St. Vincent
West Indies

ISBN/EAN: 9783337316693

Printed in Europe, USA, Canada, Australia, Japan

Cover: Foto ©Andreas Hilbeck / pixelio.de

More available books at **www.hansebooks.com**

XI. *On the Diptera of St. Vincent (West Indies).* By
Professor Samuel Wendell Williston. (*Doli-
chopodidæ* and *Phoridæ,* by Professor J. M.
Aldrich.) Communicated by David Sharp, M.A.,
F.R.S , on behalf of the Committee for investigat-
ing the Flora and Fauna of the West Indies.

[Read March 4th, 1896.]

Plates VIII., IX., X., XI., XII., XIII. and XIV.

[This paper is a list, accompanied with descriptions, of
the Diptera found in the island of St. Vincent, by Mr. H.
H. Smith, the well-known American entomologist, who
was sent to the islands by F. D. Godman, Esq., F.R.S.,
to assist the Committee in its investigations.   Some
general remarks by the Author will be found at the end
of the paper.   A second memoir, treating of the Diptera
of the neighbouring island of Grenada, will, it is hoped,
be almost immediately ready for publication, the present
instalment having been in the hands of the Committee
for upwards of two years.—D. S.]

CECIDOMYIIDÆ.

Diplosis.

Loew, Dipt. Beitr., iv., 20, 1850.

1. *Diplosis pictipes,* n. sp.

♂. Face yellow. Antennæ as long as the wings, yellow, the
joints alternately double, with their petioles as long as the thickened
portion. Mesonotum opaque red ; two slender stripes and the
middle portion behind yellow. Abdomen reddish-yellow. Legs
black ; the distal two-fifths of the front femora, the immediate
tip of the hind femora, the tip of the hind tibiæ ; a broad ring on
the second, third, and fourth joints of all the tarsi, and the
terminal portion of the fifth joint, light yellow. Wings with
black hair, forming irregular markings ; third vein gently curved,
terminating just beyond the tip of the wing. Length 1½ mm.

Four specimens.

2. *Diplosis*, sp. (Pl. VIII., fig. 1, wing.)

♂. Antennæ about as long as the wings ; all the joints single, the petioles a little shorter than the thickened portion. Yellow, the mesonotum somewhat brownish, the abdomen, tibiæ, and tarsi infuscated. Wings nearly hyaline, black haired. Length 1½ mm.

3. *Diplosis*, sp.

♂. Very much like the preceding species, but with each alternate joint of the antennæ double.

4. ? *Diplosis*, sp. (Pl. VIII., fig. 2, wing.)

Two specimens, with the antennæ incomplete, I refer doubtfully to this genus. The antennæ are not petiolated, and resemble those of *Asphondylia*, but have the joints provided with long hairs, as in this genus.

WINNERTZIA.

Rondani, Dipt. Ital. Prodri, 1856.

1. *Winnertzia*, sp. (Pl. VIII., fig. 3, wing.)

Two specimens, male and female ; both injured.

MIASTOR.

Meinert, Natur. Tijdschr., 3 R., iii., 156, 1864.

1. *Miastor*, sp. (Pl. VIII., figs. 4, wing ; and 4*a*, part of antenna.)

A single specimen of a species which seems to present all the essential characters of this genus. The wings have the first and third veins distinct, but lack the posterior forked cell. The legs are short and not slender. The tibiæ are as long as the first two joints of the tarsi together, and the first joint is a half longer than the second.

HAPLUSIA.

Karsch, Revision der Gallmücken, p. 15, 1878.

1. *Haplusia*, sp. (Pl. VIII., fig. 5, wing.)

A single specimen of a minute species shows evident relationship to this genus, though I am not fully satisfied that it should be located in it.

The neuration is very nearly the same as that of the type species (comp. Karsch, *l. c.*, fig. 1). The first joint of the tarsi is about one-third of the length of the second joint, which is as long as all the other joints together. The fifth joint is widened, somewhat disk-like, and is as long as the preceding joint. The head is wanting. The colour of the remainder of the insect is light yellow, with the mesonotum brown. Length about ½ mm.

TRICHOPTEROMYIA, n. g.

Allied to *Diomyza* (in Schiner's sense), but the first and third longitudinal veins are not crowded together anteriorly, the third vein terminating at the tip of the wing. Wings broad, very hairy; proximal section of the third vein straight, the distal section nearly straight; prefurca of forked cell scarcely longer than the sixth vein. Antennæ with the joints distinctly petiolate; the distal portion of the antennæ in both specimens is wanting. Metatarsi longer than the following two joints together.

The genus *Diomyza* is, as yet, not well known, and I do not feel quite sure of its distinctive characters. As Schiner defines it, it differs from *Lasioptera* only in the elongate metatarsi. However, there has been much confusion in the application of the name *Diomyza*, as Karsch has shown (Revision der Gallmücken, p. 13), and it may be that the name will have to be abandoned. The present genus seems to be the only other one known with elongate metatarsi, in which the fifth vein is forked.

1. *Trichopteromyia modesta*, n. sp. (Pl. VIII., figs. 6, wing; 6*a*, tarsus; 6*b*, part of antenna.)

♀. Reddish-yellow, opaque; the pleuræ, venter, and legs yellow; the front and tip of abdomen blackish, the metanotum brownish. Antennæ brownish-yellow, with black hair. Wings hyaline beneath the dense blackish hair. Length nearly 2 mm.

Two specimens.

MYCETOPHILIDÆ.

MACROCERA.

Meigen, Illiger's Mag., ii., 261, 1803.

1. *Macrocera concinna*, n. sp. (Pl. VIII., fig. 7, wing.)

♂, ♀. Yellow. Mesonotum with three brown stripes; wings cinereous, with a large central brown spot, a spot at the tip of the thickened first vein, the tip of the wing and a small cuneate spot in the first basal cell. Length 4–5 mm.; of the antennæ, male, 16 mm.; female, 7 mm.

♂. Head light yellow, the ocelli black. Antennæ about four times the length of the body; brownish, toward the base brownish-yellow. Palpi brown. Mesonotum yellow, with three brown stripes, the middle one extending to the collar, the lateral ones abbreviated in front and turned downwards to connect with a vertical brown stripe on the pleuræ. Pleuræ light yellow, with a brown spot in front of the halteres, in addition to the vertical stripe, which extends to the middle coxæ. Scutellum and metanotum brown. Abdomen yellow, the proximal segments somewhat infuscated toward their base; hair black. Legs light yellow; tarsi infuscated; front tibiæ suddenly dilated at their tip. Wings cinereous hyaline; a dark brown spot at the junction of the third and fourth veins, extending back to the angle of the posterior basal cross-vein; a similarly coloured spot at the tip of the first vein, reaching across the third longitudinal vein; the tip of the wing is broadly brownish, and there is a small brown spot in front of the fourth vein, opposite the tip of the auxiliary vein; anterior cells yellowish; anterior branch of the third vein oblique and pallid.

♀. In the single female specimen, the colour is more reddish-yellow, the abdomen is red with the posterior margin of the segments yellow. Antennæ only about twice the length of the body.

Seven specimens. Sea level, and 1000 feet. This species seems to be related to *M. inconcinna*, Loew, but differs especially in the markings of the thorax.

PLATYURA.

Meigen, Illiger's Mag., ii., 264, 1803.

TABLE OF SPECIES.

1. *Platyura parva*, n. sp.

♂. Antennæ brownish-yellow, shorter than the thorax. Posterior part of the mesonotum, the narrow lateral margins, and three slender stripes, brown or black ; elsewhere the thorax is yellow, save two spots on the pleuræ, and the metanotum for the greater part, which are black. Abdomen cylindrical, black, the venter and immediate base yellowish. Coxæ and legs yellow ; the terminal portion of the tibiæ, and the tarsi, brownish ; metatarsi about three-fourths of the length of the tibiæ ; all the tibiæ with a single spur and without spines. Wings lightly tinged ; the anterior branch of the third vein terminates in the first vein near its tip. Length 2½-3 mm.

Two specimens.

2. *Platyura ignobilis*, n. sp. (Pl. VIII., fig. 9, wing.)

♂. Base of antennæ and the face yellow ; front and occiput blackish. Thorax reddish-yellow, the dorsum with black hair arranged in distinct rows. Scutellum and metanotum brownish. Abdomen brownish-yellow, with black hair. Legs yellow, the tarsi infuscated ; front metatarsi not more than three-fourths the length of the tibiæ. Wings uniformly subinfuscated ; the anterior branch of the third vein is nearly rectangular, terminating in the costa. Length 3-4 mm.

3. *Platyura pictipennis*, n. sp. (Pl. VIII., fig. 10, wing.)

♂, ♀. Front and face yellowish or brownish, the palpi darker coloured. Antennæ brownish, about as long as the thorax, moderately compressed. Thorax yellow; the dorsum, save a yellowish spot or stripe in the middle, and the yellow lateral margins, brown or black ; disk and sides of the metanotum brown. Abdomen brown or blackish-brown, the posterior margin of each segment yellow. Legs, including the coxæ, yellow, the distal portion of the tibiæ, and the tarsi, brownish ; tibiæ without spines ; front tibiæ and metatarsi of nearly equal length, the hind metatarsi shorter than their tibiæ ; all the tibiæ with a single spur. Wings nearly hyaline, with markings as follows : a large brown spot, reaching from the costa to the fifth vein, over the prefurca ; another of about the same size in the outer part of the first posterior cell ; and smaller ones in all the cells on the posterior side of the wing ; the anterior branch of the third vein runs into the costa a little beyond the tip of the first vein. Length 3-3½ mm.

Six specimens.

4. *Platyura fasciventris*, n. sp. (Pl. VIII., fig. 11, wing.)

♀. Head and basal joints of the antennæ reddish-yellow, the distal joints of the antennæ black or brownish-black; the oval ocellar spot black. Front broad, the orbits emarginate. Thorax reddish-yellow; the dorsum red, with four brown stripes, sometimes feebly marked or obsolete. Abdomen red, or reddish-yellow, with a black band of variable width at the posterior part of each segment; venter yellow. Coxæ and femora light yellow; tibiæ yellow, the tarsi brownish; tibiæ without spines; metatarsi about as long as their tibiæ; all the tibiæ with a single terminal spur. Wings uniformly brownish; anterior branch of the third vein oblique, terminating in the costa. Length 5–6 mm.

Three specimens. The antennæ are about as long as the dorsum of the thorax.

CEROPLATUS.

Bosc., Actes de la Soc. d'Hist. Nat. de Paris, i., 1, 42, 1792.

1. *Ceroplatus longimanus*, n. sp. (Pl. VIII., fig. 12, wing.)

♂. Mesonotum with yellow and black stripes. Abdomen black, with yellow lateral spots. Length 6 mm.

Face yellow, very narrow. Palpi and first two joints of the antennæ yellow; remainder of the antennæ dark brown. Antennæ about as long as the dorsum of the thorax. Front narrow, the sides gently convex, black, except on the lowermost portion; the two large ocelli about equidistant from each other and from the margins of the eyes. Occiput black. Thorax yellow; the dorsum with three broad black stripes, enclosing two narrow yellow stripes, which are convergent posteriorly; the median stripe enclosing a slender yellow stripe, which does not reach beyond the middle; a large rounded spot on the mesopleuræ, another below it on the mesosternum, and the sides of the metanotum, dark brown or black, the middle of the metanotum brownish; scutellum brown. Abdomen slender, cylindrical, dark brown; each segment, save the first and last, with an elongate yellow spot on each side, reaching two-thirds of the way to the hind margin; genital organs yellow. Coxæ light yellow, the hind pair with a brown spot; femora yellow, the base of the middle and hind pairs brown; tibiæ yellowish-brown; tarsi brown; no bristles on the front femora; front metatarsi about two and a-half times the length of the tibiæ ; middle metatarsi a fourth or a third longer than the tibiæ ; the hind pair scarcely longer ; hind tibiæ with two spurs. Wings tinged with brownish ; the anterior branch of the third vein runs into the costa.

One specimen. " Cliff over mountain stream, under overhanging rock, Sept. 1000 feet."—H. H. Smith.

NEOGLAPHYROPTERA.

Osten Sacken, Cat. Dipt., p. 10, 1878, vice *Glaphyroptera*, Winnertz, Pilzmücken, 145 (781), 1863 (preoc.).

1. *Neoglaphyroptera nitens*, n. sp.   (Pl. VIII., fig. 13, wing.)

♂, ♀. Mesonotum shining black ; wings infuscated. Length 4 mm.

Front black or blackish, yellow on the lower part. Face yellow. Antennæ blackish, the basal joints yellowish, about as long as the thorax. Mesonotum, scutellum, and metanotum shining black, the bristles of the same colour. Pleuræ yellow in front ; reddish-brown behind. Abdomen slender ; shining black or deep brown, the proximal segments in front yellow or yellowish ; venter yellow. Tuberculum of halteres black. Coxæ yellow ; femora nearly of the same colour ; hind femora at the tip blackish ; tibiæ brownish-yellow ; tarsi brown ; front tibiæ shorter than the metatarsi ; middle tarsi nearly a half longer than their tibiæ ; hind tibiæ and tarsi of nearly equal length. Wings infuscated, the apex tinged with blackish ; a brown spot at the origin of the cross-vein. Middle and hind tibiæ with stout spurs.

Six specimens. 1000–1500 feet. In some of the specimens the face is brown, the front wholly black, the posterior part of the pleuræ black, and the abdomen, for the greater part, of the same colour. The species must be nearly related to *N. ventralis*, Say, but the infuscated wings and the absence of a distinct terminal fascia, seem ample to distinguish them.

2. *Neoglaphyroptera concinna*, n. sp.

♀. Mesonotum reddish-yellow. Length 4 mm.

Antennæ about as long as the thorax, brown or blackish, the basal joints yellow. Front and face, like the thorax, reddish-yellow. Bristles and very short hair of the thorax black. Abdomen reddish-yellow ; each segment with a large, subtriangular, black spot, the base directed posteriorly and the apex reaching nearly or quite to the anterior margin ; last segment wholly black. Legs yellow, the tarsi brownish ; front metatarsi longer than the tibiæ ; middle tarsi a third longer than the tibiæ ; hind tarsi of about the same length as the tibiæ. Wings tinged with brownish ; an indistinct band across the outer part, and a similar spot at the base of the anterior forked cell.

Four specimens.

MANOTA, n. g.

Head flattened, placed rather high as regards the thorax ; face and front broad, the antennæ situated high up, directed upwards and forwards ; composed of sixteen joints closely united, the basal joints a little differentiated from those of the flagellum. Three ocelli of nearly equal size, situated near the vertex, in a gently curved line, the lateral ones about as far from the inner borders of the eyes as from the middle one. Palpi composed of three joints, elongate, the terminal joint slender and directed angularly backwards. Dorsum of thorax moderately convex ; scutellum with short bristles. Abdomen slender, flattened cylindrical. Femora stout, flattened ; front and middle tibiæ with one, the hind tibiæ with two spurs ; hind tibiæ and metatarsi with a row of short bristles on the outer side ; all the tibiæ without long bristles ; coxæ elongate. Wings longer than the abdomen ; auxiliary vein rudimentary ; the first vein terminates before the middle of the wing ; third vein not furcate ; fourth vein wanting, save the distal portion of its branches ; fifth vein furcate near the basal portion of the wing ; the costa extends a considerable distance beyond the termination of the third vein.

As in the following genus, the proximal portion of the two outer veins is so wholly obliterated that it is impossible to trace them.

1. *Manota defecta*, n. sp.   (Pl. VIII., fig. 14.)

♂. Antennæ brown, densely pubescent, reaching nearly to the middle of the abdomen if bent backward. Face and front brownish-yellow. Mesonotum reddish or yellowish-brown, finely white pubescent. Pleuræ a little lighter coloured. Coxæ and femora light yellow, the middle coxæ near the upper part with a small, oval, black spot; tibiæ yellow, the tarsi more brownish. Abdomen brown or blackish above. Wings tinged with brownish. Length 2–2½ mm.

Six specimens.

PROBOLÆUS, n. g.

Proboscis more than half of the length of the body, slender, directed downwards and forwards, composed of five slender bristles; palpi wanting. Antennæ sixteen-jointed, compressed, the joints closely set together; first two joints only a little differentiated from the others. Head composed almost wholly of the eyes; face very narrow; front narrow below; eyes pubescent. Thorax strongly convex, nearly bare, a few short bristles on the sides. Scutellum small, with about six small bristles. Abdomen slender, elongate, longer than the wings; male organs composed of a pair of simple, fleshy forceps. Four anterior legs very slender; hind legs stouter and much elongate, the femora thickened, and the tibiæ clubbed. Neuration defective; third vein entirely separated from the first, and without anterior branch; proximal portion of the fourth and fifth veins wholly invisible; sixth vein complete. The costa reaches a considerable distance beyond the tip of the third vein.

This genus is remarkable in the apparently entire absence of the palpi. The closest examination of our three specimens has failed to reveal any trace of them. The labium, or sheath for the other mouth-parts, is quite rudimentary. In the wings there is not the faintest trace of the proximal portions of the fourth and fifth veins; those portions that are present are by no means weak. An equally minute examination fails to show the ocelli, though I will not be positive that they are not present. The presence of tibial spurs, the moderately elongate coxæ, and the general relationship to other species of the family, especially *Gnoriste*, seem to prove the correct location of the genus here.

1. *Probolæus singularis*, n. sp. (Pl. VIII., figs. 15, wing; 15*a*, head; 15*b*, mouth-parts; 15*c*, hypopygium.)

♂. Front, face and occiput black. Antennæ brown, the basal joints somewhat yellowish. Mesonotum opaque deep reddish-brown, the humeri and postalar callosities yellowish. Pleuræ brown or yellowish-brown, shining. Abdomen black, the first segment and a posterior band on the second, third and fourth segments yellow. Halteres yellow. Wings nearly hyaline, lightly clouded on the outer part. Legs, including coxæ, light yellow; the tarsi and the thickened portion of the hind tibiæ infuscated or blackish. Length 4–5 mm.

Three specimens. " Forest, 1800 feet, west slope of Sonfriere, Sept. 23."—H. H. Smith.

NEOËMPHERIA.

Osten Sacken, Cat. Dipt., 1878, p. 9, vice *Empheria*, Winnertz, Pilzm., 102 (738), 1863 (preoc.).

1. *Neoëmpheria maculipennis*, n. sp. (Pl. VIII., fig. 16, wing.)

♂. Wings with brown markings; anterior branch of third vein situated a little beyond the furcation of the fourth vein. Length 5 mm.

Antennæ about as long as the head and thorax together; the basal joints light yellow, the remainder with a brownish tinge. Palpi brown; front and face yellow; mesonotum, except the lateral margins, light brown, with black hair and bristles; indistinctly striped; moderately shining. Pleuræ, coxæ and femora light yellow. Scutellum, except at its base, light yellow, and with two bristles on its margin. Abdomen light yellow, each segment with a large black or brown spot, not reaching the hind margin. Tibiæ and tarsi yellow, but appearing blackish from the abundant, short, black hair; front tarsi more than twice the length of their tibiæ. Wings nearly hyaline, with the following markings: the tip of the subcostal cell and the submarginal cell beyond the anterior branch of the third vein, and the proximal end of the first posterior cell, brown; a more distinct brown spot clouding the costal cross-vein, the basal section of the third vein, the base of the first posterior cell, and, more diffusely, along the posterior branch of the fourth vein, to connect with a spot running from the first posterior cell into the hindmost posterior cell; a smaller brownish spot in the axillary angle; costal and subcostal cells yellowish; costa produced beyond the tip of the third vein; anterior branch of the third vein situated a little beyond the furcation of the fourth vein.

Four specimens. 1000 feet.

Sciophila.

Meigen, Syst. Beschr., i., 245, 1818.

1. *Sciophila diluta*, n. sp. (Pl. VIII., fig. 17, wing.)

♂. Reddish yellow; abdomen brown. Length 3 mm.

Antennæ about as long as the head and thorax together, somewhat compressed; light brown, the basal joints yellow. Front and face brown or brownish-yellow, palpi brown. Thorax, coxæ and femora reddish or luteous yellow; mesonotum brownish-yellow, with black hair and bristles. Abdomen brown or yellowish-brown, with black hairs. Tibiæ brown; tarsi blackish; front metatarsi a trifle shorter than their tibiæ; hind tarsi scarcely longer than the tibiæ. Wings tinged with brownish; the costal vein terminates at the tip of the third vein; first submarginal cell very short; furcation of the fifth vein very nearly opposite the origin of the third vein.

Two specimens.

Phthinia.

Winnertz, Pilzmücken, 143 (779), 1863.

1. *Phthinia fraudulenta*, n. sp. (Pl. VIII., fig. 18, wing.)

♂. Brown or blackish and luteous; wings hairy; the auxiliary, first and third veins with distinct, short, bristly hairs. Length 2½–3 mm.

Antennæ brown or blackish, the basal joints somewhat yellowish; the joints of the flagellum closely set together, somewhat compressed. Front and face black or brownish-black. Mesonotum reddish-brown, shining, with black hair; pleuræ and coxæ yellow. Abdomen reddish-brown or blackish, black at the tip; venter yellow. Legs yellow, the tarsi brownish, becoming black at the tip; spurs of tibiæ stout; hind tibiæ with two rows of spines; front metatarsi distinctly shorter than their tibiæ; hind tarsi longer than their tibiæ. Wings tinged with blackish, due to the easily perceptible pubescence.

Two specimens.

Mycetophila.

Meigen, Illiger's Mag., ii., 263, 1803.

Table of Species.

1. Mycetophila insipiens, n. sp. (Pl. VIII., fig. 19, wing.)

♀. Antennæ about as long as the thorax, yellow ; brownish toward the end. Front and face yellow. Mesonotum yellowish-red. Abdomen reddish-yellow ; each segment broadly brown on its posterior part. Legs, including the coxæ, light yellow ; front tibiæ about one-third of the length of the tarsi, and shorter than the metatarsi ; middle tibiæ with two large and one small bristles on the inner side; middle and hind tibiæ with spines on the outer side ; hind metatarsi distinctly shorter than the remaining joints of the tarsi together. Wings tinged with yellowish ; a small brownish cloud on the basal section of the third vein. Length 2½ mm.

Six specimens.

2. Mycetophila dolosa, n. sp.

♂. Antennæ brown, somewhat compressed, the basal joints yellowish. Front and face brown. Mesonotum dark brown, opaque, with a thin yellowish sheen in some reflections. Abdomen dark brown or black, the venter yellow. Pleuræ yellowish-brown. Coxæ and legs light yellow, the tarsi appearing blackish from the hair ; front tibiæ less than half of the length of the tarsi, and a little longer than the metatarsi ; hind tibiæ with two rows of spines on the outer side ; middle tibiæ with spines on the inner side ; hind metatarsi nearly as long as the following joints together. Wings tinged with brownish. Length 2½–3 mm.

3. Mycetophila nodulosa, n. sp. (Pl. VIII., fig. 20, wing.)

♂. Antennæ brownish-yellow, the basal joints yellow ; longer than the head and thorax together. Front and face light

ochraceous yellow. Palpi brown. Mesonotum light ochraceous
yellow, lightly white pruinose on the sides, and with blackish and
yellow hair. Pleuræ brownish-yellow. Abdomen reddish-brown ;
pubescence chiefly black. Legs yellow, the coxæ and femora light
yellow, the broad hind femora at the tip brown. Front tibiæ about
one-third of the length of the tarsi, and shorter than the metatarsi ;
middle tibiæ with spines on the inner side ; hind tibiæ with two
rows of spines on the outer side. Wings lightly tinged ; the outer
part of the first section of the fourth vein, the anterior cross-vein,
and the base of the second of the third vein, thickened, forming a
straight spindle-shaped mass. Length 2½ mm.

Six specimens.

SCIARA.

Meigen, Illiger's Mag., ii., 263, 1803.

TABLE OF SPECIES.

1. *Sciara germana*, n. sp.   (Pl. VIII , fig. 21, wing.)

♂, ♀. Head black, opaque, thinly greyish dusted. Antennæ black, with white pubescence ; first joint of the flagellum somewhat yellowish. Thorax and halteres black ; mesonotum moderately shining, with three rows of short black bristles ; pleuræ whitish dusted. Abdomen black or deep brown, venter on the sides yellow or red in the female ; male forceps large. Legs pitchy black. Wings blackish in front and along the veins, the cells posteriorly subhyaline. The first vein reaches a little beyond the furcation of the fourth vein ; the third vein reaches nearly to the tip of the wing. Length 5-7 mm.

Numerous specimens. It is possible that this is the same as *S. nigra*, Wiedemann, but the description is too brief to afford any certainty that such is the case. It is evidently closely related to *S. thomæ*, of Europe. The origin of the third vein is a little before the middle of the first vein.

2. *Sciara concinna*, n. sp.

♀. Front below the eyes and the face, brownish-red ; vertex and occiput black, somewhat shining. Antennæ black, shorter than the abdomen ; basal joints yellowish ; proximal joints of the flagellum with black pubescence, that of the distal joints whitish. Thorax black ; humeri yellowish ; mesonotum moderately shining. Abdomen black, with black hairs ; venter yellow. Coxæ and femora yellow ; tibiæ brownish ; tarsi black. Wings uniformly smoky or blackish ; origin of the third vein a little before the middle of the first, which reaches as far as the furcation of the fourth vein ; prefurca of fourth vein distinctly longer than the anterior branch ; tip of the third and of the posterior branch of the fourth veins equidistant from the tip of the wing. Length 2½-3 mm.

Numerous specimens. The male differs only in having the antennæ as long as the body.

3. *Sciara debilis*, n. sp.   (Pl. VIII., fig. 22, wing.)

♂. Vertex shining black, with black hair ; front and face reddish-brown ; palpi yellow. Antennæ as long as the body, luteous yellow, but obscured by the black pubescence. Thorax light yellow, except the mesonotum and scutellum, which are shining black ; humeri luteous. Abdomen black, with black hair ; hypopygium yellowish. Coxæ and femora light yellow ; tibiæ and tarsi brown. Wings smoky ; the third vein arises from beyond the middle of the first vein, which does not reach as far as the furcation

of the fourth ; tip of third and of the posterior branch of the fourth
vein equidistant from the tip of the wing ; prefurca of fourth
vein longer than its branches ; furcation of fifth vein beyond the
origin of the anterior cross-vein, acute. Knob of halteres brown.
Length 2½ mm.

Eight specimens.

4. *Sciara delectata*, n. sp.

♂ . Antennæ black, with grey and black pubescence, the scape
and first one or two joints of the flagellum yellow. Front and
face brownish-yellow, the occiput yellow. Thorax yellow, tho
mesonotum with two elongated brown spots, and a median, less
conspicuous brown stripe. Abdomen yellow ; each segment with
a broad brown posterior band ; hypopygium large, light yellow, the
forceps brownish. Legs light yellow, the tarsi infuscated. Wings
nearly hyaline ; neuration nearly as in *S. debilis*. Length 2 mm.

Six specimens. Sea level, 1000.

5. *Sciara*, sp.

♀ . Light yellow ; bristles and hair black, rather strong.
Each segment of abdomen with a broad, posterior, dark-brown
band. Tarsi infuscated. Wings nearly hyaline ; the first vein
terminates nearly opposite, or a little before the furcation of the
fourth vein ; the third takes its origin a little beyond the middle
of the first vein ; tip of third and the posterior branch of the
fourth vein nearly equidistant from the tip of the wing. Length
3 mm.

One specimen ; antennæ wanting.

6. *Sciara zygoneura*, n. sp. (Pl. VIII , fig. 23, wing.)

♂ . Occiput and vertex shining black ; front below the
eyes, and the face, opaque black. Scape and first three or four
joints of the flagellum yellowish ; distal three joints white with
white pubescence ; remaining joints black, with black pubescence.
Thorax black ; mesonotum shining, with two rows of short black
bristles ; scutellum shining black, with bristles on its border.
Venter and first two segments of the abdomen yellow ; remainder
of abdomen black or deep brown with yellow incisures ; ovipositor
black, lamellæ yellowish ; knob of the halteres brown. Legs
yellow, including the coxæ ; terminal joints of the tarsi blackish ;
the tarsi and tibiæ obscured by short black hairs. Wings lightly
brownish ; origin of third vein near the outer fourth of first vein ;

termination of first vein at some distance before the furcation of the fourth ; prefurca of fourth vein about as long as the posterior branch ; anterior branch strongly curved forward in its anterior portion, as in species of *Zygoneura*. Length 2 mm.

Eight specimens. There are not more than one or two joints of the flagellum which are yellow in some specimens ; apparently, also the number of white joints at the tip may be limited to one. The humeri are some-times red. The abdomen, when not drawn out, appears almost wholly black in some specimens.

ZYGONEURA.

Meigen, Syst. Beschr., vi., 304, 1830.

1. *Zygoneura sciastica*, n. sp.   (Pl. VIII., figs. 24, wing ; 24*a*, part of antenna.)

♂. Dark brown, or blackish brown, opaque. Antennæ as long as the body, its pubescence in some reflection grey. Legs luteous yellow ; tibiæ infuscated ; tarsi blackish. Wings nearly hyaline ; neuration as in the figure. Length 1–1½ mm.

One specimen.

SIMULIIDÆ.

SIMULIUM.

Latreille, Hist. Nat. Crust. et Ins., xiv., 294, 1804.

1. *Simulium tarsale*, n. sp.   (Pl. VIII., figs. 25, wing ; 25*a*, front tarsus of ♂.)

♀. Abdomen black, the proximal segments opaque, the distal four segments shining. Length 2 mm.

Front and face black, with a light grey reflection. Antennæ yellow ; the distal joints somewhat brownish. Mesonotum deep black ; in front, opaque with a silvery shimmer, and with sparse, short, curly, golden-yellow tomentum ; behind, shining. Pleuræ black, whitish pruinose. Abdomen black, the basal segments opaque, the distal four segments somewhat shining, and with a delicate whitish pruinosity. Legs reddish-yellow ; tarsi black, except that the proximal half of the middle and hind metatarsi light yellow ; first and third joints of the front pair each with two long hairs ; second and third joints of the same pair dilated, the fourth and fifth very small ; hind metatarsi elongate and stout, the following two joints a little dilated, the fourth and fifth small. Wings hyaline, veins yellow.

Three specimens.

BIBIONIDÆ.

SCATOPSE.

Geoffroy, Hist. Nat. d. Ins., ii., 545, 1764.

1. *Scatopse pygmæa.* (Pl. VIII., fig. 26, wing.)

Scatopse pygmæa, Loew, Centur., v., 13.

Hab. District of Columbia.

♂. Black, but little shining, the margins of the mesonotum, the scutellum, the pleuræ in part, femora in part, knob of halteres, and tip of abdomen somewhat lighter coloured or brown. The tibiæ in part, and the tarsi, yellow or yellowish. Antennæ black, stout, the joints closely united, and gradually increasing in width to very near the tip. Wings greyish hyaline, the anterior thickened veins dark brown, the others light yellowish ; the short veins do not reach nearly to the middle of the wing ; the short prefurca of the forked cell takes its origin nearly opposite the connecting cross-vein of the subcostal cell ; the branches of the forked cell are very long and strongly curved away from each other near the margin of the wing. Length 2 mm.

One specimen. Loew's description agrees well with this specimen, still, the identity cannot be positively stated without comparison of specimens from the United States.

BLEPHAROCERIDÆ.

PALTOSTOMA.

Schiner, Verh. Zool.-Bot., Ges., 1866, p. 931.

1. *Paltostoma schineri,* n. sp. (Pl. VIII., figs. 27, wing ;
    27a, hypopygium ; 27b, head of ♂.)

♂. Mesonotum without black spots. Length 2¼-3 mm., of wings 5-6 mm.

Front yellow or yellowish-red ; in width a little less than one-third of the head ; facets of the eyes uniform in size. Antennæ brown or blackish, finely pubescent, composed of thirteen joints, of which the first two are swollen, and the third somewhat dilated. Palpi small, for the most part concealed. Proboscis nearly four times as long as the vertical diameter of the head. Eyes pubescent. Thorax yellow or yellowish-red, the mesonotum a little darker in front, the pleuræ with patches of silvery lustre. Abdomen dark brown, the basal segments more or less yellowish. Legs yellow, the femora with blackish bands on the distal half, the tarsi blackish towards the tip ; hind tibiæ with spurs. Wings pure hyaline.

Four specimens. The present species, though seeming to agree closely in its structural characters with *P. superbiens*, Schiner, differs, aside from the markedly smaller size, in the absence of black spots on the mesonotum. It is not at all improbable that our specimens are conspecific with those mentioned by Osten Sacken (Cat. Dipt., 197♂, 17,218) as occurring in Mexico.

Sackeniella, n. n.—Since the appearance of my paper (Kansas Univ. Quart., i., p. 119) in which I described a new genus of this family, I have discovered that the name *Snowia*, there used, has been previously employed for a genus of Lepidoptera. I here therefore substitute *Sackeniella* in honour of Dr. C. R. Osten Sacken.

CULICIDÆ.

MEGARRHINA.

Rob. Desvoidy, Essai, etc., in Mem. de la 'Soc. d'Hist. nat. de Paris, iii., 412, 1827.

1. *Megarrhina portoricensis.*   (Pl. VIII., fig. 28, head of ♂ ; 28*a*, wing.)

Megarrhina portoricensis, Roeder, Stett. Ent. Zeit., 1885, p. 337.—Porto Rico.

Two specimens, male and female. Sea level.

ÆDES.

Meigen, Syst. Beschr., i., 13, 1818.

1. *Ædes pertinans*, n. sp. (Pl. VIII., figs. 29, antenna; 29*a*, hypopygium.)

♂, ♀. Face, basal joints of antennæ and base of proboscis yellowish; antennæ and proboscis otherwise nearly black, the former only a little more hairy in the male than in the female, the terminal joint of the male only a little longer than the preceding ones. Mesonotum brown, thickly covered with dark brown squamulæ; pleuræ yellow, with white tomentum. Abdomen deep brown, with brown squamulæ; venter yellow, with white squamulæ; male forceps small, yellow. Legs deep brown; the femora, and, in a less degree, the tibiæ showing the yellow ground-colour on the underside. Wings nearly hyaline; veins uniformly brown squamulate. Length 3 mm.

Six specimens. Sea level and 1000 feet.

2. *Ædes perturbans*, ♂, ♀. (Pl. VIII., fig. 30, head of ♀.)

♂, ♀. Head black. Antennæ brown; plumosity of the male long, abundant and black; terminal joint as long as the seven or eight preceding it together, and clothed with short hair; in the female the joints are more slender, and the terminal one is not longer than the two preceding it taken together, the verticils of moderate length. Proboscis black, as long as the abdomen; palpi brown. Thorax yellow, the mesonotum a little darker, and clothed with brown squamulæ. Abdomen yellowish, brownish-yellow or brown, the terminal segments and the hypopygium brown or blackish; clothed above with brown squamulæ. Legs brown or blackish, the femora, for the most part, yellow, and with a purplish or greyish reflection in some lights; in some specimens the tibiæ largely yellowish beneath the tomentum. Veins of the wings uniformly dark-brown squamulate. Length 4–5 mm.

Eight specimens.

HÆMAGOGUS, n. g.

Allied to *Ædes*. Palpi short in both sexes; five-jointed, the first and fifth small, the second nearly as long as the third and fourth together. Anterior claws of male inequilaterally unipectinate; of the female simple.

1. *Harmagogus splendens*, n. sp.   (Pl. IX., figs. 31, head
     of ♀ ; 31*a*, palpus ; 31*b*, claw of ♂ ; 31*c*, wing.)

♀. In ground-colour deep black, the base of the femora, and
the coxæ in part, somewhat yellowish Occiput, mesonotum and
scutellum wholly covered with brilliant green and coppery squamulæ; pleuræ densely snow-white squamulate. Abdomen brilliant
steel-blue, in some reflections black; a spot on the sides of each
segment snow-white. Legs blue, like the abdomen, shining black
in some reflections; the undersides of the femora, towards the
base, with white squamulæ. Wings hyaline, somewhat brownish
in front, squamulæ black, evenly distributed. Length 5 mm.

Eight specimens.   1000 feet.   The single male
specimen was injured after the drawings were made. It
does not appear to differ, however, from the female. The
colouring must be much like that of *Culex cyaneus*, save
of head and thorax.

CULEX.

1. *Culex mosquito.*

Culex fasciatus, Wiedemann (*nec* Fabricius), Auss.
     Zw. Ins., i., 8.
Culex mosquito, Rob. Desvoidy, Culicides, etc., 390;
     Guerin et Percheron, Genera, etc., Dipt., pl. ii,
     fig. 1; Macquart, Hist. Nat. Dipt., i., 35; F. Lynch,
     A., Dipt. Argent. Culicidæ. 60, pl. iii, fig. 1.
Culex frater, Rob. Desvoidy, Culicides, etc.

A single female specimen, to which Lynch's description applies well, and whom I follow in the above-quoted
synonymy.   That *C. fasciatus*, Fabricius, is different
from *C. fasciatus*, Wiedemann, seems evident, but that
the present species is the same as the latter is not so
fully apparent to me. Wiedemann says that "An den
vordern Fusswurzeln ist die äusserste Basis der ein-
zelnen Glieder schneeweiss," while it is only the first
joint that is thus marked in this species.

2. *Culex*, sp.

Several specimens of a luteous species, which are too
ill-preserved to describe.

CHIRONOMIDÆ.

CHIRONOMUS.

Meigen, Illiger's Mag., ii., 260, 1803.

1. *Chironomus spilopterus*, n. sp. (Pl. IX., fig. 32, wing.)

♂, ♀. Face and front yellowish brown. Basal joint of antennæ brownish-yellow ; flagellum brownish, the plumosity of the male blackish grey. Mesonotum brown or yellowish-brown, lightly whitish dusted ; in well-preserved specimens brown vittate on the sides, and in front in the middle. Pleuræ black, in part luteous. Scutellum yellow or yellowish-brown. Abdomen black, with yellowish hair ; in the male, slender ; in the female, broader, and with a whitish posterior margin to the segments. Legs yellow, with rather abundant yellow hair ; femora in part brown or brownish ; front tibiæ not more than one-half of the length of the front metatarsi. Wings whitish hyaline, with pale blackish spots, which are more distinct when seen obliquely, and situated as follows : One near the base, another near the middle, and a third near or at the tip of the first posterior cell ; a streak near the middle, and a spot near the tip of the cell in front of the forked cell ; a spot on the posterior branch of the furcation, and one or two in the anal angle. Length 1¾-2¼ mm.

Eight specimens.

2. Chironomus anonymus, n. sp.

Cairon, (Cairon)

♂. Head red, or reddish-yellow, the front more yellow. Antennæ brown, the first joint red ; plumosity at the tip blackish. Mesonotum light brownish-red ; two stripes and the humeri yellow ; scutellum light yellow. Pleuræ light brownish or reddish-yellow. Metanotum brown. Abdomen blackish, the first segment and the distal part of the next two or three segments yellow or yellowish. Legs yellow ; the immediate tip of the tibiæ and the tip of all the tarsal joints dark brown ; proximal end of the front tibiæ also brown ; front tibiæ about one-half of the length of their metatarsi, and not longer than the second joint. Wings nearly hyaline. Length 4–5 mm. 1 Type AMNH 1 cotype nme L H.

tenebreon. 3. Chironomus (longimanus,) n. sp. (Pl. IX., fig. 33, wing.)
pleurus (Kieffer) 1906. presee, Meigen

♂. Head yellow. Antennæ, save the basal joint, black or deep brown, the plumosity greyish-black. Thorax light yellow : a blackish-brown stripe, running from in front of the root of each wing, and joining in the middle in front, forming a V-shaped figure ; below these stripes the sides of the mesonotum are of a purer yellow ; the metanotum and a spot below the halteres blackish. Abdomen yellow ; a black band on the posterior margin of the first and second segments ; the fourth segment, the posterior, or greater part of the fifth segment, and the hypopygium, black or dark brown. Legs yellow ; the base and tip of the four posterior femora, and the proximal end of their tibiæ brown ; front legs much elongate, the metatarsi about one-fourth longer than their tibiæ. Wings nearly hyaline. Length 3–4 mm.

Numerous specimens.

4. Chironomus lugubris, n. sp.

♂. Similar to Ch. longimanus, but differs in lacking the brown stripes of the mesonotum, which is uniformly light yellow, in the abdomen being uniformly brown, and in the femora being wholly light yellow. Length 3–4 mm.

Six specimens.

5. Chironomus innocuus, n. sp.

♂. Head and basal joints of the antennæ light yellowish ; palpi brown ; antennæ brown. Thorax light yellow ; mesonotum with a broad brown stripe in the middle in front, and, on either side, an oval brown spot, the three separated, and the middle stripe bisected, by a slender yellow stripe. Scutellum light yellow. Metanotum brown; halteres brown. Abdomen black, with black hair; the seventh and eighth segments light yellow, with yellow hair. Legs light yellow; the extreme tip of the four posterior tibiæ black; distal joints of the front tarsi infuscated, as also the front tibiæ; front metatarsi about one-third longer than their tibiæ. Wings hyaline. Length 3-4 mm.

6. *Chironomus*, n. sp.

♂. Light yellow, the antennæ brownish, and, rarely, the posterior part of the abdomen also brownish. Extreme tip of the four posterior tibiæ black; front metatarsi about one-fourth longer than their tibiæ. Wings hyaline; anal angle only feebly indicated. Length 2-2½ mm.

Orthocladius.

Van der Wulp, Tijdschr. voor Entom., xvi., lxx., 1874.

1. *Orthocladius debilis*, n. sp.   (Pl. IX., fig. 34, wing.)

♂. Red or reddish-yellow. Plumosity of the antennæ brownish-black. Mesonotum with three shining brown spots or stripes, narrowly separated. Abdomen slender; each segment with a brown posterior band. Legs yellow; front femora brown on the distal end; front tibiæ light yellow on the proximal half or two-fifths, dark brown on the distal portion, about one-third longer than the corresponding metatarsi; front tarsi infuscated; the four posterior femora somewhat infuscated distally. Wings hyaline. Length 2½-3 mm.

Tanypus.

Meigen, Illiger's Mag., ii., 261, 1803.

1. *Tanypus flaveolus*, n. sp.

♂. Posterior forked cell not petiolate; wings hairy; front metatarsi nearly as long as their tibiæ. Light yellow; antennæ brownish, the plumosity grey; abdomen somewhat infuscated toward the tip; legs light yellow throughout, with rather abundant light yellow hair; wings hyaline, clothed moderately densely with grey hair. Length 1½-2 mm.

2. *Tanypus indecisus*, n. sp.   (Pl. IX., fig. 35, wing.)

♂, ♀. Wings hairy ; posterior forked cell not petiolate ; front metatarsi shorter than their tibiæ. Head and basal joint of the antennæ reddish-yellow ; palpi and the remainder of the antennæ brownish-yellow ; antennal plumosity of the male grey, towards the tip blackish. Thorax reddish-yellow ; bare, opaque, with three slender, reddish-brown stripes in front, separated by ashy intervals ; on each side posteriorly with an elongate brown spot, the middle of which is ashy ; scutellum light yellow ; metanotum brownish-red. Abdomen slender ; opaque brown, the posterior angles and borders of the segments ashy ; the yellow of the venter some-times encroaches upon the brown of the dorsum ; sixth and seventh segments more distinctly yellow ; the seventh and eighth segments with the posterior portion blackish. Legs yellow, less hairy than in *T. flaveolus.* Wings hyaline, moderately hairy. Length 1½-2¼ mm.

CERATOPOGON.

Meigen, Illiger's Mag., ii., 1803.

TABLE OF SPECIES.

1. Two subcostal cells, that is, the third vein is either contiguous or connected by a cross-vein with the first
vein 3
One subcostal cell ; the third vein is distinctly separated
from the first throughout its course, and is not connected with it by a cross-vein 2
2. A small, round, black spot just back of the tip of the
third vein . . . . *punctipennis*, n. sp.
No such spot . . . . *venustulus*, n. sp.
3. Metatarsi shorter than the following joint ; wings hairy . . 4
Metatarsi much longer than the following joint. 6
4. Antennæ not longer than the mesonotum ; wings densely
hairy . . . . *criophorus*, n. sp.
Antennæ distinctly longer than the mesonotum 5
5. Abdomen banded ; hind metatarsi about one-half the
length of the following joint . . . *propinquus*, n. sp.
Abdomen not banded ; hind metatarsi about one-third the
length of the following joint ; tarsi very slender
flavus, n. sp.

6. The posterior branch of the fourth vein arises before the
   origin of the anterior cross-vein ; wholly deep black,
                                             longicornis, n. sp.
   The furcation of the fourth vein occurs beyond the cross-
   vein 7
7. Wings bare, or hairy at the tip only 8
   Wings hairy throughout, or nearly so 13
8. Black species ; mesonotum shining . . . . . *thirsites*, n. sp.
   Mesonotum not shining 9
9. Abdomen opaque black, with a slender yellow median
   stripe and incisures . . . . *lituratus*, n. sp.
   Abdomen without distinct markings 10
10. Wings with distinct markings; first and third veins indis-
    tinctly separable 11
    Wings without distinct markings . . . . *sequax*, n. sp.
11. Wings with three blackish spots along the costa, the other
    markings pale or obsolete . . . . *decor*, n. sp.
    One blackish spot on the costa at the tip of the first vein,
    the other markings distinct 12
12. Dorsum of thorax light opaque yellowish . *phlebotomus*, n. sp.
    Dorsum of thorax with numerous, rounded, dark brown
    spots on a yellowish-grey ground . . *maculithorax*, n. sp.
13. Deep black ; mesonotum shining . . . . . *pygmæus*, n. sp.
    Thorax yellow or brownish-yellow . . . . . . *lotus*, n. sp.

1. *Ceratopogon maculithorax*, n. sp.   (Pl. IX., fig. 36,
                        wing.)

♀. Wings hairy at the tip ; third vein contiguous with the
first, terminating at or near the middle of the wing : fourth vein
with a prefurca, though indistinct ; metatarsi as long as the following joints together. Proboscis, palpi, face, front and basal
joint of antennæ yellowish-brown ; proboscis slender ; second
joint of palpi thickened. Antennæ yellow, not as long as the
thorax. Mesonotum opaque yellowish-grey, with numerous, small,
rounded, dark-brown spots on a yellowish-grey ground, hair not
abundant or long, yellow. Scutellum yellow on the sides, brown
in the middle. Halteres light yellow. Pleuræ black and luteous,
lightly greyish pruinose. Legs yellow ; all the femora, and the
front and hind tibiæ with a broad blackish ring ; the immediate
tip of the femora also blackish. Wings with pale brown markings
with hyaline or whitish spots and streaks ; a spot at the tip of the
first and third veins blackish. Length 2 mm.

One specimen.

2. *Ceratopogon pygmæus,* n. sp.   (Pl. IX., fig. 37, wing.)

♀. Shining black : wings hairy ; first and third veins closely approximated, terminating before the middle of the wing. Metatarsi nearly as long as the following joints together. Black : antennæ brown ; scutellum and halteres yellow, genital organs and legs luteous. Mesonotum shining. Abdomen opaque. Wings hyaline, sparsely hairy. Length 1 mm.

Three specimens.   Sea level.

3. *Ceratopogon venustulus,* n. sp.   (Pl. IX., figs. 38, wing ; 38*a*, front leg ; 38*b*, palpus.)

♀. The third longitudinal vein terminates in the costa towards the tip of the wing, distinctly separated from, and not connected by a cross-vein with, the first longitudinal vein ; front femora with spines on the inner underside ; claws not denticulate, and without pulvilli ; wings bare. Deep black. Antennæ reddish-brown, slender ; if turned backward, reaching about to the middle of the mesonotum. Mesonotum deep shining black. Abdomen opaque, black, elongate. Halteres black. Legs black ; the base of the femora, and the tibiæ more or less yellowish ; first two or three joints of the tarsi yellow or luteous ; hind tibiæ with fine, not very long, black hairs on the outer side ; metatarsi slender, as long as the three following joints together. Wings nearly hyaline, bare. 1¼–1½ mm.

Five specimens.   Sea level. May.   In one of the specimens, the legs are yellow throughout, but I do not distinguish other differences. It is possible that this species is the same as *C. trivialis,* Loew, but the difference in size and the colour of the tarsi render the identity doubtful.

4. *Ceratopogon punctipennis,* n. sp. (Pl. IX., fig. 39, wing.)

♂, ♀. Wings bare : one subcostal cell, the third vein is well separated from the first, and terminates beyond the middle of the wing ; prefurca of fourth vein obsolete or nearly so ; first joint of the tarsi elongate, fourth short, fifth elongate ; pulvilli wanting. Plumosity of the male antennæ yellow ; terminal joints in both sexes black, the basal joint reddish. Face and proboscis dark brown : palpi slender, the second joint elongate. Thorax black ; mesonotum opaque, with whitish pubescence, variable in different lights. Abdomen deep brown or black, with a whitish, variable pruinosity. Femora and tibiæ yellowish-brown or reddish-brown ; tarsi yellow, the tip of each joint brown or black ; all the femora on the upper side distally, and all the tibiæ on the outer side, most conspicuous in the hind pair, with black bristles. Wings nearly hyaline ; a rounded blackish spot back of the third vein at its tip, and a smaller one nearly opposite on the fourth vein. Length 3 mm.

5. *Ceratopogon eriophorus*, n. sp. (Pl. IX., figs. 40, tarsus ; 40*a*, antenna ; 40*b*, palpus.)

♂. Wings densely hairy ; the third vein scarcely distinguishable from the first, and terminating before the middle of the wing ; metatarsi about one-half of the length of the following joint, the last joint not elongate ; pulvilli hairy. Face, antennæ and palpi brown or black ; second joint of the latter much thickened, the third slender. Antennæ yellow, somewhat infuscated distally. Mesonotum dark-brown or black, opaque, and with abundant, light yellow hair ; scutellum like the mesonotum. Halteres light yellow : pleuræ yellowish-brown. Abdomen stout, dark brown, the incisures narrowly yellowish : clothed with light-yellow hair. Legs yellow, with abundant, rather long, yellow hair. Wings hyaline beneath the dense, dark-coloured hair. Length 1½-2 mm.

Four specimens. 1000–1500 feet.

6. *Ceratopogon propinquus*, n. sp. (Pl. IX., figs. 41, tarsus ; 41*a*, wing.)

♂. Wings hairy ; the third vein terminates about the middle of the wing, and is indistinctly separated from the first vein : fourth vein with a prefurca, though indistinct ; first tarsal joint about one-half of the length of the second joint, the last joint not elongated ; pulvilli hairy. Head and antennæ yellow, the latter somewhat infuscated distally, the plumosity blackish-grey. Second and third joints of the palpi enlarged. Metanotum opaque brown, more yellow.sh near the middle in front : rather thickly, light-yellow, hairy. Abdomen slender, with abundant, and long, yellow pile ; anterior segments yellow, with a broad black band, which becomes successively broader till the last segments are wholly black. Legs yellow, with long yellow hair ; the tip of the middle and hind femora, at least, and the proximal end of their tibiæ blackish. Wings nearly hyaline beneath the rather abundant hair. Length 2¼ mm.

One specimen.

7. *Ceratopogon flavus*, n. sp. (Pl. IX., figs. 42, wing ; 42*a*, tarsus.)

♂. Wings hairy ; the third vein terminates distinctly before the middle of the wing, and is very close to the first vein ; fourth vein with a prefurca, though indistinct ; first joint of the tarsi about one-third of the length of the second joint, the fifth a little shorter than the fourth : pulvilli hairy. Face, proboscis, palpi, and antennæ yellowish, the last brownish toward the extremity ; the plumosity blackish-grey. Thorax yellow, the mesonotum brownish-yellow, opaque, with light-coloured hair. Abdomen slender, in large part brown or blackish, its base and tip yellow ; hair of the venter long. Legs yellow, with long yellow hair ; the tarsi a little infuscated. Wings hyaline beneath the hair. Length 2 mm.

Ten specimens. Sea level, and 1000 feet.

8. *Ceratopogon longicornis*, n. sp. (Pl. IX., figs. 43, wing ; 43*a*, antenna.)

♀. Wings bare ; the third vein terminates in the costa much beyond the middle of the wing : two submarginal cells. The posterior branch of the fourth vein arises before the anterior cross-vein ; femora without spines. Antennæ slender, much elongate, if turned back, reaching to near the middle of abdomen, the distal four joints nearly equal in length to all the preceding together. Mesonotum deep shining black throughout : pleuræ lightly pruinose. Abdomen elongate, shining. Legs black or deep reddish-brown ; femora not thickened ; metatarsi slender, as long as the three following joints together. Wings nearly hyaline, narrow, with no perceptible anal angle. Length 1½–2 mm.

Three specimens. 500 feet.

9. *Ceratopogon thersites*, n. sp. (Pl. IX., fig. 44, wing.)

♂. Two subcostal cells ; the third vein terminates beyond the middle of the wing ; wings bare ; prefurca of the fourth vein very short ; first joint of the tarsi elongate, last joint not elongate ; pulvilli hairy. Abdomen black, not shining, elongate, yellow at tip and on the venter. Thorax black or reddish-brown, the mesonotum shining moderately through the sparse yellowish pubescence or pollen. Legs yellow ; the tarsi blackish at tip. Wings hyaline. Antennæ brown or blackish, yellowish at base. Palpi and proboscis brown. Length ½–¾ mm.

Eight specimens. Sea level, and 1000 feet.

10. *Ceratopogon lituratus,* n. sp.

♀. Two subcostal cells ; the third vein terminates beyond the middle of the wing ; prefurca of fourth vein short ; wings a little hairy on the distal margin ; first joint of the tarsi much longer than the second, the last joint not elongate. Proboscis yellow ; labium brown ; face elsewhere, basal joints of the antennæ, and the frontal triangle, yellow. Antennæ brown or blackish on the distal portion, yellowish on the proximal part ; about as long as the mesonotum. Occiput yellow. Mesonotum opaque brown, the humeri and sides in front, the post-alar callosities, and the scutellum, light yellow ; halteres light yellow. Abdomen opaque blackish-brown ; the first segment, except a small spot on each side, the last segment, and a slender median stripe and the narrow posterior margin of each segment, light yellow. Legs yellow. Wings hyaline. Length 1 mm.

Four specimens.

11. *Ceratopogon decor,* n. sp. (Pl. IX., fig. 45, wing.)

♀. Wings sparsely hairy ; the third vein terminates a little beyond the middle of the wing, and only a short distance from the tip of the first vein ; fourth vein with a prefurca ; metatarsi longer than the following joint ; pulvilli hairy. Antennæ yellow, somewhat longer than the mesonotum ; face, proboscis, and palpi brownish-yellow. Mesonotum brownish-yellow, opaque ; the humeri, pleuræ, and a part of the scutellum light yellow ; pleuræ, in part, black. Abdomen black, with yellowish incisures. Legs yellow ; all the femora at the tip, and a median ring on the hind pair, black Wings nearly hyaline, with three blackish spots along the costa, one at the outer part of the subcostal cell, another near the middle of the first posterior cell, and the third, less distinct, across the middle of the costal and first basal cell ; posterior part of the wings with paler markings, which, however, become distinct when seen obliquely. Length 1½–2 mm.

Three specimens.

12. *Ceratopogon phlebotomus,* n. sp. (Pl. IX., figs. 46, wing ; 46a, palpus.)

♀. Third vein very close to the first, terminating in the costa about the middle of the wing ; wings infuscated, with whitish spots, hairy at the tip ; metatarsi distinctly longer than the following joint, about as long as the next two or three together ; pulvilli wanting. Antennæ, face, proboscis and palpi black or dark brown, the antennæ not as long as the thorax. Thorax black ; mesonotum opaque yellowish pollinose, with three slender indistinct lines ; in the middle behind, whitish ; pleuræ lightly whitish pruinose. Abdomen opaque black, the anterior segments somewhat luteous ; the posterior margin of the segments very narrowly whitish, perhaps due to the drying. Legs luteous. Wings rather broad, tinged with brownish, leaving six or seven rounded, hyaline or whitish spots in the cells ; tip of the costal cell blackish. Length 1–1½ mm.

Four specimens, one of which bears the following label, apparently in Mr. H. H. Smith's handwriting : "This is the common 'sand-fly' about the southern end of the island, but is not very troublesome. Bites late in the afternoon, before sunset; sometimes during the heat of the day."

13. *Ceratopogon lotus,* n. sp.   (Pl. IX., fig. 47, wing.)

♂. Two subcostal cells ; the third vein unites with the costa a little beyond the middle of the wing; wings hairy ; metatarsi as long as the three following joints together. Antennæ brown, yellowish towards the proximal end. Proboscis yellowish. Mesonotum brownish yellow, with yellowish hair. Abdomen black or brownish black. Legs yellow, a little infuscated towards the tip of the tarsi ; with light coloured hair ; pulvilli wanting. Wings hyaline beneath the light coloured pubescence ; posterior branch of the fourth vein indistinct in its proximal part. Length 1–1¼ mm.

Two specimens.   1000 feet.

14. *Ceratopogon sequax,* n. sp.   (Pl. IX., fig. 48, wing.)

♂. Two subcostal cells ; the third vein terminates distinctly beyond the middle of the wing ; wings bare ; prefurca of anterior fork short ; metatarsi as long as the two following joints together. Antennæ dark-brown ; yellowish on the proximal portion, the plumosity yellowish. Palpi and proboscis yellowish-brown. Thorax brown, the scutellum and sides of dorsum more yellowish ; only a little shining. Abdomen slender, dark brown. Legs luteous or yellow, with long hairs on the tibiæ. Wings hyaline. Length 1½ mm.

PSYCHODIDÆ.

PSYCHODA.

Latreille, Precis, etc. 1796.

1. *Psychoda alternata.* (Pl. IX., fig. 49, wing.)

Psychoda alternata, Say, Long's Exped., App., 358 ; Compl. Wr., i., 242 ; Wiedemann, Aus. Zw. Ins., i., 23 ; Williston, Entom. News, iv., 114 ; Banks, Can. Entom., xxvi., 330.

Hab. New England States ; Pennsylvania ; South Dakota ; Kansas.

A single, injured specimen seems to belong to this species, though I cannot be sure of the identity without examining better preserved specimens.

2. *Psychoda antennalis,* n. sp.

♂ . Black or dark brown, with dark hair. Antennæ stout, the joints moniliform, about as long as the thorax. Wings with a distinct picture formed by the hairs, which are black, save an apical white fringe, and two subconfluent spots of the same colour beyond the middle on the outer side of two spots of denser black hair. Front legs black, the base of the metatarsi and the middle joints white. Length 1–1¼ mm.

3. *Psychoda pallens,* n. sp. (Pl. IX., figs. 50, hypopygium ; 50a, wing.)

♂ . Wholly light-yellow, with white or yellowish-white hair. Hair of the wings not long ; at the tip a minute blackish spot ; furcations approximated to the base of the wing. Antennæ rather slender, not as long as the mesonotum, with rather long verticellate hairs. Legs moderately long ; tarsi rather stout. Length 1–1¼ mm.

k. *Psychoda angustipennis*, n. sp. (Pl. IX., fig. 51, wing.)

♀. Yellow, with nearly white hair. Wings very narrow, acutely lanceolate, covered uniformly with long black hair ; a small tuft of white at the extreme tip ; another larger one on each side beyond the middle, and yet another toward the base on the posterior margin ; hair ou the posterior margin long and abundant. Antennæ light-yellow, about as long as the mesonotum ; sixteen-jointed, the basal joints darker, the following ones slender. Thorax and abdomen light reddish-yellow, the hair of the abdomen slightly intermixed with blackish. Legs rather stout, light-yellow ; the terminal joints of the tarsi somewhat infuscated. Length 1–1½ mm.

Pericoma.

Walker, Ins. Brit., ii., 256, 1856.

1. *Pericoma albitarsis*, n. sp. (Pl. IX., fig. 52, wing.)

♂, ♀. Black or brown, with black or dark-brown hair. All the tarsi white. Antennæ slender, rather longer than the thorax ; brownish-yellow or brown, sixteen-jointed. Palpi elongate. Hair of the wings uniform in colour and uniformly distributed ; that along the hind border rather short. Terminal joints of the tarsi rather short, slightly infuscated. Length 1–1¼ mm.

Ten specimens.

TIPULIDÆ.

Geranomyia.

Haliday, Ent. Mag., i., 154, 1833.

1. *Geranomyia pallida*, n. sp. (Pl. IX., fig. 53, wing.)

♂, ♀. Front and vertex brownish-yellow, whitish pruinose. Antennæ brown, the basal portion more or less yellow. Rostrum yellowish at the base, brownish on the distal part; nearly as long as the thorax and abdomen together. Thorax and abdomen light-yellow, the mesonotum in some specimens yellowish-red. Knob of halteres yellow. Legs yellow. Wings hyaline ; stigma distinct,

brownish ; termination of the auxiliary vein at a distance beyond
the origin of the second longitudinal vein about equal to the length
of the first section of the third vein. Length 5 mm.

Three specimens, leeward side, and at an altitude of
1000 feet.

2. *Geranomyia,* sp.

♀. Yellowish-red, the mesonotum with three, rarely distinct,
slender, brownish stripes. Antennæ somewhat infuscated. Head
black, whitish pruinose. Antennæ yellowish, or yellowish-brown.
Proboscis black. Legs red : the tarsi luteous. Wings nearly
hyaline ; stigma small, distinct ; the auxiliary vein terminates
opposite the origin of the second longitudinal vein. Knob of
halteres brown. Proboscis as long as the abdomen. Length 5 mm.

Six specimens.

3. *Geranomyia rostrata.*

Limnobia rostrata, Say, Journ. Acad. Nat. Sci. Phil.,
 iii., 22 ; Wiedemann, Auss. Zw. Ins., i., 35.

Geranomyia rostrata, Osten Sacken, Proc. Acad. Nat.
 Sci. Phil. 1859, 207 ; Monogr., etc., iv., 79.

Hab. Atlantic States ; Canada ; Cuba.

Two specimens, male and female, which agree fairly
well with Osten Sacken's description and observations.
The brown stripes of the dorsum of the thorax are well
marked, but the tip of the tibiæ is not black, and there
are but four brown spots along the front border of the
wing, as Wiedemann describes.

RHIPIDIA.

Meigen, Syst. Beschr., i., 153 (122), 1818.

1. *Rhipidia bipectinata,* n. sp. (Pl. IX., fig. 54, wing.)

♂. Antennæ long, bipectinate ; thorax without brown
stripes ; wings clouded, unspotted. Length 5 mm.

Rostrum palpi and antennæ black, the last long-bipectinate,
beginning with the second joint of the flagellum. Mesonotum
light opaque yellow in front ; in the middle, in front of the suture,
brownish ; behind the suture, with two large brown spots.
Pleuræ brown ; a longitudinal, more blackish stripe, just below

the root of the wings. Metanotum brown. yellowish on the sides.
Abdomen dark brown, the forceps reddish. Halteres with a
brown knob. Legs brown, the base of the femora yellowish.
Wings nearly uniformly clouded with blackish, the stigma darker :
termination of the auxiliary vein nearly opposite the proximal
end of the submarginal cell.

One specimen. 1000 feet. In this specimen the
anterior cross-vein is situated nearly opposite the middle
of the distal cell.

2. *Rhipidia unipectinata*, n. sp. (Pl. IX., fig. 55, antenna.)

♂. Brown spots along the anterior border of the wing : antennæ
long-uninectinate; halteres brown ; thorax with a brown stripe and
a lateral brown spot. Length 5 mm.

Rostrum, palpi and antennæ black. Flagellum of antennæ,
except the terminal joints, unipectinote, the pectinations beginning
with the first joint and increasing in length to the seventh. Thorax
yellow ; the dorsum with a median brown stripe, and, on
either side behind, a rounded yellow spot, leaving a yellow space
between them ; these brown spots are continued on the scutellum,
enclosing a small yellow spot. Pleuræ with a slender, longitudinal
brown stripe. Halteres brown. Metanotum brown. Abdomen,
brown, the venter yellowish. Legs brown, the femora lighter
coloured toward the base ; second, third, and fourth joints of the
hind tarsi light yellowish. Wings with a blackish tinge, with
inconspicuous darker clouds along the anterior margin and on the
cross-veins : before and beyond the dark-brown stigma, a rounded,
more hyaline spot ; apical portion of the costa more distinctly
clouded ; insertion of the auxiliary vein a little beyond the middle
of the prefurca.

One specimen. 1000 feet.

3. *Rhipidia costalis*, n. sp. (Pl. IX., fig. 56, antenna.)

♂. Antennæ bipectinate ; thorax not striped ; costa with
brown spots or clouds. Length 5 mm.

Palpi, rostrum and antennæ black, the latter bipectinate, but
the pectinations shorter and more slender than in *R. bipectinata*.
Thorax brownish-yellow, the mesonotum opaque yellowish-red,
with a spot in front, and two behind the suture, faintly brownish.
Knob of halteres brownish. Abdomen reddish, with brown
posterior borders to the segments ; forceps red. Legs brown ; the

tip of the slightly clavate femora yellow : base of femora yellowish. Wings tinged with brownish ; four large brown spots or clouds along the costa, the outermost one confluent with a brown cloud at the origin of the third vein ; the outer cross-veins with brown clouds, and the distal costal portion more distinctly clouded ; between the brown spots along the costa, the intervals are more purely hyaline ; termination of the auxiliary vein at or before the middle of the prefurca.

Two specimens. 1500 feet.

4. *Rhipidia subpectinata,* n. sp. (Pl. IX., fig. 57, wing ; Pl. X., fig. 57*a*, antenna of ♂.)

♂. Antennæ subpectinate in both sexes. Mesonotum conspicuously lighter coloured on the sides ; wings with small dark spots. Length 4 mm.

Head ochraceous yellow. Antennæ yellow, slightly brownish at the tip. Palpi brown or blackish. Mesonotum on the upper surface yellowish-brown, or brownish-yellow, forming a long, subtriangular figure, the margins of which are dark brown ; just outside or below this line, conspicuously light yellow, extending in a nearly equal width from the root of one wing to that of the other ; below the light yellow band, near the upper part of the thorax, a narrow, longitudinal, nearly black stripe. Scutellum and metanotum light yellow ; the former with two spots, the latter with a median stripe and a lateral spot pale brown. Legs yellow, the two or three terminal joints of the tarsi black. Wings nearly hyaline, with small brown spots, as shown in the figure.

Two males and two females. 1000 feet. The female scarcely differs from the male.

LIMNOBIA.

Meigen, Syst. Beschr., i., 92, 1818.

1. *Limnobia insularis,* n. sp. (Pl. X., fig. 58, wing.)

♂. First longitudinal vein recurved to the second near its tip ; femora without brown rings. Length 6 mm.

Front black. Antennæ, palpi and rostrum brown. Thorax brownish red, the mesonotum shining ; pronotum long, somewhat lighter coloured ; mesonotum with inconspicuous, narrow, brown stripes. Abdomen and halteres dark brown. Wings infuscated, strongly so along the costa distally. Legs dark brown, the tarsi more yellowish, except the terminal joints, which are blackish.

One specimen. 1000 feet.

RHAMPHIDIA.

Meigen, Syst. Beschr., vi., 281, 1830.

1. *Rhamphidia albitarsis.*   (Pl. X., figs. 59, wing; 59a, hypopygium.)

Rhamphidia albitarsis, Osten Sacken, Berl. Ent. Zeitschr., xxxi., 184, 1887.

Hab. Porto Rico.

Two specimens, male and female, agreeing well with the description.

ELEPHANTOMYIA.

Osten Sacken, Proc. Acad. Nat. Sci. Phil., 1859.

1. *Elephantomyia longirostris,* n. sp.

♂. Proboscis about one and a-half times the length of the body; wings with a brown stigma and brownish clouds along the cross-veins. Length of body 6 mm, of proboscis 8½ mm.

Head yellow. Proboscis very distinctly longer than the body, finely pubescent. Antennæ brownish-yellow ; basal joints yellow, the verticils black. Thorax yellow ; a rather broad, brownish stripe along the middle, and a shorter, similarly coloured one on each side. Halteres yellow. Abdomen light yellow, with a broad, brown band on the posterior part of each segment ; forceps brownish. Wings lightly 'tinged with brownish ; with distinct brownish or brown clouds along the distal part of the costa, and along the cross-veins. Legs yellow ; femora brown at tip ; neuration as in *E. westwoodi*, O. S.

This species is evidently closely allied to the type of the genus, and I at first believed that it was the same, but the more elongate proboscis and the brownish clouds of the wings seem sufficient to separate them.

ATARBA.

Osten Sacken, Monogr., etc., iv., 127, 1868.

1. *Atarba puella,* n. sp.   (Pl. X., figs. 60, wing; 60a, hypopygium.)

♂, ♀. Antennæ short and slender, not as long as the mesonotum, the first two joints thickened ; in the male, the following joints slender, and each, except the distal ones, with two long hairs. Front, and basal joints of the antennæ yellow, the remainder of the antennæ and the palpi brown. Thorax yellow, the mesonotum brown, the metanotum brownish. Abdomen brownish-yellow, the male organs more yellowish. Legs brownish throughout, the tarsi finely pubescent. Wings nearly hyaline ; no stigma. Length 3–4 mm.

Twelve specimens. This and the following species differ from the type of this genus, as described by Osten Sacken, in the structure of the antennæ and in some peculiarities of the neuration, but the differences will not justify generic separation. Both species have distinct empodia, and there appears to be a minute spur on the middle tibiæ.

2. *Atarba pleuralis*, n. sp. (Pl. X., figs. 61, antenna ; 61*a, b*, genitalia ; 61*c*, wing.)

♂. ♀. Front yellow. Antennæ and palpi blackish. Mesonotum brownish-red ; the colour in shape of an elongated triangle, the base of which is the scutellum ; the lateral margins of the mesonotum show a slender, dark-brown stripe ; immediately below which the colour is light yellow, extending over the dorso-pleural suture. Pleuræ dark-brown, with a longitudinal stripe above the base of the coxæ : or, the pleuræ may be otherwise described as having two dark brown stripes enclosing a light yellow one. Abdomen brownish-red, with a narrow, dark-brown band on the posterior margin of each segment, and with a median, indistinct brownish stripe. Coxæ light yellow ; femora yellow, with a brown ring just before the light yellow tip, which colour extends narrowly on the base of the tibiæ ; tibiæ and tarsi brown. Wings tinged with brown ; stigma dark-brown ; the marginal cell is shorter and wider than in *A. puella*. Length 4–5 mm.

Six specimens.

TEUCHOLABIS.

Osten Sacken, Proc. Acad. Nat. Sci. Phil., 1859.

1. *Teucholabis complexa*. (Pl. X., fig. 62, wing.)

Teucholabis complexa, Osten Sacken, Proc. Acad. Nat. Sci. Phil., 223, 1859 ; Monogr., etc., iv., 129.

Hab. District of Columbia ; New York ; Illinois.

Sixteen specimens. The description of this species applies so well to these specimens that there can be but little doubt of the identification. The brown stripes of the mesonotum are only feebly indicated in most of the specimens ; the posterior part of the abdominal segments is yellow, and the tibiæ are brownish.

2. *Teucholabis annulata*, n. sp.   (Pl. X., fig. 63, wing.)

♂, ♀. Front black ; palpi brown ; rostrum and first joint of the antennæ yellow; flagellum brown or black. Mesonotum shining, with three broad, more or less confluent, shining, deep broad stripes, the middle one not reaching the suture, the lateral ones not extending far in front of it ; elsewhere the mesonotum, like the scutellum and anterior part of the metanotum, is light yellow. Pleuræ dark yellow or brown ; when seen obliquely, with a silvery sheen. Posterior part of metanotum brown. Abdomen yellow, with a broad brown band on the anterior part of each segment. Legs yellow ; all the femora brown at the tip, and with a brownish ring beyond the middle ; all the tibiæ and the first three tarsal joints brown at the tip, the last two joints of the tarsi black. Wings hyaline ; the stigma and a cloud at the end of the costa—sometimes obsolete—brown. Length 7–8 mm.

Twelve specimens. In one female the abdomen is black, with a narrow yellow posterior margin to the segments ; in others brown, with a broader yellow border. The neuration is very much like that of *T. complexa* ; both the second and third veins are curved less, and the second vein extends further towards the tip of the wing.

ELLIPTERA.

Schiner, Wien. Ent. Monatschr., vii., 222, 1863.

1. ? *Elliptera*, sp.   (Pl. X., figs. 64, wing ; 64*a*, genitalia.)

♀. Head brownish, or brownish-yellow, including rostrum and palpi. Antennæ yellow, the first two joints red. Mesonotum brownish grey, with four narrow, brownish stripes ; humeri and sides of prothorax light yellow. Pleuræ yellow, obscurely brownish in places. Abdomen light luteous yellow. Legs yellow ; the tip of femora, tibiæ, and the distal joints of the tarsi brownish. Wings hyaline ; stigma faintly brown. Length 5 mm.

One specimen. The present species can hardly be a true *Elliptera*, because the anterior veins do not show the approximation characteristic of that genus, but it seems to agree in all other respects. The antennæ are sixteen-jointed, the joints oval in shape ; the thorax is gently convex, the pronotum small, the abdomen is elongate, etc. The neuration is shown in the figure. There are no spurs to the tibiæ.

DIOTREPHA.

Osten Sacken, Cat. Dipt., xxviii., 1878.

Wings very slender ; great cross-vein near their proximal third ; three posterior cells ; no discal cell. Antennæ sixteen-jointed, simple. Rostrum projecting, nearly as long as the head. Neck slender. Mesonotum but little convex, elongate and slender ; metanotum elongate. Legs slender, distinctly pubescent ; tibiæ without spurs. Abdomen very slender ; male forceps obtuse ; upper valve of ovipositor smal' and gently curved.

1. *Diotrepha mirabilis.* (Pl. X., figs. 65, wing ; 65*a*, hypopygium.)

(?) *Diotrepha mirabilis*, Osten Sacken, Cat. Dipt., 1878, p. 220.

♂, ♀. Proboscis, palpi, and antennæ brownish. Antennæ microscopically pubescent, and with verticils of short hairs ; in length the antennæ would reach to about the suture, if bent backwards. Thorax yellowish-brown, or brownish-red. Abdomen yellowish-brown, the posterior margins of the segments, or, the posterior segments, wholly brown ; in some specimens the abdomen is deep brown throughout. Legs light yellow ; the tibiæ and the tarsi more nearly white ; the tip of all the femora and tibiæ dark-brown. Wings nearly hyaline ; a fringe of hairs along the posterior margin. Length of body, 7 mm. ; of wings, 5 mm.

Hab. St. Vincent, Georgia, Texas, Cuba.

Eight specimens. "This species is abundant in forest glen, 1000 feet, near a stream, Sept. Alights on the lower side of leaves."—H. H. Smith.

2. *Diotrepha concinna*, n. sp. (Pl. X., fig. 66, wing.)

♀. Differs from *T. mirabilis* in the darker colour, the proboscis, palpi, and antennæ being blackish ; in the legs being light yellow, and in the absence of the brown tip to femora and tibiæ ; and in the neuration as shown in the figure. The wings are uniformly and distinctly tinged with brown. Length 6 mm.

One specimen. Sea level.

MONGOMA.

Westwood, Trans. Ent. Soc. London, 1881, p. 364.

Antennæ sixteen-jointed, if bent backward, reaching about to the base of the wings ; second joint a little shorter than the first, both thickened : the following joints slender, distinctly separated, finely pubescent. Rostrum rounded, a little prolonged, but shorter than the head ; palpi inserted towards its base, rather slender, the ultimate joint shorter than the penultimate, the two together about equal to the antepenultimate joint. Front rather narrow ; vertex but little developed. Legs very long and slender, finely pubescent ; tibiæ without spurs ; ungues simple ; no empodia. Male forceps not large, in the dry specimen showing two obtuse, fleshy lobes. Valves of the ovipositor small, slender, arcuated. Auxiliary vein nearly as long as the first longitudinal vein, joining the costa in an acute angle ; the subcostal cross-vein at some distance before the tip. The second longitudinal vein arises at some distance before the middle of the wing, with a strong curve backward ; nearly opposite the distal end of the discal cell, it gives off an oblique branch to the costa : marginal cross-vein long and oblique, sometimes joining the proximal end of the anterior branch. The beginning of the third vein in the same straight line with the first section of the second vein, terminating in the fourth vein at the proximal end of the discal cell. Anterior cross-vein wanting. Anal cell narrowed in the margin. Seventh vein very short.

This singular genus is remarkable, if my interpretation of the neuration is correct, in the entire absence of the first posterior cell, the second submarginal cell lying in contact with the discal cell and the second posterior cell, through the absence of the small cross-vein and the greater part of the third vein. It is difficult to see how there can be any other interpretation, as the branch of the second vein that takes the place of the small cross-vein cannot possibly be that cross-vein, for, in that case, it would arise from the second vein—an impossibility. Furthermore, this interpretation seems probable from a study of the neuration in *Paratropesa*, where the first posterior cell begins at the outer end of the discal cell. The relationship seems to be with that genus, but I cannot agree with Osten Sacken in considering the anterior branch of the second vein an adventitious cross-vein. There are two submarginal cells present, as in *Gonomyia*. Aside from the fact that there are only three posterior cells present, which may or may not be a generic character, the shortness of the seventh longitudinal vein is sufficient for the separation of the genus.

The foregoing, without change, was written in the belief that our specimens represented a new genus. A more careful search of the literature, however, revealed to my surprise the congenerousness of the species, especially *M. albitarsis*, Dol., included in the genus *Mongoma*. The species hitherto made known—seven or eight in all—are from Java, Sumatra, the Philippine Islands, Borneo, Madagascar, and Southern Africa. Its occurrence in the western continent is of great interest.

1. *Mongoma manca*, n. sp.

♂, ♀. Front and basal joints of the antennæ brownish red ; flagellum of antennæ and the palpi brown or black. Thorax, light brownish-red, the metanotum sometimes a little darker, and the pleuræ more yellow. Halteres yellow. Abdomen brown or brownish-red, the terminal segments more reddish. Legs brownish: base of femora and the distal joints of the tarsi more yellowish. Wings nearly hyaline ; stigma small, rounded, brownish. Length 7-8 mm.

Six specimens. Forest, 2000 feet, July.

2. *Mongoma pallida*, n. sp. (Pl. X., fig. 67, wing.)

♂, ♀. Wholly light yellow, the front and outer joints, the antennæ, only, brown or brownish; the legs a little darker. Wings pure hyaline, with light-coloured veins ; no stigma ; the distance between the junction of the marginal cross-vein and the origin of the anterior branch of the second vein greater than in *M. manca*, nearly as great as the length of the anterior branch itself. Length 5 mm.

Four specimens. 1000-1500 feet. In addition to the smaller size, much lighter colour, and more hyaline wings, the species will be readily distinguished by the shorter outer submarginal cell. In the present species, its inner end, in all the specimens, is opposite the inner end of the second posterior cell; in *M. manca* the proximal end is, in every case, at a considerable distance proximad to that of the posterior cell.

ERIOPTERA.

Meigen, Illiger's Mag., ii., 1803.

1. *Erioptera caloptera.*

Erioptera caloptera, Say, Journ. Acad. Nat. Sci. Phil.,
    iii., 17; Compl. Wr., ii., 44; Wiedemann, Auss.
    Zw. Ins., i., 23; Osten Sacken, Proc. Acad. Nat.
    Sci. Phil., 1859, 226; Monoghr., iv., 161, pl., iv.,
    f. 15.

Hab. Atlantic States; Kansas; Colorado; Canada;
Cuba.

One specimen, which scarcely differs from others
from Kansas.

2. *Erioptera annulipes*, n. sp.

♀. Legs conspicuously white and black annulate. Length
3–3½ mm.

Head brown or blackish. Antennæ brown, not longer than the
mesonotum. Thorax and abdomen yellowish-brown, the latter
posteriorly more yellow. Legs conspicuously white and dark-
brown annulate, the femora, t biæ. and tarsi each with three brown
rings; a fourth brown ring on the femora is more or less indistinct.
Wings nearly hyaline, the costa with four brown spots intercalated
with as many white ones; the outer posterior margin also with
alternating white spots.

Two specimens.

EPIPHRAGMA.

Osten Sacken, Proc. Acad. Nat. Sci. Phil., 1859.

1. *Epiphragma sackeni*, n. sp.   (Pl. X, fig. 68, wing.)

♂. Head black in ground-colour, opaque yellowish-grey pollinose; brown on the lower part of the broad front. First two
joints of the antennæ brown, the third and fourth yellow;
remainder of the antennæ blackish; if bent back, the antennæ
would reach about to the root of the wings. Mesonotum ochraceous, with slender, dark-brown markings. Metanotum deep brown
or blackish, somewhat darker than the pleuræ. Halteres yellow,
the knob brownish. Abdomen dark brown, the venter yellowish.

Basal half of the femora yellow; the distal part with two dark-
brown bands, and two, narrower, yellow bands, the second yellow
band at the tip; tibiæ and tarsi brownish, with a narrow yellow
band at the base of the tibiæ (middle and front legs wanting).
Wings with uniform brown spots, located as in the figure: separated from the infuscation of the rest of the wing by narrow,
hyaline, or light-yellow margins.   Length 7 mm.

One specimen.   1500 feet.

Tipula.

Linne, Anim. per Sueciam observata, 1736.

1 *Tipula subinfuscata*, n. sp.   (Pl. X., fig. 69, wing.)

♂. ♀.   Antennæ black, or black and yellow: wings uniformly
subinfuscated.   Length 12 mm.

Antennæ in the male black, the proximal three or four joints
yellow, about as long as the front femora; in the female, yellow,
with the proximal end of the sixth and following joints black, and
only about as long as the mesonotum.   Thorax light yellow, the
mesonotum brownish.   Front, rostrum and palpi yellow, the last a
little brownish at the tip.   Halteres brown.   Abdomen reddish-
yellow, the lateral margins of all the segments, a part of the sixth
segment, and all of the seventh, black (in the female specimen the
abdomen is wanting).   Legs yellow, the tip of the tibiæ, and the
tarsi for the greater part, black.   Wings uniformly tinged with
brown, the costal cell and the stigma pale brown.

I can find no description which will apply to this
species, though that of *T. infuscata*, Loew, will nearly
do so.   The colour of the antennæ in the female will at
once distinguish the two.

Pachyrrhina.

Macquart, Hist. Nat. Dipt., i., 88, 1834.

1. *Pachyrrhina elegantula*, n. sp.   (Pl. X., fig. 70, wing.)

♀.   Stripes of the mesonotum brownish red, lateral margins
with three opaque black spots.   Length 14 mm.

Front and rostrum light opaque orange-yellow, the former with an angular spot posteriorly, not continued into a stripe, subshining bluish. Antennæ yellow, the terminal joints brownish. Pronotum light opaque yellow in the middle, black on the sides; mesonotum opaque yellow, with light brownish-red, shining stripes; the lateral ones curve strongly outward in front, and terminating in an opaque black spot; a similar spot just back and below these, and a third velvety black spot immediately above the root of the wings, extending narrowly into the suture. Scutellum shining brownish-red. Metanotum yellow, with a stripe of the colour of the scutellum, expanded triangularly behind. Pleuræ light sulphur-yellow, with shining reddish spots. Abdomen light opaque orange-yellow; the first four or five segments with inconspicuous brownish bands. Knob of halteres brown. Coxæ, femora, and tibiæ yellow, the two latter black at the tip; tarsi black, the proximal joints somewhat yellowish. Wings with a brownish-yellowish tinge; costal cell yellow; stigma pale brown.

♂. Antennæ darker, the basal three or four joints yellow. Markings of thorax; abdomen and legs somewhat darker.

One male and two females. The species seems nearest allied to *P. consularis*, O. S., but will be at once distinguished by the colour of the thoracic stripes and the additional black spots.

POLYMERA.

Wiedemann, Auss., Zw. Ins., i., 57, 1828.

1. *Polymera albitarsis*, n. sp. (Pl. X., figs. 71, part of antenna ♂; 71*a*, antenna ♀; 71*b*, wing.)

♂, ♀. Front, pa'pi and rostrum brown. Antennæ brown, the basal joints yellowish. Thorax brownish-yellow, the pleuræ in the middle blackish. Abdomen dark brown. Legs luteous, the base of the femora yellow; tarsi white, except the metatarsi of the two anterior pairs, the proximal end of the second joint of the same pairs, and of the metatarsi of the hind pair, which are brown. Wings distinctly tinged with brownish. Length 6-7 mm.

Four specimens. Hitherto, only South American species of this genus have been made known, from which the present species seems distinct. The male antennæ were originally described as having twenty-eight joints, and the true number, sixteen, was not known till specimens were examined by Loew. The joints in this sex are very closely united, and it is only by close examination that the number can be made out. From *P. fusca*, Wiedemann, and *P. obscura*, Macquart, which seems to be a distinct species, the present appears to be so closely allied, that the short descriptions will hardly distinguish them. However, Wiedemann figures the female antennæ as elongate, like those of the males, but with simple, not constricted joints. In the present species, the female antennæ are short, in fact not longer than the thorax, and are of the ordinary Tipulid structure; that is, the joints are oval, slightly hairy, and are easily distinguishable. The first joint is not cylindrical, and is not provided with short, closely-set hairs, as is described. The figure given by Macquart shows short and abundant hairs on the swellings of the male antennæ, very different from the long, delicate hairs of the present species.

Species Incertæ Sedis.

Two species of *Tipulidæ*, represented by single, more or less mutilated specimens, I cannot locate. I give figures herewith, which will, I believe, render the identification not doubtful. One of them (Pl. X., figs. 72 and 72*a*) possibly represents a new genus. The tip of the antennæ is broken off, otherwise the specimen is complete. If the antennæ are but 14-jointed, the species would be located in *Rhipidia*, from which, however, the structure of the male organs show distinct differences, and the antennæ are hardly sufficiently pectinated. If there are sixteen joints, Schiner's and Osten Sacken's tables will carry the species to *Antocha*. This genus and *Thaumastoptera* are almost the only ones in this group which I do not know. Still, the neuration is sufficiently distinct to render its location with *Antocha* practically out of the question.

DIXIDÆ.

DIXA.

Meigen, Syst. Beschr., i., 216, 1818.

1. *Dixa claculus*, n. sp.   (Pl. X., fig. 73, wing.)

♂. Head black, lightly greyish-pruinose; palpi and rostrum a little reddish. Antennæ black, the basal joints somewhat reddish. Thorax yellow, the mesonotum with three dark-brown stripes, the median one abbreviated posteriorly, and divided by a slender line; the lateral ones begin a little before the termination of the median one. Scutellum and mesonotum brownish-yellow. Abdomen dark-brown. Legs brown or yellowish brown; the tip of the hind tibiæ and their tarsi blackish; the femora, for the greater part, yellowish; hind tibiæ thickened at the tip. Length of body 2 mm., of wings 3 mm.

Four specimens. This species must be closely allied to *D. clavata*, Loew, from Massachusetts, and I was, at first, inclined to identify it with it. · It differs from the description, however, in several important points. The pleuræ are immaculate yellowish, the legs are darker coloured, and the wings are uniformly tinged with brownish, not hyaline, with markings.

RHYPHIDÆ.

RHYPHUS.

Latreille, Nat. Hist., etc., xiv., 291, 1804.

1. *Rhyphus dolorosus*, n. sp.   (Pl. X., fig. 74, wing.)

♀. Front and occiput black, somewhat greyish-pruinose. Mesonotum yellow with three brown stripes; wings broadly clouded on the distal and posterior margin, with two conspicuous brown spots in front, and narrow brown clouds on the cross-veins. Length of body 4 mm., of the wings 5 mm.

F.o it a little narrower below, the ocelli situated wholly in front of a line drawn through the angles of the eyes. Face more yellowish. Eyes reaching to the oral margin below. Palpi and proboscis black. Antennæ black, the two basal joints yellowish. Mesonotum opaque yellow with three brown or brownish-red stripes, the middle one abbreviated posteriorly the lateral ones in front ; bristles very short, hair-like. Pleuræ yellow, with obscure brownish spots. Metanotum and halteres yellow. Abdomen deep brown or black, the basal segments with obscure yellow markings. Legs yellow ; the tip of hind femora and tibiæ, and the distal joints of all the tarsi brown or blackish. Wings broadly clouded with brown at the tip and along the posterior margin, the inner portion subhyaline ; two dark-brown spots in the marginal cell, separated by a yellow spot : costal cell yellowish ; the cross-veins with narrow, dark-brown clouds.

One specimen. Allied to *R. fenestralis*, but differs in tl e abdomen and wings.

STRATIOMYIDÆ.

SARGUS.

Fabricius, Ent. Syst. Suppl., 566, 1798.

1. *Sargus lucens.*

Sargus lucens, Loew, Centur., vii., 11.—Cuba.

Six specimens.

HERMETIA.

Latreille, Hist. Nat. des Crust. et Ins., xiv., 338, 1804.

1. *Hermetia illucens.*

Musca illucens, Linné, Syst. Nat., ii., 979. (For remaining synonymy, see Osten Sacken, Cat. 46,
and Williston, Trans. Amer. Ent. Soc. xv., 245.)

Hab. Southern United States ; Mexico ; Brazil ; West Indies.

Eight specimens. Quite like others from the United States and Brazil.

PELAGOMYIA.

Williston, Manual. N. A. Diptera, 48, 1896.

1. *Pelagomyia albitalus,* n. sp. (Pl. X., fig. 75, head of ♂.)

♂. Front and face deep shining green, with long and abundant, erect black hair. Eyes thickly pilose. Antennæ black ; second joint a little shorter than the first, the third joint about twice the length of the first two together, gradually tapering, the annuli closely set together ; style distinctly differentiated, and extending at an angle with the third joint ; its first joint small ; second joint thickened, spindle-shaped, finely and densely hairy, terminating in a slender bristle about as long as the thickened portion of the style ; altogether, the style is shorter than the third antennal joint. Thorax shining metallic, deep green, with blue reflections and erect black pile. Abdomen elongated, of equal width, black or brownish black, the second, third, and fourth segments with a narrow posterior margin of golden or silvery pubescence, forming an interrupted band. Femora black ; tibiæ light yellow with a broad brown ring beyond the middle ; the hind pair with the distal two-thirds brown ; tarsi light yellow or yellowish-white, the distal three joints of the four anterior ones, the tip of the meta-tarsi, and the remaining joints brown or brownish. Wings hyaline on the basal anterior portion ; clouded behind, and blackish on the outer half. Length 9 mm.

Two males and one female. The female differs in being of a larger size (12 mm.) in the absence of metallic coloration, in the more reddish-brown colour of the abdomen, and in the lighter coloured wings. It may be an immature specimen. I at first identified this genus as *Chromatopoda*, Brauer, but it will be at once distin-guished by the structure of the second antennal joint.

AOCHLETUS.

Osten Sacken, Biol. Centr. Amer. Dipt., 38, i., 1883.

♂. Holoptic, the upper eye-facets moderately enlarged and sharply distinguished from those of the lower portion. Antennæ situated a little below the middle of the eyes in profile, shorter than the head ; annuli of the third joint closely united, the first one small and short, the sixth elongate and with several minute bristles at the tip. Scutellum with two slender spines. Abdomen slender, composed of five segments. Veins of the wings on the outer posterior part weak or evanescent, the beginning of the second and fourth ones arising from the discal cell apparent, the first and third only faintly indicated by folds.

1. *Aochletus bistriatus*, n. sp. (Pl. X., fig. 76, antenna.)

♂. Face black, moderately shining ; on either side silvery pubescent. Antennæ black ; the first and second joints, for the greater part, reddish. Mesonotum black, moderately shining ;

finely pubescent; with two yellow stripes, acuminate in front, and connected with the yellow post-alar callosities behind. Scutellum wholly yellow. Pleuræ yellow, the mesosternum black. Abdomen black or dark-brown, with a red band across each of the three anterior segments. Legs yellow, the tarsi infuscated toward the tip. Wings hyaline. Length 5 mm.

One specimen. 1500 feet.

Cyphomyia.

Wiedemann, Zool. Mag., i., 3, 55, 1819.

1. *Cyphomyia lasiophthalma*, n. sp.

♂. Eyes markedly pilose. The small vertical triangle black; frontal triangle and face shining metallic black, densely clothed with white pile, intermixed with black hairs. Antennæ black, the base of the third joint red. The narrow inferior occipital orbits white pubescent. Mesonotum shining violet-black, with three stripes of white pubescence, and with long, erect, black pile. Scutellum like the mesonotum, with long black pile and white pubescence; spines as long as the scutellum, somewhat divergent, reddish at the distal end, and clothed with black pile. Pleuræ with white pile. Tegulæ yellow. Abdomen shining metallic blue, with erect black pile, and four sharply marked, white pubescent spots. Legs black; the knees and base of hind metatarsi reddish; four anterior metatarsi, except their tip, light yellow. Wings nearly hyaline.

♀. Antennæ a little longer, the third joint about equal to half the width of the head. Front and face shining blue-black, clothed with close-lying, nearly white pile, the face nearly bare in the middle. Occipital orbits a little broader than in the male, white pubescent. Pile of mesonotum and scutellum dusky, that on the spines white; the spines are wholly of the colour of the mesonotum, and are shorter than in the male. Abdomen, as usual, with six spots. Length 7 mm.

Two specimens. 1500 feet. The species is allied to *C. marginata*, Loew, one of the few known species with long-pilose eyes. The front of the female is narrow and without elevations of any kind.

CHORDONOTA.

Gerstæcker, Linn. Ent., xi., 311, 1857.

1. *Chordonota leiophthalma*, n. sp.

♂. Eyes bare, closely contiguous, the upper part with the facets markedly enlarged, those of the lower half small, the two sets separated by a distinct line. Occiput concave, wholly invisible from the side. Ocellar triangle small, black: frontal triangle small, silvery, the silvery pubescence extending a little way along the facial orbit. Antennæ red, the upper margin and the distal portion of the third joint black. Mesonotum black, with a strong purple reflection, beneath the short, dense, black pubescence; two narrow, silvery, or light golden, pubescent stripes on each side, and an indication of a fifth in the middle. Scutellum like the mesonotum and with silvery pubescence near its margin. Pleuræ black. Abdomen shining metallic blue or purple, the fourth and fifth segments each with a spot of silvery pubescence on each side. Legs black, the metatarsi a little reddish. Wings tinged with blackish, the stigma luteous. Length 7 mm.

Two specimens. This species, structurally and in appearance, resembles *C. nigra*, Willist., but will be at once distinguished by the bare eyes, distinctly vittate mesonotum, and shorter pile.

SPECIES INCERTÆ SEDIS.

A small species, represented by a fragment only, belonging among the Pachygastrinæ, perhaps to *Pachygaster*.

TABANIDÆ.

TABANUS.

Linné, Fauna Suecica, 1761.

1. *Tabanus alcis*, n. sp. (Pl. X., fig. 77, antenna.)

♀. Brown; wings with brown spots; upper angle of the third antennal joint drawn out into a long process. Length 13–14 mm.

Eyes bare; no ocellar tubercle. Front narrow, cinnamon-brown; callus very small, shining red. Antennæ yellow, with black hairs; slender; the upper process of the third joint drawn out into a long process, the annulate portion slender, and curved. Face of the colour of the front, bare. Palpi yellow, with black hairs. Mesonotum cinnamon-brown, or darker brown, with two slender yellowish stripes. Pleuræ more whitish. Abdomen brown; on the sides in front yellow; the segments with a median, posterior triangle of light golden hair, which extends outward, forming a narrow hind border. Legs reddish or brownish-yellow. Wings subhyaline, the anterior part to the tip of the second vein luteous; the distal costal portion and the posterior margin clouded with blackish; a large spot covering the cross-veins at the outer part of the discal cell, and extending into the first posterior cell, and another large one on the furcation of the third vein, reaching to the costa, brown.

Three specimens. It is not impossible that this is the same as *T. parallelus*, Walker.

2. *Tabanus*, sp. (Pl. X., fig. 78, antenna.)

♂. Frontal triangle yellow; face brownish-red, thickly grey pollinose; palpi light yellow; all clothed with white hair. Antennæ yellow; third joint angular above, but not drawn out into a process. Mesonotum black, not shining, greyish pollinose, and with yellowish-white pile; pleuræ ochraceous yellow, with white pile. Abdomen brownish-red and brown, opaque; the segments with a narrow, light yellow, hind border. Legs yellow; tarsi infuscated distally. Wings hyaline; the furcation of the third vein with a stump. Eyes bare; no ocelli. Length 10 mm.

One specimen.

LEPTIDÆ.

CHRYSOPILA.

Macquart, Dipt. du Nord de la France, 1827.

1. *Chrysopila ludens.*

Chrysopila ludens, Loew, Wien. Entom. Monatschr., v., 34.

Hab. Cuba (Loew).

Six specimens agree sufficiently well with the description of this species. In those that are well preserved, there is a golden pubescence on the abdomen, and the hind femora may be in large part black. With these specimens, there are several others in which the thorax is yellow, with the mesonotum brownish. The abdomen, in all the specimens, is in large part black.

2. *Chrysopila atra*, n. sp. (Pl. X., fig. 78*bis*, wing.)

♂. Deep black; wings hyaline, with two dark-brown spots on the costal margin. Length 5 mm.

Deep black throughout, with black pile. Face cinereous pruinose. Mesonotum and abdomen opaque velvety. Wings hyaline, the apical third in front clouded; the stigma, a spot across from the costa to the second vein on the distal part of the auxiliary vein, and a cloud on the humeral cross-vein, dark-brown.

One specimen.

ASILIDÆ.

OMMATIUS.

Wiedemann, Auss. Zw. Ins., i., 418, 1828.

1. *Ommatius marginellus.*

Ommatius marginellus (Fabricius), Wiedemann, Auss. Zw. Ins., i., 421; Dipt. Exot., i., 223, pl. vi., fig. 5; Macquart, Dipt. Exot., i., 2, 134; Schiner, Verh. zool. bot. Gesellsch, 1866, 682.

? *Ommatius tibialis*, Say, Journ. Acad. Phil., iii., 49; Compl. Wr., ii., 63; Wiedemann, Auss. Zw. Ins., i., 422; Williston, Trans. Amer. Ent. Soc. xi., Pl. ii., fig. 12 and xii., 76.

Ommatius Saccas, Walker, List, ii., 474.

Ommatius vitreus, Bigot, Ann. Soc. Ent. Fr., 245, 1875.

Hab. West Indies; South America; ? North America.

Thirty specimens. The only difference which these specimens present from others, both male and female, from Brazil, are the yellow bristles of the hind femora. Others in my collection from San Domingo agree in this respect with the Brazilian ones. That all are of the same species, I have no doubt. That *O. tibialis* is the same species, I am not so confident. The distinctive characters pointed out by Schiner, though I do not think that they are of much importance, are present in North American specimens. The posterior part of the mesonotum and the scutellum also seem to be more hairy in *O. tibialis*. In all the specimens, the colour of the legs varies much. There are no structural differences in any of the specimens, and, in some of the San Dominican specimens, the colour of the bristles of the hind femora varies. Taking the above facts into consideration, I believe that all the names above given, and probably others, represent a single species of wide distribution. *O. tibialis* occurs through all of the Eastern United States, as far as the Rocky Mountains.

ERAX.

Macquart, Dipt. Exot., i., 2, 107, 1838.

1. *Erax rufitibia.* (Pl. X., fig. 79, wing.)

Erax rufitibia, Macquart, Dipt. Exot., 3rd Suppl., 27. Pl. ii., fig. 11 ; Walker, List, vii., 623 ; Roeder, Stett. Ent. Zeit., 339, 1885.

Hab. Brazil ; San Domingo ; Porto Rico.

♂. Front and face light yellowish-grey ; gibbosity of the face with numerous black bristles and yellowish-white hairs. Mesonotum grey, with three broad black stripes, narrowly separated, the lateral ones narrowly divided into three spots, the hindmost one of which is small ; the middle one with an indication of a middle stripe in front. Abdomen black, not shining ; hair yellow, sparse and reclining, save on the anterior two segments ; lateral margins opaque light-grey ; sixth and seventh segments silvery ; hypopygium large, black. Wings with the costal border thickened ; furcation of third vein beyond the base of the second posterior cell. Legs black ; tibiæ except the tip, red. Length 18-20 mm.

Two males and three females, the latter showing scarcely any differences, save the usual sexual ones.

LEPTOGASTER.

Meigen, Illiger's Mag., 1803.

1. *Leptogaster roederi*, n. sp. (Pl. XI., fig. 80, wing.)

♂, ♀. Antennæ yellow, with the distal half of the third joint black ; wings blackish at the tip. Length 8-9 mm.

Front brown. Face and mystax yellow. First two antennal joints and the base of the third yellow ; remainder of the third joint and the arista black ; third joint a little shorter than the first two together, the arista a little longer than the three joints together. Mesonotum shining, dark pitchy, a little more yellowish on each side in front; on the posterior part subopaque ; sides lightly pollinose. Pleuræ brown and yellowish, light yellow pollinose. Abdomen black or brown, the posterior margin of each segment whitish, the hind angles reddish. Coxæ light yellow ; femora black or brown, with the base and a preapical ring red or yellow ; anterior tibiæ yellowish, with the distal part yellow ; hind tibiæ black or deep brown, with the proximal part yellow ; anterior tarsi yellow ; hind tarsi black. Wings pure hyaline, with the tip blackish. Empodium about half the length of the claws. Occiput without bristles.

Two specimens. In one the colours throughout are not so deep, and the tip of the wing is cinereous.

HOLCOCEPHALA.

Jœnnicke, Abhandl. Senckenb. Gesellsch, vi., 1867.

Two male specimens of a species related to *H. calva,* Loew, but with the legs nearly black, and the abdomen not clavate.

BOMBYLIIDÆ.

GERON.

Meigen, Syst. Beschr., ii., 223, 1820.

1. *Geron senilis.* (Pl. XI., fig. 81, antenna.)

Geron senilis, Fabricius, Ent. Syst., iv., 411; Syst. Antl., 135, *Bombylius* ; Wiedemann, Auss. Zw. Ins., i., 357 ; Macquart, Dipt. Exot., Suppl., i., 119.

Hab. West Indies ; Texas.

One male specimen, agreeing very well with Wiedemann's description.

THEREVIDÆ.

PSILOCEPHALA.

Zetterstedt, Ins. Lapp., 525, 1840.

1. *Psilocephala argentata.* (Pl. XI., fig. 82, antenna.)

? *Thereva argentata,* Bellardi, Saggio, ii., 90 ; Roeder, Stett. Ent. Zeit., 1885, 340.—Mexico, Porto Rico.

♂. Black ; abdomen silvery white, except a large spot on the anterior angles. Length 6-8 mm.

Frontal triangle shining black, its inferior corners and the face opaque silvery. Antennæ black ; third joint on the inner, basal portion yellowish. Checks, immediately below the eyes, shining black, with black pile. Beard white ; occiput silvery grey. Mesonotum with dusky yellowish pile, and black bristles ; on the sides, shining black ; in the middle, with two broad, narrowly separated, opaque, olivaceous grey stripes ; a narrow stripe between the two, brown. Scutellum shining black, its apical margin opaque grey, and with four bristles. Pleuræ opaque greyish-white, with white hair. Halteres brown. Abdomen silvery white, when viewed from above ; the brown or black ground-colour predominant, when seen from behind ; the first segment in the middle, and a large spot on the anterior angles of the following segments, extending nearly to the posterior margin, black. Legs, for the greater part, sordid yellow ; femora black ; the tip or distal portion of the tibiæ, and the distal joints of all the tarsi, blackish. Wings nearly hyaline ; stigma elongate.

Four specimens.   Seashore.

EMPIDIDÆ.

Hybos.

Meigen, Illiger's Mag., ii., 1803.

1. *Hybos dimidiatus.*   (Pl. XI., fig. 83, wing.)

? *Hybos dimidiatus*, Loew, Wien. Entom. Monatschr., iv., 36 (*nec* Bellardi).

Hab.   Cuba.

There are, in the collection, some twelve or more specimens, which I refer very doubtfully to this species. In the most typical, the chief differences from the description are : The presence of black hairs on the thorax, the darker colour of the front femora, and the light-brown colour of the basal portion of the wings. The distal portion of the wings is not hyaline, or even cinereo-hyaline, but is distinctly infuscated. In some of the specimens the wings are nearly uniform in colour throughout.

SYNECHES.

Walker, Dipt. Saunders, 165, 1856.

1. *Syneches pusillus.*   (Pl. XI., fig. 84, wing.)

Syneches pusillus, Loew, Centur., i., 25.

Hab. Illinois, New York.

Two specimens agree with this description. I have no specimens from the United States for comparison.

DRAPETIS.

Meigen, Syst. Beschr., iii., 1822.

1. *Drapetis xanthopodus,* n. sp.   (Pl. XI., figs. 85, antenna; 85a, wing.)

♂, ♀. Deep shining black; legs yellow; first posterior cell a little narrowed at the extremity. Length 2-2½ mm.

Antennæ, front and proboscis black; eyes contiguous below the antennæ; front very narrow or subcontiguous in both sexes. Occiput black, with black pile. Thorax and abdomen shining black, the mesonotum a little metallic; pile short, dusky. Legs, including the coxæ, yellow, the tarsi more or less infuscated: hind metatarsi brown or brownish; elongate and somewhat thickened; hind tibiæ with a short terminal spur; all the femora stout. Wings cinereous hyaline; third and fourth veins gently convergent near the margin.

Ten specimens.

2. *Drapetis flavidus,* n. sp.   (Pl. XI., figs. 86, antenna; 86a, wing.)

♂, ♀. Yellow or reddish-yellow; head and the fourth abdominal segment black. Length 2-2½ mm.

Occiput, vertical triangle and front black. Eyes contiguous below the antennæ, subcontiguous above. Antennæ yellow, the third joint sometimes brownish. Thorax reddish-yellow, the mesonotum shining, with light-coloured hair and bristles. Abdomen yellow, opaque, the fourth segment and the hair black. Legs light yellow, with light-coloured hair and bristles: hind tibiæ in the male with a stout curved spur at the tip; hind femora less thickened than the middle ones; the front pair considerably thickened. Wings hyaline; the outer portions of the third and fourth veins parallel or very slightly divergent.

Numerous specimens.

DOLICHOPODIDÆ.*

Of this family, the collection contains forty-six species, of which five only can be recognized as previously described. The study of so much material throws an interesting light on the geographical distribution of the genera. The entire absence of *Dolichopus*, of which the continent of North America contains nearly a hundred species, strongly emphasizes the fact that the genus is limited to the temperate and colder regions. On the other hand, more than half of the species in the present collection belong to the group which may be termed the *Chrysotinæ*, embracing *Chrysotus*, *Diaphorus*, and several smaller genera, while this group is represented on the continent by a considerably smaller proportion.

The discovery of a second species of the peculiar genus *Polymedon*, having identically the same habits as the Californian species, is a matter of great interest.

In the description of new species, the aim has been to give a careful review of the generic as well as specific characters in those not infrequent cases where there was possibility of an erroneous generic determination. The genera of *Dolichopodidæ* are, at least in part, in need of thorough revision, and several new ones must yet be erected for North American forms. Unwilling to undertake what should be the work of a more experienced hand, I have avoided, as far as possible, the establishment of new genera in the present article.

I am under the greatest obligation to Professor Williston, not only for the privilege of undertaking this work, but for the use of books and other valuable assistance.

GYMNOPTERNUS,

Loew, Neue Beitr., v., 1857.

1. *Gymnopternus ruficornis*, n. sp.

♂. Face of moderate width, white pollinose ; front blue-green, with white dust below ; cilia of inferior orbit white. Antennæ red, short, apex of third joint infuscated, the dorsal arista slightly pubescent. Thoracic dorsum bright green ; a blackish-bronze

---

° By Professor J. M. Aldrich.

stripe above the base of each wing, before and below this a spot with a silvery reflection when viewed from above ; pleuræ dark green, in part black, with grey dust. Cilia of tegulæ black, halteres yellow. Abdomen bright green above, the sides below white-dusted, the hairs everywhere black and rather coarse ; at the tip of the abdomen are two bristles, as long as two segments ; hypopygium blackish-green, the lamellæ rounde l, yellow, with pale brown margin fringed with yellow bristles. Fore and hind coxæ yellow, the former with very long black bristles and black hairs, the latter with a large and a smaller lateral bristle close together ; middle coxæ brown on the basal half ; femora and tibiæ light yellow, the fore tibiæ with a row of irregular but distinct bristles on the front side ; the fore tarsi are pale to the extreme tip ; middle and hind tibiæ with erect and conspicuous bristles ; they are gradually infuscated from tip of first joint. Wings rather narrow, hyaline, the fourth vein converging towards the third, toward the tip close to, and nearly parallel with it.

♀. Face nearly twice as wide, white ; no long bristles at tip of abdomen ; otherwise substantially like the male.

Length 1·6 mm.; of wing, the same.

One male, one female.

PŒCILOBOTHRUS.

Mik. Dipt. Untersuch., 1878.

1. *Pœcilobothrus unguiculatus,* n. sp.   (Pl. XI., fig. 101, last joint of ♂, front tarsus.   Pl. XII., fig. 116, tip of wing.)

♂. Face very wide, below the suture with two lateral convexities separated by a narrow groove ; colour dark brownish-green, with dense brown pollen, which appears lighter in certain directions. Palpi brown, with yellow tips ; proboscis large, blackish. Front concave, shining violet in the middle, about the edges blackish. Antennæ brownish-black, the under part a little reddish ; third joint ovate, a little pointed in an upward direction ; arista nearly basal, short, distinctly feathered. Cilia of the inferior orbit white. Thorax bronze-green, not very shining ; acrostichal bristles in two rows ; the two rows of interior dorsal bristles (Mik) are inserted upon slender longitudinal shining blue lines, expanded posteriorly. The posterior margin of the dorsum is in the form of a thin projection, running around from the root of one wing to that of the other ; above this the surface is considerably dusted. Scutellum bare, coppery. Pleuræ greenish, with white pollen.

Cilia of tegula black. Tegulæ and halteres deep yellow. Abdomen olivaceous, slightly shining, on the sides shining green, and ventrally white pollinose. Hypopygium free and rather large, but sessile ; colour black, a little dusted on the sides, the lamellæ are brown, yellowish at base, rather long and narrow, with rounded corners and a fringe of long black bristles all the way around except basally. All the coxæ brown, their tips yellow ; femora yellow, tibiæ brownish-yellow, the hind knees brown. Tips of front tibiæ light yellow ; first joint of fore tarsus of the same colour for two-thirds of its length, the remainder of the tarsus brownish-black. The joints beyond the first are short, and all are somewhat thickened ; the last is rather long, and bears a little prominence on the underside near the base ; the claw on the inner side is greatly enlarged, and bends back across this prominence as a straight spine, forming a grasping organ ; beyond this its point curves laterally, the other claw and the pulvilli are nearly normal, but the latter are inserted a little toward the side instead of exactly at the end ; the other tarsi normal, brownish-black beyond the first joint, which is short in the hind foot. Middle and hind tibiæ a little infuscated at the tip. Wings a little brownish, more so along the veins, costa a little thickened in its first part ; the fourth vein makes a gradual curve forward throughout its last section, the convexity behind (see figure).

♀. Face wider and more prominent, the two convexities uniting below. Pollen more greyish. Palpi larger. Antennæ more yellowish below. Front tibiæ yellow with brownish tip, their tarsi simple, coloured like the others. Costa very much thickened before the end of the first vein. In one of my females each posterior cross-vein has a short stump on the exterior side near the middle.

Length 4–4·5 mm. ; of wing, 4 mm.

Four males and four females. May.

HERCOSTOMUS.

Loew, Neue Beitr., v., 1857.

1. *Hercostomus latipes*, n. sp. (Pl. XII., fig. 111, tip of wing.)

♂. Face very narrow in the middle, above and below a little wider, with a median groove almost the whole length ; in colour yellowish-brown, with thick silvery pollen. Palpi and proboscis yellow or a little brownish. Front shining green. Antennæ red ; third joint brown, oval, slightly pointed, with a dorsal, moderately pubescent arista. Cilia of inferior orbit white. Thorax shining green, sometimes coppery, more so along the front margin. Small humeral bristles (Mik) numerous. Viewed from above, there is a silvery pollinose spot behind the humerus, and another behind the root of the wing. Scutellum coppery. Pleuræ mixed light and dark green, white-dusted. Tegulæ yellow, their cilia black. Abdomen coppery, on the sides more green, and ventrally somewhat white-dusted. Hypopygium large and long, yet scarcely pedunculated; the lamellæ proper are very small, yellow; the outer basal portion of each gives rise to a stout claw, twice as long as the lamella itself, black except a little at base, and curving upward toward the venter. A row of black bristles runs along the outer side of the claw two-thirds of the distance to the tip. Coxæ, legs, and feet wholly yellow, the last gradually infuscated toward the end. The fore coxæ have three large bristles, numerous black hairs, and a few smaller bristles. Middle coxæ with hair and bristles. Hind coxæ with the usual bristle. Fore tarsi widened from near the tip of the first joint, the under surface destitute of the customary black hair, therefore resembling a broad yellow sole. All the joints beyond the first are shorter than usual. Hind metatarsi shorter than following joint. Wings subhyaline, of slender outline. Fourth vein converging with the third in its last section, less so near the tip, ending distinctly before the apex. Posterior cross-vein at right angles to the long axis of the wing.

♀. Face wider, less narrowed in the middle, without groove; but little white pollinose, except on the prominent lower part, the remainder more greenish or brownish. Palpi a little larger, each with a minute bristle as well as fine hairs. The black spot overlying the transverse suture on each side of the thorax is very large, rather more so than the male. In one immature specimen the coppery colour is but little noticeable, leaving the abdomen and scutellum almost pure green.

Length 3-3½ mm.; of wing, 2¼ mm.

Seven males and five females. 500–1500 altitude.

PELASTONEURUS.

Loew, Neue Beitr., viii., 1861.

1. *Pelastoneurus lineatus*, n. sp.

♂. Front of moderate width, deep blue-green, shining. Face narrow in the middle, wider above and below, the ground colour brown, white pollinose. Palpi brownish-yellow, but little visible. Antennæ red, the first two joints short, the third large, oval, the apical half brown ; arista dorsal, black, short, curved, distinctly feathered with sparse hairs. Cilia of inferior orbit white. Thorax shining green, with a bronze median line extending to the scutellum : anteriorly this line is enclosed by the acrostichal bristles ; the small humeral bristles occupy a large area. The usual black colour accompanies the transverse suture on its upper side. In the proper light there is a silvery pollinose spot behind the humerus, another above the root of the wing, and a third behind it. Pleuræ blackish-green, white-dusted. Cilia of tegulæ black. Abdomen shining green, the sides of each segment silvery pollinose ; each incisure is covered with a broad black band. Hypopygium black, exserted, the peduncle nearly as long as a segment of the abdomen ; lamellæ small, dark-brown, with slender cilia, and on the upper side a row of equal short spines. Front coxæ yellow ; middle ones brown, except the tips ; hind ones yellow, with brown base. The front and middle ones have numerous black hairs ; the former have several bristles, the latter only one of any size ; hind coxæ with a single lateral bristle. Femora and tibiæ yellow ; the middle femora with a row of delicate, short, light-coloured cilia below. Middle and hind femora with preapical bristle. Tarsi yellow, the middle and hind ones infuscated toward the tip. Fore pulvilli enlarged ; hind metatarsi shortened. Wings slightly infuscated ; the last section of the fourth vein bends gently forward, runs nearly straight for a distance, then is gradually recurved, ending near the third, which bends back at tip.

♀. Face wider and more yellowish ; palpi and proboscis larger, yellow ; third joint of antennæ smaller, scarcely infuscated ; dorsal stripe wider ; pulvilli normal ; middle femora without cilia.

Length 4 mm. ; of wing, 3·8.

Twelve males, five females. Sea level to 1500 feet. May.

2. *Pelastoneurus argentiferus*, n. sp.

♂. Face wide, concave to the suture, convex below, the concave portion shining green, except that the sides and lower part are somewhat silvery pollinose ; this pollen covers the convex part. Palpi a little more yellowish. Front violet-green, scarcely shining. Antennæ blackish, the lower side reddish to a variable degree. Third joint short when fully developed, in some specimens shrivelled. Arista plumose, short, thick at base, rapidly tapering. Cilia of inferior orbit whitish. Thorax dark green, but little shining, acrostichal bristles in two rows, enclosing an area which is opaque as far as the middle. On each side of this, reaching to the inner dorsal bristles, is a more shining dark-blue area changing to violet posteriorly, and also spreading wider, so that most of the posterior half of the dorsum is deep violet. Viewing the specimen from above and behind, the light striking it from above and in front, four silver spots are visible—two just below the transverse suture, and behind the humeri, the others above and behind the roots of the wings. Scutellum bronze-green. Pleuræ green, white-dusted, tegulæ light-yellow, their cilia black. Abdomen bronze-green above, brighter green on the sides, below the middle of the sides white pollinose. Sixth segment entirely silvery pollinose, rather thin dorsally. Hypopygium large, blackish-green, considerably dusted, sessile, the lamellæ developed into rather long upcurved black processes, irregular in outline and with numerous black bristles of different sizes ; at the base of each of these processes, below (dorsad) is a minute, yellowish, yellow-haired appendix, —this I take to be the true lamella, homologous with that organ in *Dolichopus*, while the process just described is a development from its upper basal corner, as occurs in some other species of the family. Fore coxæ yellow, at the base very slightly infuscated, with black hairs and bristles, middle and hind coxæ brownish-black, rather largely yellow at apex. Femora and tibiæ all yellow, the middle and hind knees very slightly infuscated, middle tibiæ slightly, the hind ones strongly infuscated at tip. Front tarsi only slightly and gradually infuscated, middle ones from tip of first joint, hind ones entirely, black. Wings brownish, the fourth vein bent forward in a very gentle curve and afterward nearly straight, ending close to the third before the apex.

♀. Face wider, in the middle somewhat brownish ; palpi larger. Front blackish-brown, silver spots on thorax smaller, but still distinct. Abdomen somewhat coppery, often less bronze. Hind tibiæ less black at the tip.

Length 3·5 mm. ; of wing, 3 mm.

Eleven males and five females. May, September ; one specimen marked "Near sea by open stream."

PARACLIUS.

Bigot, Ann. Soc. Ent. Fr., 1859, p. 215.

1. *Paraclius filiferus*, n. sp. (Pl. XI., fig. 102, tip of wing.)

♂. Front of medium width, white pollinose on a green background. Palpi brownish-yellow, the extreme tips only visible, front rather wider than long, green, shining, with a violet reflection. Antennæ red; the third joint moderately large, ovate, with a blunt point, brown at the apex. Arista short, black, with moderate pubescence. Cilia of inferior orbit white. Thorax metallic-green. Acrostichal bristles rather large, in two rows, between which the colour is more coppery. A large area of small humeral bristles; on this area the colour is also somewhat coppery, and whitish dusted. Scutellum coppery. Pleuræ green, white-pollinose. Abdomen shining green, the posterior margins of the segments darker, lateral parts white-pollinose. Hypopygium large, exserted but sessile, the main part greenish-black coloured with light dust. Lamellæ yellow, brownish and rather pointed in front, with slender bristles; the upper basal corner is drawn out into a long hairy filament. All the coxæ, femora, and tibiæ red; middle coxæ with a lateral basal brown spot. Fore and middle coxæ with numerous black hairs and bristles. Lateral bristle of hind coxæ small. Middle and hind femora with a preapical bristle. Middle and hind tibiæ with large bristles arising from an outer glabrous stripe; their tarsi infuscated from tip of first joint. Hind metatarsus short. Wings a little brownish along the costal portion; venation normal; the curve of the fourth vein is almost a right angle. Posterior cross-vein somewhat curved, the convexity outward. Length 3·5 mm.; of wing, 2·8 mm.

Numerous males and females. Sea-level to 500 feet. May, September.

The female differs in having a wider and less dusted face, and somewhat darker tarsi and middle coxæ.

LEPTOCORYPHA, n. gen.*

♂. Face not reaching down to inferior corner of eye. Antennæ large; first joint with hair on the upper side, on the inner apical side projecting in a short cone; second joint transverse, attached to the first, so as to make an angle toward the side; third joint large, arista dorsal. The lower part of the joint drawn out in a point with pile on the front and lower sides. Palpi small. Acrostichal bristles in two rows. At a little distance from these, along the anterior dorsal margin of the thorax, begins an area of minute, closely-set bristles, reaching to the humeri, forming a distinctly limited triangular space on each side. Scutellum with two large

---

* λεπτός, narrow; κορύφη, apex.

bristles and two small ones, its disk large. Abdomen short, for a male, tapering, the posterior margin of each segment, with a row of large bristles, which are longest on the last segment. Hypopygium disengaged, large, bent forward under the abdomen, the lamellæ rather small. Fore and middle coxæ with bristles and hair on the front side ; the hind ones with two bristles on the outer side. Middle and hind femora with a pre-apical bristle. Hind metatarsus without bristles above. Second and third longitudinal veins straight, moderately divergent ; fourth curving abruptly forward about the middle of its last segment, then gradually curving in the other direction, so that near the extremity it has a concavity behind, ending near the third vein. Posterior cross-vein a little more than its length from the margin.

1. *Leptocorypha pavo,* n. sp.   (Pl. XII., fig. 112, wing.)

♂. Bright, metallic-green. Front wide, bright-green, a little concave. Face moderately narrow, wider above, covered with a smooth coat of whitish pollen. Palpi but little visible, yellow, with only one or two very minute bristles. Cilia of the inferior orbit whitish, no long hairs behind them. Occiput flat. Antenna large, reddish, first joint hairy above, broad at the end, drawn out on the inner corner into a cone ; second joint transverse, hairy above ; third joint very large. Viewed from the side, the last on its proximal, lower corner runs back entirely past the second joint. It is very high, rounded above, the arista dorsal rather short and stout with long pubescence, the lower distal portion of the joint drawn out into a long up-curved point, densely short, pilose on the inner and lower side. It reaches about to the middle of the arista, and beyond its end the latter has longer pubescence than before it. This third joint in outline is similar to that of some species of *Tabanus.* Thorax very bright metallic-green, somewhat whitish-dusted about the front part. The triangular areas of fine bristles above mentioned are on a bronze ground colour. Transverse suture very far forward, a black spot along its upper side. Scutellum long, nearly rectangular on its disk. Pleuræ mostly black, dusted lightly with white, around the base of middle and hind coxæ more or less yellow. That thin fold of the integument which, in many species of this family, begins just above the hind coxæ and expands upward, so as to partially embrace the first abdominal segment, is strikingly conspicuous in my specimens of this species. Halteres and tegulæ yellow. Cilia of the latter black. Abdomen bright-green, a narrow line of black along the posterior border of each segment, numerous black hairs and a

posterior row of long bristles on each segment. The bristles of
the fifth segment are a little longer than the segment. The exserted
hypopygium is large, yellow throughout, except that the pedicel
is brownish at the base, and the lamellæ are bordered with brownish. Bristles of the latter yellow, comparatively weak.   Coxæ,
femora, and tibiæ all yellow. Tarsi yellow at base, uniformly a
little brownish toward the tip, on account of the covering of
minute dark hairs. Pulvilli of ordinary size. Venation of the
wings are in the description of the genus. Length 3·25 mm.; of
wing, 3 mm.

Two specimens. St. Vincent, West Indies. Altitude,
one 500 and one 1000 ft.

ANEPSIUS.

Loew, Neue Beitr., v., 1857.

1. *Anepsius linearis*, n. sp.

♂. Thoracic dorsum shining green. Abdomen yellow and
black. Legs yellow. Front very short, opaque, greyish. Face
white, long, so narrow as to be almost invisible, still the eyes in
well-preserved specimens are not contiguous ; just below the
antennæ the face widens. Antennæ brownish or yellowish, long ;
the first joint elongate, with a few hairs above ; the second and
third of about equal size, the latter with a blunt point directed a
little upward. Arista basal, bare, its first joint thick. Cilia of
the orbit apparently wanting in all my specimens. Thorax bright
green. Acrostichal bristles in two rows. Scutellum with one
large and one minute bristle on each side. Pleuræ non-metallic,
brown, toward the coxæ, and along the hind border yellowish.
Halteres yellow. Cilia of tegulæ blackish, one or two yellow.
Abdomen elongate, laterally compressed, black, non-metallic,
second, third, and fourth segments across the dorsum yellow,
except the fore and hind margins, venter yellow. Hypopygium
small, scarcely exserted, the yellowish appendages minute. The
hairs on the sides of the abdomen and on the venter are long and
yellowish; on the dorsum they are short and brown. Coxæ and
legs light yellow, only the hind tarsi slightly infuscated. Hairs of
fore and middle coxæ sparse and delicate ; hind coxa with a single
slender blackish lateral bristle. Fore tarsi one-and-a-half times as
long as the tibiæ ; the pulvilli strongly enlarged. Middle tibia
just below the knee, with two or three weak bristles in a group ;
middle tarsi longer than their tibia. Hind femora with considerable
hair, especially on the fore side ; hind tibiæ long, a little clavate,

on the hind side below the middle with a row of small bristles. Hind metatarsus thickened, half as long as the following joint. Wings broad, yellowish ; first and second veins far from the costa, fourth only gently curved, ending behind the apex, nearly parallel to the third. Posterior cross-vein long, almost twice its length from the border ; second posterior cell large. Anal angle well developed.

♀ . Much smaller than male. First joint of antennæ not elongated. Arista scarcely thickened. Face moderately narrow, parallel, the palpi and proboscis rather prominent, brownish. Abdomen usually not compressed, the dorsum wholly brownish-black ; venter yellowish. Fore pulvilli not enlarged. Hind tibiæ as in the male, but the bristles fewer and shorter. Wings a little narrower.

Length, male, 2·6 ; female, 1·7 mm.

1000 to 1500 feet altitude. June. Numerous males and females.

Polymedon.

Osten Sacken, Western Diptera, 317, 1877.

This genus will have to be somewhat amended, as it should evidently include the following species. Baron Osten Sacken, in establishing it, had only one species, and consequently did not succeed in separating perfectly the generic and specific characters. The long cilia of the tegulæ, absence of acrostichal bristles, and large swelling of the costa, are characters that pertain only to the male of *P. flabellifer*, and are not generic. In the species here described, the hind metatarsi are in the male decidedly, in the female slightly, shorter than the following joint. Mr. Samuel Henshaw, at my request, kindly examined the types of *P. flabellifer* in the Museum of Comparative Zoology, Cambridge, Mass., and informs me that the hind metatarsi are not shorter than the following joint.

In the generic diagnosis, add " above " to the clause, " First joint of hind tarsi without bristles."

1. *Polymedon superbus*, n. sp. (Pl. XI., fig. 103, head of ♂. Pl. XII., fig. 113, wing; fig. 118, head of ♀ ; fig. 119, head of ♂.)

♂ . Head large and high. Face wide ; about half-way to the lower corner of the eye it is bent backward obliquely and grows

gradually wider ; beyond the lower corner of the eye it hangs
down in a thin sheet, rounded below, about as far as its own width.
The mouth parts hang down behind this. The whole face is
silvery white. The proboscis and palpi are brown. Front somewhat excavated, deep metallic-blue, approaching violet in colour,
very slightly dusted in the middle ; along each side and across
behind the ocelli white pollinose. Antennæ situated far above the
middle of the face, directed strongly upward, as compared to the
head alone ; the latter, however, stands in an oblique position,
strongly receding below, so that the antennæ are in reality directed
straight forward. Immediately below their origin there is an
angle in the profile of the head, and it begins to recede. First
joint of the antennæ long and slender, yellow, with hairs above,
the second projects considerably in a rounded curve over the inner
edge of the third ; it is also yellow. Third joint large rounded, a
little longer than high, with a slight point. The arista is dorsal,
thick, short, nearly bare, curved downward, brown in colour.
Third joint of antennæ brown at the tip. Cilia of inferior orbit
white. Occiput dark-green, dusted on each side. Dorsum of
thorax shining metallic-green, in an oblique view, more blue or
violet, darker and more bluish near the borders. Acrostichal
bristles two rowed ; a considerable area of small humeral bristles.
The transverse suture is wholly bronze-black, which colour extends
narrowly toward the anterior. Just below this is an elongate
silvery pollinose spot, reaching forward to a point above the
humerus. Pleuræ greenish-black, covered with bluish white dust.
Tegulæ infuscated, with black cilia. Halteres yellow. Scutellum
shining bluish-green, with a very large and a very small bristle on
each side. Between the corner of the scutellum and the root of
the wing is an excavated area, black, with a handsome silver spot.
Abdomen bluish-green, with rather long bristles bordering the
segments behind. When viewed in the proper light, each segment
beyond the first is white pollinose on the anterior half, except in
the middle of the dorsum. Toward the venter this pollen becomes
dense and silvery. In the same light the posterior half of each
segment is deep metallic violet-blue. Hypopygium large, exserted,
turned under the venter. It is opaque-black, except some of the
inner parts, which are brownish or yellowish. The lamellæ are
large, parallelogram shaped, somewhat oblique, black. Along
the upper margin of each are two slender curved yellow bristles,
some distance apart. Fore and middle coxæ with a few hairs and
bristles ; hind ones with a single lateral bristle. Fore coxæ yellow,
the others brownish-black. Femora and tibiæ yellow. Tarsi
blackened from the middle of the first joint, middle tarsi a little

crooked near the middle. Hind metatarsi three-fourths the length of the following joint, with a small but distinct bristle on the underside. Wings a little smoky ; venation much as in *Tachy trechus* (Loew, Mon. N. A. Dol., Pl. III., 6) ; the third vein, how-ever, is bent backward by a very gentle curve, beginning before the middle of the wing ; the fourth vein runs in a straight line past the cross-vein for a distance about equal to the length of that vein, then bends forward in a gentle curve and is almost straight for the rest of its course, but with a slight convexity forward. It ends some distance before the apex, near the third vein. Costa scarcely swollen before the end of the first vein. Fifth vein attenuated near the end, obsolete before the border.

♀. Face white pollinose of about the same width as in the male, ending in a point below, which reaches fully to the lower edge of the eyes. Palpi and proboscis rather small, brownish. First joint of the antennæ shorter than in the male, all the joints blackened along the upper border. Middle tarsi simple : hind metatarsi but little shorter than the following joint. General colour of thorax and abdomen deep blue, verging into green, shining.

Length 4–4·75 mm. ; of wing, 4·2 mm.

Eleven males and eight females ; one label reads, "Richmond Valley, Forest. 1800 feet, December 31. On stones along stream ; " another, "This species lights on rocks in the beds of mountain streams above 1000 feet. Very wary."

The green, blue, and silver colours of this species are so changeable in different lights that they are difficult to describe. There will be no difficulty in recognizing the insect.

DIAPHORUS.

Meigen, Syst. Beschr., iv., 1824.

1. *Diaphorus opacus*, Loew.

This species was based by Loew on a single male specimen from New York, and a female from Pennsyl-vania was doubtfully referred to it. The length of these specimens is 3 mm. I have numerous representatives of a species from St. Vincent, West Indies, which agree substantially with the description, but are only 2 mm. long ; in the males also the hairs on the underside of the middle femora seem to be less conspicuous. It would not be safe to describe the species as new without comparison with the types of *opacus* ; for the present I consider it a small form of the latter.

In the West Indian specimens, it is difficult to separate *Diaphorus* from *Chrysotus*. When the face and front are parallel, I have followed the general rule of referring all to *Chrysotus* that did not show in the male sex elongated front pulvilli or large bristles at the end of the abdomen.

2. *Diaphorus approximatus*, n. sp.

♂. Face white pollinose, rectangular, the ground colour blackish ; the eyes approximated on the front so as almost to touch, the two frontal triangles and the narrow strip connecting them whitish pollinose. Antennæ short, third joint crescent shaped, with apical arista ; second joint with several radiating black hairs of moderate length. Cilia of inferior orbit white. Dorsum of thorax green, dusted with yellow, not very shining ; pleuræ black with grey dust. Halteres and tegulæ yellow, the cilia of the latter brown, sometimes a little mixed with white. Abdomen shining dark-green, with black hairs above, which change to reddish on the sides ; hair of the venter long, delicate, pale. The four bristles at the apex of the abdomen are small. Hypopygium concealed. Coxæ black ; femora brownish-black, yellow at tip ; on the outer and lower edge of the fore femora, near the tip is a row of long hairs. Tibiæ yellow, tarsi infuscated from the tip of the first joint, pulvilli of fore tarsi enlarged. Wings slightly brownish, very broad ; the greatest width is about the middle ; the third vein toward the tip curves noticeably backward. Length 3 mm.; of wing, 2·5 mm.

Numerous males. Sea level to 1000 feet. May. The tegular cilia seem to be pale in some lights and brown in others.

3. *Diaphorus parvulus*, n. sp.

Minute, shining green ; legs yellow ; cilia of tegula and of inferior orbit pale ; eyes of male broadly separated.

♂. Face blackish ; with grey dust ; palpi brownish-yellow,

front shining green, broader than face ; antennæ black, third joint
rather large, with subapical arista. Cilia of inferior orbit white.
Thorax shining green, a little dusted ; bristles black ; pleuræ
black, with thin grey dust. Abdomen shining bronze-green,
venter yellowish ; the black bristles at apex not present ; hypopygium concealed, the tips of two small, yellow appendages
visible ; hair of abdomen black, below somewhat reddish. Fore
coxæ yellow, with yellow hairs ; middle coxæ pale at tip, the basal
half or more blackish ; hind tibiæ yellow with dark base. Femora,
tibiæ and tarsi yellow, the last one or two joints of the tarsi
infuscated ; the femora sometimes have a brownish tinge. Fore
tarsi one and a-half times the length of the tibiæ, with enlarged
pulvilli; the other pulvilli of equal size scarcely enlarged. The
erect lateral bristle of the middle tibiæ very large. Wings
yellowish, with yellow veins and the usual configuration.

♀. Antennæ, particularly the third joint, smaller. Pulvilli
plain : otherwise as in the male.

Length 1·2 mm. ; of wing, the same.

Three males, three females, 1500–2000 feet. May,
July.

4. *Diaphorus dimidiatus*, n. sp.

Light green, whitish pruinose ; basal half of abdomen yellow.

♂. Face and front concolorous, bluish-green with grey dust ;
lower part of the face rather narrow, palpi rather large, pale
yellow, with black hairs; antennæ blackish, third joint very short,
with dorsal arista ; cilia of lateral and inferior orbit pale, the
lower ones long. Thorax light green, somewhat bluish, wholly
pruinose with white ; in the middle of the dorsum a little shining ;
pleuræ concolorous with the dorsum, opaque ; halteres large, pale
yellow; tegulæ pale yellow with black cilia. Second and third
segments of the abdomen light yellow, with black hairs ; fourth
and fifth segments shining green, a little coppery ; the four apical
bristles large ; hypopygium concealed, with scarcely visible
appendages. Fore coxæ pale yellow, with long black bristles and
a few small black hairs on the front side ; middle coxæ black with
yellow tip, with rather coarse black bristles on the front side ;
hind coxæ brownish-yellow, more black at base, purer yellow at
tip, with a single lateral bristle. Femora, tibiæ and tarsi yellow,
the last two or three joints of the tarsi infuscated ; the fore tarsi
are longer than the tibiæ, with pulvilli as long as the third
joint ; middle tarsi proportionally a little shorter, their pulvilli

almost the same size. Middle tibiæ on the outer front edge with two bristles besides the one at the tip ; hind tibiæ slender, with a few small bristles behind. Wings rather narrow, subhyaline, with yellow veins. The anterior end of the large cross-vein is in the centre of the wing. Length 2 mm.; of wing, 1·8 mm.

Five males. May. This species belongs to the group of *D. hoffmanseggii*, Meig., of Europe, and *D. satrapa*, Wheeler, of Nebraska, but is readily distinguished by the characters given.

5. *Diaphorus contiguus*, n. sp.

Brownish, opaque species, or sometimes slightly shining ; femora black, tibiæ yellow ; cilia of inferior orbit and of tegulæ blackish ; eyes of male broadly contiguous.

♂. Face opaque, blackish, short ; palpi brown ; antennæ very short arista sub-apical ; ocellar tubercle prominent ; cilia of inferior orbit almost black, yet in certain lights rather brownish. Dorsum of thorax opaque-brown, the ground colour being blackish and the thick dust light-brown. Pleuræ black with thinner and greyer dust ; halteres and tegulæ yellow, the latter with black cilia. Abdomen opaque-black with black hairs ; the apical bristles large ; appendages of the hypopygium not or scarcely visible. Coxæ and femora black, the latter with yellowish tips. Front femora along the lower and outer edge with a row of long hairs ; middle and hind femora with a few rather long hairs near the tip on the fore side ; tibiæ yellow, with only few and weak bristles, except at tip. Fore tarsi once and a half as long as the tibiæ, the pulvilli large ; middle tarsi scarcely longer than the tibiæ, the pulvilli small ; all the tarsi infuscated from about the third joint. Wings very broad near the base on account of the extraordinary development of the anal angle ; first vein farther from the margin than usual.

♀. Face and front of equal width, the face remarkably broad and short, greyish brown ; the large palpi of the same colour ; front opaque-brown ; front femora destitute of long hairs ; bristles of posterior tibiæ stronger than in the male ; wings, although very broad, not quite so much so as in the male.

Length 2 mm. ; of wing, 1·8 mm.

Eleven males, seven females. May.

6. *Diaphorus flavipes*, n. sp.

Pure green, lightly dusted ; cilia of tegulæ and inferior orbit pale ; legs yellow ; eyes of male contiguous.

♂. Face short, small, greyish pollinose; antennæ small, brownish, second and third joints short but rather large, with almost apical arista. Eyes contiguous for a moderate distance; palpi and proboscis yellow; cilia of inferior orbit white. Thorax green, slightly dusted, the smaller bristles of a rusty reddish colour, the larger ones at the tips the same, but black at base; pleuræ blackish, grey-dusted. Halteres large, pure sulphur yellow, tegulæ brownish-yellow with yellow cilia. Abdomen shining bronze-green, venter yellowish; hairs of abdomen yellow, the apical bristles not present; hypopygium concealed, only some minute yellow appendages visible. Coxæ femora, tibiæ and tarsi yellow, the middle coxæ largely blackish at base and the tips of the tarsi a little brownish; bristles of tibiæ extremely small and weak, except at the tips of the posterior ones. Fore tarsi longer than tibiæ, pulvilli enlarged; pulvilli of middle tarsi scarcely at all enlarged. Wings yellowish, with yellow veins, widest about the middle.

♀. Front as wide as the face below, a little wider above, shining green, with yellow dust below and at the sides; thorax shining green with yellow dust, the larger bristles scarcely reddish at 'tip; yellow hair of the abdomen rather dense near the tip; bristles of the posterior tibiæ larger than in the male; pulvilli small.

Length 2–2·4 mm.; of wing, 2 mm.

Numerous males and females. March to September. Sea-level to 2000 feet.

7. *Diaphorus dubius*, n. sp.

Greenish-bronze, moderately shining; eyes of male not approximated; femora black, tibia yellow.

♂. Face obscurely dusted with greenish-white, parallel; front green, shining only in a band across the vertex, the remainder yellowish dusted; antennæ black, the third joint very short, subreniform, with apical arista; cilia of inferior orbit pale, palpi and proboscis blackish, the former of ordinary size. Thorax bronze-green, a little shining; the pleuræ blackish, with white dust, more conspicuous posteriorly; halteres and tegulæ yellow, the tegular cilia black. Abdomen bronze-green with a coppery reflection, sometimes scarcely at all green; its hairs are black, on the lower side less so and longer; the four stout black hairs at the apex are well-marked in some specimens, in others not. Hypopygium concealed, its appendages small and inconspicuous. Coxæ and femora black, trochanters and tips of femora reddish; the fore coxæ with black hairs on the front side, middle coxæ with a few coarse blackish hairs in front, hind coxæ with a single lateral bristle ; near the end of each femur, on the outer side, are three or four larger hairs ; on the anterior side of the middle tibia just below the knee, is a single erect bristle, on the posterior side of the hind tibiæ are two or three small bristles. The pulvilli of the fore tarsi are enlarged ; fore and middle tarsi infuscated from the tip of the first joint, the length of the former exceeding that of their tibiæ ; hind tarsi shorter than their tibiæ, the infuscation beginning near the base. Wings of only ordinary width, subhyaline, the fourth vein ending exactly in the apex, the outline is more rounded before the apex than behind it.

Length 2·4–2·7 mm. ; of wing, the same.

Numerous males and females. 500–1500 feet altitude.

This species differs from *sodalis*, Loew, by its smaller size and black hairs on the fore coxæ. The female of *dubius* differs from the male in having a slightly wider face, smaller antennæ, shorter and thicker abdomen, the femora without longer hairs, and the tibiæ with stronger bristles. In a large series of specimens I notice considerable variation : some of the specimens if alone would no doubt be referred to *Chrysotus*.

CHRYSOTUS.

Meigen, Syst. Beschr., iv., 1824.

1. *Chrysotus excisus*, n. sp.

♂. Eyes broadly contiguous on the face, with an area of enlarged facets ; front broad, short, deep bluish-green to bronze-green in colour ; palpi and proboscis blackish. Antennæ black, the third joint very large, kidney-shaped, hairy along the outer part ; arista apical, arising from a deep notch in the joint. In some specimens this peculiarity is but little developed ; in others it is very distinct ; in some specimens the point below the notch is longer than the one above, giving the arista a subapical position. Cilia of inferior orbit small, brownish. Dorsum of thorax bright bluish-green, sometimes more bronze or coppery ; pleuræ black ; tegulæ and halteres yellow to brown, the former with black cilia. Abdomen short, thick, black, scarcely with a green reflection ; hypopygium concealed, sometimes with a minute brownish appendage or two barely visible. Feet black ; from the knees down sometimes more brownish than black, with close black hair. Fore tarsi longer than the tibiæ ; the middle and hind femora have near the tip below a few bristles ; the latter not ciliated. Wings almost hyaline, rather small in size, of the usual shape.

♀. Face blackish, of ordinary structure ; third joint of antennæ not so large nor so deeply notched as in some of the males ; halteres yellow.

Length 1·7–2·1 mm. ; of wing, the same.

Numerous males and females. 500–2000 feet altitude.

2. *Chrysotus proximus*, n. sp.

Differs from the preceding species only in having the legs from the knees down light yellow ; some of the males have the third joint even larger ; the average size is smaller. In some specimens the trochanters also are yellow. Length 1·6–2 mm.; of wing, the same.

Numerous specimens, as above,

3. *Chrysotus flavus*, n. sp.

Wholly pure yellow species; eyes of male contiguous on the face.

♂. Palpi large, about half as long as the face, yellow ; eye contiguous, leaving a blackish triangle below the antennæ ; front very broad at vertex, narrow towards the antennæ, dark in colour, probably metallic in living specimens ; antennæ rather large, the third joint a little elongated with a subapical brownish arista ; the colour of the antennæ is wholly yellow ; cilia of lateral and inferior orbit yellow. Thorax with pleuræ wholly yellow, the bristles blackish, but in a strong light more yellowish. Cilia of tegulæ brown ; below the tegula a small blackish spot. Metanotum strongly developed. Abdomen yellow, the dorsum blackish except at base ; the first segment has a row of long hairs, black above, at the sides yellow. The hair of the dorsum is blackish, of the rest yellow. The abdomen as a whole is short, the hypopygium concealed, a few minute yellow organs visible. Legs from coxa to tarsus wholly pure yellow, with yellow hairs and bristles ; middle and hind tibiæ rather bristly, the hind tarsi with small bristles below. Wings almost hyaline ; fourth vein perfectly straight in its last segment, ending behind the apex.

♀. Face very narrow, white pollinose ; palpi long, broader than in the male, resting on the very large yellow proboscis.

Abdomen only a little blackish above, but still with black hairs.

Length 1·6 mm. ; of wing, 1·6 mm.

One male, one female. 1000 feet.

4. *Chrysotus albipalpus,* n. sp.

Minute blackish species, the male with contiguous eyes and large white palpi.

♂. Eyes briefly contiguous or just touching on the face, with some very large facets at this point ; the palpi are large, snow-white ; the front, and also the facial triangle below the eyes yellow-dusted on a green colour. Antennæ small, black, the third joint not enlarged, rounded, with apical arista. Cilia of inferior orbit white and rather long. Dorsum of thorax green, somewhat golden, moderately shining ; a dark stripe along the lateral edge. Pleuræ black with white dust ; tegulæ somewhat infuscated, with black cilia ; halteres yellow. Abdomen dark green, scarcely shining, short, somewhat clubbed toward the apex. Hypopygium concealed, some small dark processes slightly visible, more remote than usual from the apex of abdomen. Coxæ and femora black, the former with pale hairs ; tibiæ varying from yellow to brown ; bases of tarsi concolorous with tibiæ, tips darker. Pulvilli of fore tarsi considerably, of the middle tarsi less, enlarged. Wings tinged with brown, considerably rounded behind, fourth vein ending in the apex.

♀. Face of moderate width, white pollinose, tibiæ usually light-yellow. Otherwise substantially as in the male.

Length 1·5 ; of wing, 1·3 mm.

Numerous specimens. May, June. 500–1500 feet.

The variability of this species is somewhat puzzling ; in some specimens the abdomen is deep violet, in others the halteres are yellowish-white.

5. *Chrysotus niger,* n. sp.

Palpi brownish : eyes not quite contiguous ; face and front opaque black, the latter a little greenish. Dorsum of thorax black, scarcely greenish. Pleuræ, abdomen, coxæ, and femora black, the coxæ with brown hairs. Halteres black, the stem brown : tibiæ and tarsi blackish, sometimes more brownish, in the female yellowish-brown and the femora brown. Otherwise as the preceding species. Length 1·3 mm.

Seven males, six females.

6. *Chrysotus hirsutus,* n. sp.

♂. Palpi prominent, pale yellow ; eyes contiguous on the face, leaving a whitish-dusted triangle below the antennæ ; front shining green ; antennæ small, black, with apical arista ; cilia of lateral and inferior orbits white. Dorsum of thorax bright green ; pleuræ blackish, with dense whitish dust ; cilia of tegulæ brownish-yellow ; tegulæ and halteres yellow. Abdomen shining green at the base, more blackish posteriorly, with black hairs ; hypopygium concealed, only a small appendage or two, with rather long yellow hairs visible. Fore coxæ yellow, dark at base, with a group of brown bristles near the tip ; middle and hind coxæ blackish, with yellow tip. Fore femora, tibiæ, and four joints of tarsi yellow, the last tarsal joint blackened, with enlarged pulvilli ; the fore femora are a little thickened, and on the underside have a row of brownish hairs ; the tibiæ on the underside have a row of long, closely-appressed hairs. The middle femora have a row of hairs, like the front ones ; their tarsi are blackened from the tip of the first joint, and the pulvilli are small. The hind femora are thickened, the apical third infuscated. The row of hairs below ends near the tip, with four or five coarse bristles ; knees yellow ; hind tibiæ yellow with a brown stripe down the whole length of the outer side, upon which is situated a dense row of bushy brown hairs ; these hairs continue down the tarsus, becoming smaller beyond the first joint : the tarsi are very short and tapering, the first joint about two-thirds as long as all the rest ; they are gradually infuscated beyond the first joint. Wings hyaline ; fourth vein a little bent just beyond the posterior cross-vein, ending in the apex ; the curve before the apex is but little fuller than that behind it.

♀. Face rather broad, white pollinose ; fore coxæ with rather numerous yellowish hairs ; femora not perceptibly thickened, these and the tibiæ without rows of hairs ; hind femora with two or three pre-apical bristles, only its tip infuscated. The hind tibiæ have several stout bristles, and the metatarsus is scarcely half as long as the following joints, all of which are plain.

Length 1·6 mm. ; of wing, 1·4 mm.

Numerous males and females. March, May. Sea-level to 1000 feet.

This species will probably form a new genus. I place it here provisionally, on account of the male eyes.

7. *Chrysotus longipalpus*, n. sp.

♂. Palpi pale yellow, toward the tip whiter, almost as long as the head is high, proportionately rather narrow ; face slender in the middle, where the eyes almost touch, light dusted on the triangle below the antennæ ; front deep violet, not very shining ; antennæ yellow or brownish-yellow, last joint hairy, with sub-apical arista ; cilia of inferior orbit pale. Dorsum of thorax green, moderately shining. Pleuræ black, with delicate pale dust. Cilia of tegulæ blackish or brownish; halteres yellow. Abdomen bluish-black, somewhat shining, with black hairs ; hypopygium concealed. Coxæ yellow, the middle ones dark at base ; femora and tibiæ yellow, in some ill-preserved specimens the hind ones a little brownish ; the first joint of the fore tarsi is about as long as all the rest; the second, third, and fourth joints are slightly compressed, from the tip of the first joint all are infuscated. Hind femora with about three pre-apical bristles in a row, the tibiæ rather hairy, and the tarsi infuscated from the tip of the second joint. Wings hyaline, of the ordinary type, fourth vein ending in the apex.

♀. Palpi normal, face violet, like the front ; only the fourth and fifth joints of the tarsi, with extreme tips of the preceding, are infuscated.

Length 1 mm. ; of wing, 1 mm.

Nine males, three females. May. 500–1500 feet.

8. *Chrysotus picticornis*.

Loew, Monogr., ii., 184 ; Wheeler, Psyche, June, 1890, p. 358.

Numerous specimens ; both sexes. May. Sea-level to 500 feet.

9. *Chrysotus acutus*, n. sp.

♂. Eyes contiguous for a considerable distance on the face ; palpi dark ; front opaque black ; antennæ black, rather large, the third joint large. with dense brown hair. drawn out in an acute point, before the tip of which the arista is inserted. Thorax green, moderately shining, sometimes considerably dulled and more brownish ; pleuræ black. Halteres and tegulæ, with the tegular cilia, black. Abdomen black ; hypopygium concealed. Coxæ brown, the anterior ones with blackish hairs ; femora brown, varying somewhat in depth of colour the hind ones with a row of four or five small pre-apical bristles; tibiæ yellow, the hind ones a little darker; tarsi yellow, fourth and fifth joints of the fore ones black, the posterior ones gradually infuscated from the tip of the first joint. On the front side of the fore tibia is a row of small but distinct white hairs. Wings somewhat infuscated, of the usual shape, fourth vein ending very slightly before the exact apex. Length 1·1 mm.; of wing, 1 mm.

Seven males. 500–1000 feet.

10. *Chrysotus inermis*, n. sp.

♂. Face of moderate width, parallel, blackish-green, but little dusted; palpi dark; front shining green, slightly dusted; cilia of inferior orbit brownish-yellow; antennæ black, the third joint short, a little hairy, with apical arista. Dorsum of thorax shining green, thinly covered with yellow dust; pleuræ black, yellowish dusted; cilia of tegulæ brown, halteres yellow. Abdomen rather dull coppery colour, verging into blackish, the hairs brownish; hypopygium concealed. Coxæ yellow, the middle ones black nearly to the tip, the fore and middle ones with yellow hairs; femora and tibiæ yellow; the middle tibiæ with an erect bristle below the knee, the hind ones with two or three small bristles behind, otherwise the tibiæ are free from bristles except at apex; tarsi yellow, only a little infuscated at the extreme tip; fore pulvilli large, middle ones only a little larger than the hind ones. Wings yellowish, the fourth vein ending in the apex, posterior crossvein short, located before the middle.

♀. Face green, white-dusted; proboscis, cilia of inferior orbit and those of the tegulæ paler than in the male; venter slightly yellowish at base.

Length 1·6–2 mm.; of wing, 1·5–1·8 mm.

Seven males, numerous females. May and July. 500–2000 feet altitude.

The females of this species so closely resemble those of *Diaphorus flavipes*, that they can scarcely be separated, I could find no distinct differences.

11. *Chrysotus apicalis*, n. sp.

♂. Front shining green, wide; face of same colour with a little pollen, narrowed in the middle, owing to an area of enlarged facets in the eye; eyes somewhat emarginate at the level of the antennæ; palpi yellow; antennæ black, the first joint bare, this and the second of ordinary structure; the third joint crescent

shaped, in its vertical diameter very large, on the apical side near
the middle suddenly drawn out into a long, narrow point ; arista
inserted just before, or in some cases almost exactly at, the apex
of the prolongation, moderately long, pubescent ; the whole inner
and lower surface of the third joint is light pilose. Cilia of the
inferior orbit white, a considerable amount of long white hair
behind them. Thorax golden-green on the middle, more or less
covered with pollen, around the margins more pollinose ; acrostichal bristles few, in two rows ; the small humeral bristles number
only about half-a-dozen on a side ; about the base of each large
bristle is a black dot. Pleuræ greenish-black, dusted with white.
Tegulæ and halteres light yellow, cilia of the former whitish.
Abdomen dark green, more or less thickly dusted, sometimes with
a bronze reflection. Seen from above, the first segment is very
broad with parallel sides ; the rest are successively narrower,
rapidly tapering. The green colour ends with the fifth segment,
the following one is black. From the side, the abdomen is slender
the dorsum and venter nearly parallel to the fifth segment. The
following two are somewhat excavated on the under side, but only
the tips of one or two small organs are visible. Coxæ black,
about the apex sometimes slightly yellowish. The front and
middle ones with a few black hairs and bristles on the front side :
hind ones with one lateral bristle. Front and middle femora
yellow, with more or less of a blackish tinge along the upper side.
The middle ones are lighter-coloured than the front ones. Hind
femora wholly greenish-black. All the tibiæ-yellow, tarsi-yellow,
gradually infuscated from the tip of the first joint. Pulvilli of
ordinary size. In one single specimen out of fifty examined there
is, on the middle of the lower surface of one of the hind
metatarsi, a slender erect bristle. This is probably abnormal.
Venation normal, the same as figured by Loew for *C. obliquus*
(Mon., N.A. Dol., Pl. VI., 31).

♀. Face rather wide, not narrowed in the middle ; this and the
front often with a steel-blue reflection, somewhat dusted with
white or yellowish. Below the middle of the face the contour is
interrupted by a suture, except in the middle : below this the face
is more prominent. The oral cavity and the proboscis are much
larger than in the male. Palpi large, flat, yellow, sometimes
brownish, with white or yellow pollen. Proboscis projecting
below the head, black. Antennæ as in the male, but the third
joint not at all drawn out, simply crescent-shaped, at most a little
triangular. Arista apparently apical. Behind the orbital cilia
but a few hairs. Colour of thorax and abdomen more opaque than

in the male. Fore and middle femora yellow, hind ones slightly yellow at base and tip.

Length 2 mm.; of wing, 1·8 mm.

Numerous specimens. Sea level to 1000 feet. May.

ASYNDETUS.

Loew, Centur., viii., 58, 1869.

1. *Asyndetus fratellus*, n. sp. (Pl. XII., fig. 114, tip of wing.)

♂. Green, thickly dusted, not shining except on femora and slightly on abdomen. Face very broad, the sides parallel, covered with opaque, whitish dust. Palpi rather large, with black hairs and whitish-dusted. Front very broad, like the face in colour but a very little less dusted. showing more of the underlying green. Antennæ black, short, the second and third joint together nearly circular in outline. Arista dorsal. Orbital cilia black above, white below. Thorax heavily dusted with brownish, not at all shining, a single scattering row of very minute acrostichal bristles. On each side of the broad, median dorsal stripe is an ill-defined, light-blue dusted stripe, so that the brown colour appears to form three broad longitudinal bands, the lateral ones so wide as to extend down over the pleuræ for some distance, the blue colour reaches the corners of the scutellum, and the latter is wholly blue, except a narrow trace of brown along the posterior border. It has two large bristles. Pleuræ brownish above, fading into light blue below. Tegulæ yellow, their cilia whitish. Halteres yellow. Abdomen moderately elongate, tapering, green. but little shining. Behind each incisure the colour is deep blue and more metallic. The hair of the abdomen is black, and conspicuously coarse and long. Hypopygium small, embedded, with four bristles pointing backward. These are about as long as the fifth segment. Legs robust, black, bristly, the coxæ whitish from the overlying dust, front and middle ones with numerous bristles on the front side, the hind one with a single lateral bristle. Femora all somewhat thickened, dark green rather shining, with rows of moderate bristles on the under side. These structures are not raptorial, since they are rather weak and the tibiæ lack the corresponding development. Knees narrowly yellow. Tibiæ fuscous, the front ones a very little lighter, simple, with strong bristles. Tarsi black, simple. Pulvilli of all the feet much elongated, yellow. Wings slightly greyish, fading into hyaline posteriorly and apically. The first longitudinal vein ends about one-third of the way to the apex. Its end is a trifle beyond the large cross-vein. Second and third veins close together diverging uniformly through their whole course, the latter ending rather far from the apex. The costal vein ends with the third longitudinal instead of continuing to the fourth. The fourth longitudinal vein becomes gradually weaker beyond the posterior cross-vein for about three-fifths of its course. It then curves suddenly forward for a short distance, curves back again into its original direction, and ends in the apex. The whole portion beyond the first curve is very delicate and transparent, and sometimes the section running forward is entirely obsolete.

♀. Face scarcely wider than the male. Pulvilli of usual size. Abdomen even less metallic than in the male, without the terminal bristles, otherwise appearing much the same. The tibiæ and tarsi are sometimes lighter in colour than in the other sex.

Length 2·3 to 2·5 mm. ; of wing, 2 mm.

Eleven males and twenty females. Several specimens are labelled " May," and one " Seashore."

This species is closely allied to *A. interruptus*, Loew, but the latter is over 5 mm. long. The colour of the thorax seems by the description to be different also.

LYRONEURUS.

Loew, Wien. Ent. Monatsch., i., 37, 1857.

1. *Lyroneurus simplex*, n. sp. (Pl. XII., fig. 117, wing ♂.)

♂. Front bright bluish-green, brownish-black along the borders ; face green, brownish dusted, but somewhat silvery pollinose from above, a very little narrowed in the middle. Palpi yellow, with long black bristles, proboscis black. Antennæ black, very short; the third joint crescent-shaped, hairy, with a long slender subapical arista. Cilia of the inferior orbit and another row behind them white. Thorax metallic-green brown-dusted. Acrostichal bristles in a single row. Eight or ten small humeral bristles. A brownish-black stripe along the transverse suture, running forward to the humerus. Just below, a spot is silvery when viewed from above. Pleuræ green, white pollinose, more silvery from above. Halteres and tegulæ yellow ; cilia of the latter yellowish. Scutellum with the usual small and large bristles ; between the scutellum and wing is a concave area, black, with a silvery spot. Abdomen green, considerably dusted, rather elongated, scarcely tapering. Hypopygium concealed, only a few minute yellow and black parts visible. A few moderately long bristles at the end of sixth, as of the other segments. Front coxæ green at base, changing through brown to yellow at the tip, considerably white pollinose. A row of black bristles at the tip, and a few fine yellowish hairs on the front side. Middle and hind coxæ blackish, the former has a number of stout bristles on the fore side, one near the base is more lateral and quite prominent. Hind coxæ with a single lateral bristle. Trochanters all yellow. Femora all dark-green, somewhat shining; the front and middle ones broadly, the hind ones slightly, yellow at the knee. Tibiæ all yellow, the hind ones a little infuscated at the tip. Front and middle tarsi elongated, slender, yellow, infuscated from the tip of first joint; hind ones shorter and thicker, wholly infuscated. First joint longer than the following one, on its under surface with a long slender upright bristle. Front pulvilli a little enlarged. Wings large, wide toward the apex, yellow before the third vein. The first and second veins are rather far from the costa, and enter it at a less acute angle than usual. The third vein runs close to the second to its end, then turns with a strong curve backward, reaching the margin just before the apex. The last section of the fourth vein in the shape of a gentle double curve, ending just behind the apex.

♀. Front as in the male. Face rather wide, the suture distinct, less pollinose than in the male. Hind metatarsus without the bristle. Wings of the ordinary width, not yellow before the third vein; venation exactly like that of *Eutarsus aulicus*, Meig., in Loew's Monograph, pl. vi., 28 *c*.

Length 3·5–5·5 mm.; of wing, 3–4·3 mm.

Numerous specimens of both sexes. Sea level to 1500 feet. March and May. One specimen labelled "Forest by stream."

The venation of the male varies from that described to a form like that of the female.

Eutarsus.

Loew, Neue Beitr., v., 1857.

1. *Eutarsus sinuatus*, n. sp. (Pl. XI., fig. 104, wing. Pl. XII., fig. 110, ♂ wing; fig. 115, ♀ wing.)

♂. Face exceedingly narrow, almost linear; silvery pollinose on a dark ground colour. Palpi small, yellow. Front narrow, of same colour as face. Antennæ situated high up, the front therefore short and the face long. They are very short, the third joint especially small, all yellow but the tip of third joint. Arista sub-apical, brown, the basal joint somewhat incrassated. Cilia of inferior orbit delicate, of a whitish colour. Dorsum of thorax yellow in front, the posterior part and scutellum shining light-green. Acrostichal bristles two-rowed. The green colour extends forward about to the transverse suture. Farther than this it extends only in three fading and irregular streaks. Laterally it does not reach the bases of the wings. Pleuræ plain yellow ; a dark spot below and one behind the wing. Cilia of tegulæ yellowish. Metanotum yellow. Abdomen blackish, not shining, more brownish at the base, scarcely tapering. Hypopygium almost wholly concealed, the length of a few scattered yellowish bristles along the venter is noticeable. In some specimens not fully coloured the abdomen is more yellow at base. All the coxæ, legs, and feet light-yellow. Tarsi scarcely at all infuscated. Front ones very long and the pulvilli much enlarged and elongated. Hind metatarsus shorter than the following joint, with a minute bristle below. Front coxæ with fine yellow and black hair and black bristles. Middle coxæ with numerous bristles as in the pre-ceding species. Hind coxæ with one lateral bristle. Wings yellow before the third vein. Venation as figured. The second vein is normal for half its course, then runs farther from the costa, makes a wide sweep, and joins the costa nearly at a right angle. The third vein a little wavy before the end of the second, beyond that bent strongly backward. Fourth vein normal, its last section straight.

♀. The face moderately narrow, excavated, black with white pollen. Front somewhat wider, black with less pollen. Palpi almost concealed, brown. Antennæ scarcely infuscated at the tip, the arista yellowish. Thorax as in the males. Abdomen yellow, the posterior margin of each segment shining black. On the second segment an anterior black crossband, narrow, enlarged in the middle ; third segment with a wider band, more enlarged ; fourth segment chiefly black ; fifth with only an indistinct band of yellow. Legs and feet as in the male, except that the pulvilli of the front feet are of the normal size. Wings but slightly yellow. Veins straight and almost uniformly divergent : only in the second there is an almost imperceptible trace of two sinuations, at the places where these occur in the male. This vein ends nearer the apex than in the male.

Length 2·3–2·6 mm. ; of wing, 3·2 mm.

Numerous males and eight females. 500 to 1500 feet altitude.

SYMPYCNUS.

Loew, Neue Beitr., v., 1857.

1. *Sympycnus falco*, n. sp.

♂. Face blackish, the eyes nearly or quite contiguous about the middle; front blackish; antennæ black, third joint short, pointed, with a subapical arista. Cilia of inferior orbit pale. Dorsum of thorax green, but little shining; pleuræ black with greenish-grey dust; halteres yellow; cilia of tegulæ black, still rather brown at tips, and the lower two or three hairs yellow. Abdomen dull green, with blackish hairs; on each side of the first segment is a row of half-a-dozen long brownish hairs; the hypopygium projects in a sort of rounded knob behind the abdomen, its short, stout, brown grasping organs mostly concealed, and lying in front of the organ proper. Coxæ varying from yellow to brown in different specimens, the middle ones darker than the others, the front ones with yellow hairs and a few slender brownish bristles; femora, tibiæ and tarsi yellow; the fore femora have a short row of brown bristles on the hind side near the tip, the fore tibiæ on the front side with only delicate irregular hairs, in part rather long; the fore tarsi are longer than the tibiæ, the last joint rather long with a projection on the under side near the base; the inner claw folds back to meet this, thus forming a clasping organ; all the tarsi are only gradually infuscated near the tip. Wings slightly yellow, slender, the posterior cross-vein before the middle; from the cross-vein, the second and fourth veins are parallel, while the third converges toward the fourth in the latter part of its course.

♀. Face moderately narrow, black, with white pollen; fore femora and tarsi plain; venter brownish near the base; lateral bristles of first abdominal segment shorter.

Length 1·6–2 mm.; of wing, the same.

Four males, six females. 1000–3000 feet altitude.

2. *Sympycnus similis*, n. sp.

♂. Differs from the foregoing species chiefly in having on the front side of the fore tibiæ a row of four very stiff, stubby bristles of moderate length. The coxæ and wings are also a little darker, and the hypopygium projects a little more behind. Length 1·6 mm.; of wing, 1·7 mm.

One male. 1000 feet altitude.

NEURIGONA.

Roudani, Prod. Dipt. Ital., 142, 1850.

1. *Neurigona signifera*, n. sp.

♂. Face very narrow. Immediately under the antennæ is a triangular portion, yellow. Below this there is only a narrow groove between the eyes to below the middle, from this point the face protrudes as a narrow, whitish wedge, slightly wider at the bottom. Palpi yellow. Proboscis brownish. Front greenish-brown, a little dusted, converging below. Antennæ yellow, third joint with a short point, arista yellow. Inferior orbital cilia whitish. Occiput green with white dust. Thorax dark yellow, glabrous, with black bristles. Acrostichal bristles small, in two rows. On each side of the acrostichal bristles in front an area of small bristles, bounded by the humeri and the anterior margin. The characteristic flat bare disk of the back part of the dorsum is of a beautiful greenish-blue colour, which extends to the disk of the scutellum. Sides and border of the scutellum yellow. Two very large bristles between two very minute ones on the border. A very large bristle behind the root of the wing. Pleuræ deep-yellow, imperceptibly dusted, a dark spot above the middle coxa. Tegula, cilia whitish. Abdomen slender, yellow, the segments beyond the second successively shorter. The second segment bears near its anterior margin an opaque black band, emarginate behind in the middle and rounded at each end It is about half as wide as the segment. The following segments have similar bands, less emarginate and occupying more of the width of the segment, to the fifth, which is wholly black across the dorsum; like the others it is yellow along the ventral side. Hypopygium shining black, turned under, club-shaped, not much exserted, the appendages not distinct. All the coxæ yellow; front ones long, with black hairs and mixed brownish and yellowish bristles; middle ones with black hairs; hind ones with a single bristle on the outer side. Legs yellow, simple, the bristles small. Tarsi a little infuscated toward the tip. Wings a little yellowish, fourth vein in its last segment only very gently curved, almost perfectly parallel with the third.

♀. Face narrow, strongly protruding below, yellow, and yellow pollinose. Palpi larger than in the male. Third joint of antennæ small, exceedingly short, almost kidney-shaped.

Length 3·5 mm.; of wing, 3·4 mm.

Seashore to 1500 feet altitude. Two males and two females.

CŒLOGLUTUS,* n. g.

♀. First joint of antennæ bare, the second short, with a prolongation along the inner side of the third ; the latter somewhat crescent or kidney-shaped, with a subdorsal arista. Face narrow, more so a little below the antennæ. Ocellar tubercle distinct, the ocellar and lateral bristles strong. Thorax elongated, the wings attached far behind the middle. Acrostichal bristles in two rows. Small humeral bristles covering an area of half the length and almost all the width of the dorsum, comparatively large. A large concave surface begins at the middle of the dorsum and extends to the scutellum including half the width. Scutellum with only two bristles. Latero-dorsal thoracic bristles large. Fore and middle coxæ with considerable hair on the front side, hind coxa with a single lateral bristle. Hind metatarsus half the length of the following joint. Wings hyaline the apex a little pointed. After the anterior cross-vein, the fourth vein runs somewhat backward, diverging but little from the fifth, to the posterior cross-vein ; thence it runs in a direct line toward a point a little before the apex, near the margin it curves gently backward again, and ends in the apex. Posterior cross-vein short, four times its length from the margin. Sixth vein perceptible.

1. *Cœloglutus concavus*, n. sp.   (Pl. XI., fig. 105, wing.)

♀. Face white-pollinose, front more thinly so, showing a little green. Antennæ yellow, except the third joint which is brownish, the inner side of the second is as long as the first joint, the ocellar bristles are long, and curve back more abruptly than usual. Cilia of inferior orbit white. Proboscis rather prominent, brown, the palpi yellow. Dorsum of thorax violet-green, the concavity more pure green. Pleura likewise violet-green, whitish-dusted. Halteres, tegulæ and tegular cilia yellow. Above the root of the fore coxa are two white bristles. Abdomen rather broad and flattened, blackish-green with black hairs and, especially on the sides, some white ones; the ovipositor is black. Fore coxæ yellow, elongated, with a groove on the outer side ; the fore side has numerous black hairs but no bristles. Middle and hind coxæ close against each other, rather distant from the front ones: the middle ones are blackish with yellow tip, hairy in front; the hind ones yellow a little darker at base, with a whitish lateral bristle. Femora and tibiæ yellow, the extreme tips of middle and hind tibiæ blackish. Tarsi infuscated from the tip of first joint, the front ones less so. Wings a little greyish, with yellow veins as figured. Length 2·2 mm.; of wing, 2·1 mm.

A single female.

---

c   κοῖλος, concave ; γλουτός, rump.

ACHALCUS.

Loew, Neue Beitr., v., 1857.

1. *Achalcus sordidus*, n. sp. (Pl. XI., figs. 107, wing of ♂; 107*a*, wing of ♀.)

Minute, blackish, non-metallic, the male with an opaque brown or yellow spot in the first posterior cell.

♂. Face narrow, more so in the middle, where the eyes are almost contiguous. Antennæ short, third joint a little pointed, with an apical, or perhaps subapical, arista. Front wide. Thorax and abdomen blackish, non-metallic. Hypopygium concealed, but rather large, hence the abdomen scarcely tapering. Legs dull brown or yellowish, variable according to the age of specimen when captured. Wings slightly brownish, slender; sixth vein wanting, first very short, ending but little beyond the fork of the second and third; third ending a little before the apex; fourth sinuous, as figured, along its front side, near the end, a large yellow or brown opaque spot. The hind margin sinuous, and fringed with delicate hair. Acrostichal bristles in two rows.

♀. Face wider, not narrowed; antennæ a little shorter, venation simple.

Length 0 7 mm.

Two males and four females. Altitude 500–1000 feet. The specimens are so badly shrivelled that a complete description is impossible. The size, colour, and especially the venation, are sufficient to distinguish the species.

XANTHOTRICHA, n. g.*

Small species, with yellow or brownish bristles and hair; legs yellow; face in male rather narrow; antennæ small, the first and second joints united to form a sort of cup, in which the third is inserted, like an acorn; first antennal joint bare above; arista apical or subapical; hypopygium exserted, small or large; dorsum of thorax convex behind; hind metatarsus short; acrostichal bristles two-rowed. First longitudinal vein very short, sixth wanting; fourth vein straight beyond cross-vein.

1. *Xanthotricha cupulifera*, n. sp. (Pl. XI., figs. 106, wing; 106*a*, hypopygium.)

Metallic-green, legs and all the bristles yellow.

♂. Face narrow, wider above, in a certain reflection violet, without dust; front wide, rather short, violet, proboscis and palpi

Ξανθός, yellow; τρίχος hair.

yellow ; antennæ pure yellow, with long brownish arista ; cilia of inferior orbit yellow. Thorax shining green, somewhat bluish, decidedly globose above on the anterior part. Scutellum short and wide, crescent-shaped, with one pair of bristles (the outer pair are microscopic). Pleuræ black, the posterior margin, tegulæ, and halteres light yellow ; cilia of tegulæ yellow. Abdomen shining bluish green, the venter yellow, sixth segment wholly yellow. First joint of hypopygium yellow, small, lying along the basal and dorsal (outer) surface of the second ; the latter brown, elongated, tapering, at its apex with a pair of minute, delicate yellow lamellæ, fringed with light yellow hairs. The interior organs, arising from the basal portion, are three in number—a long, straight, sharp, yellow central one (penis ?), and two slender bare yellow filaments ; the former is about as long as the hypopygium itself, the latter are much longer, somewhat crooked in the described specimen. Coxæ and all the legs pure light yellow, almost destitute of bristles. Wings hyaline, the veins yellow.

♀. Somewhat smaller, otherwise not materially different. Length 1·2-1·5 mm.

One male, numerous females. May, March. Two other males, more shrivelled and discoloured, are considerably darker than the perfect specimen here described.

2. *Xanthotricha minor*, n. sp.

Resembles the preceding, except in the following respects : The general colour is somewhat darker, the venter and sixth segment not yellow, male hypopygium blackish, the delicate parts shrunken and difficult to make out, but apparently without the long filaments so characteristic of the preceding ; pleuræ wholly bluish black ; the posterior cross-vein is shorter, in consequence of the fact that the fourth vein bends back to meet it, forming a distinct angle at this point. The last character is sufficient to separate the two species. Length 1·2 mm.

One male, two females. 500 feet.

3. *Xanthotricha singularis*, n. sp.

Still a third species of this minute genus differs from the first in its extremely small size, in its colour, which is in general the same as the second, and in the singular structure of the male hypopygium. This bears a close resemblance to the ovipositor of a female, extended to its full length and bent under the abdomen. Only by using a power of several hundred diameters could I ascertain that this structure really belonged to a male instead of a female. The females of the species, however, do not have such extended ovipositors; so the resemblance is rather to what one might suppose the female to be than to the female itself. This hypopygium is black, minutely yellow at tip. The wings of this species resemble those of the first, but are a little more rounded. Length 1 mm.

Six males, three females. May. 500 feet.

GNAMPTOPSILOPUS.

Aldrich, Kans. Univ. Quart., 1893.

1. *Gnamptopsilopus bicolor.*

Loew, Neue Beitr., viii., 96 ; Monogr., ii., 280 (*Psilopus*).

A single female. May.

Gnamptopsilopus flavidus, n. sp. (Pl. XII., fig. 109, wing.)

Slender, yellow, a broad stripe on the thorax, all the scutellum, and the hind margins of the abdominal segments bright-green. Cilia of tegulæ yellow.

♂. Face bright-green with thin white dust. Palpi and proboscis yellow. Front bright-green. Antennæ yellow, very small, arista dorsal. Thorax yellow, the scutellum violet, a green stripe upon the dorsum of the thorax is as wide as the scutellum behind and tapers in front to a rounded point at the margin. Metanotum yellow. Scutellum with only one pair of large bristles, the outer pair being very small. Abdomen yellow, the first segment above with a very narrow green border behind ; the following three segments almost half green ; the fifth a little more than half, and the sixth entirely, green. Venter wholly yellow ; near the hind margin of each segment are placed several large bristles. Hypopygium embedded, yellow ; only two small yellow, hairy, palpus-like organs are visible. Feet wholly yellow, the tarsi only moderately infuscated. Fore coxæ on the front side with a single longitudinal row of minute black hairs, and about three bristles at the end. Front femora near the base with six short thorn-like bristles. Front tarsi nearly three times the length of the tibiæ. Middle tibiæ and metatarsi with two rows of close short cilia, one on the front and one on the upper side ; as these cilia project in nearly the same direction, the effect is like a single somewhat tangled row. Hind tarsi as long as the tibiæ. All the legs are destitute of large bristles. Wings slender, hyaline. Costa noticeably ciliated along the middle, in the neighbourhood of the first vein. Third vein at its tip recurved forward. Posterior cross-vein oblique, less than half its length from the border. Fork of fourth vein making scarcely a right angle at its origin.

♀. Thorns of the fore femora larger. Middle tibiæ and tarsi simple. Abdomen, except the first segment, with more green on the dorsum, and shorter than in the male.

Length 4·5 mm. ; of wing, the same.

Sea level to 500 feet.   Six males and eight females.

3. *Guamptopsilopus flavicornis*, n. sp.

♀. Small, bright green, base of abdomen yellow, antennæ. yellow, the third joint sometimes brownish, arista dorsal or subdorsal. Face moderately narrow for the genus, blue or green, white-dusted.   Front shining green, excavated. dusted below. Antennæ yellow, the third joint sometimes brownish ; the arista dorsal or subdorsal. Thorax bright green. Scutellum with two large bristles, the outer pair minute, oppressed, or absent. Pleuræ green, white pollinose, the posterior border yellow. Tegulæ and halteres yellow. Abdomen green, the venter dorsum of first and proximal half of second segment yellow. Still in some cases the posterior margin of the first segment green. On the lateral angle of the first segment one or two long black bristles. Remainder of abdomen with small sparse black hair. Legs including coxæ, yellow, the tarsi slightly infuscated. Fore coxæ with three yellow bristles, hind with one. Fore metatarsus scarcely shorter than tibia, middle one but little shorter, whole hind tarsus four-fifths the length of its tibia. The legs have no bristles of any size ; at the tips of the middle and hind tibiæ, and on the fore side of the same near the base are very small ones. Wings hyaline, the veins yellow ; third vein recurved at tip, branch of fourth vein making a right angle at its origin. Posterior cross-vein oblique, two-thirds its length from the margin. Length 1·8 mm. ; of wing, 2 mm.

Three females.   One specimen has the third joint of the antennæ brownish-black, and the outer pair of scutellar bristles visible though minute, the other two have the antennæ wholly yellow, and no second pair of bristles whatever.   This does not seem to indicate a specific difference.

PSILOPUS.

Meigen, Syst. Beschr., vi., 1824.

1. *Psilopus chrysoprasius.*

Walker, List, &c., iii., 616 ; Loew, Neue Beit., viii., 90 ; Monogr., ii., 266.

Numerous specimens. Sea level to 500 feet. May.

2. *Psilopus caudatulus.*

Loew, Neue Beitr., viii., 93 ; Monogr., ii., 271.

Four males, two females. May.

3. *Psilopus bellulus,* n. sp.

Shining dark green, cilia of tegulæ black ; wings with a dark spot along the apical part of the front side.

♂. Face bright-green slightly white-dusted, with a deep transverse impression below the middle, bare. Palpi black ; proboscis brown. Front shining green with sparse and very delicate white hairs, especially towards the sides. Antennæ black ; small, the arista dorsal not long. Thorax shining green with erect and rather long bristles. Scutellum with four bristles. Pleuræ green, white-dusted. Tegulæ and their cilia black ; halteres fuscous with a yellow knob. Abdomen shining green, somewhat coppery, with a broad black band across each incisure ; on each side of the first segment a tuft of white hair, and a few more white hairs on the ventral surface, except these, the hair and bristles of the abdomen are all black. Bristles before the incisures rather long and erect. Hypopygium black, the lamellæ whitish or greyish. Coxæ, femora and hind tarsi including the extreme tips of the hind tibiæ, black. Tibiæ yellow. Fore and middle tarsi a little infuscated toward the tip ; still the fourth joint of the middle tarsus is covered with white hair, and hence almost white in colour. Fore coxæ with white hairs and two black bristles. All the femora with white cilia below, longest on the front ones near the base. Front tibiæ on the upper side with a row of four successively longer bristles, the last conspicuously long and two-thirds of the way to the end. Bristles of the other tibiæ inconspicuous, the hind tibiæ rather hairy. Tarsi simple, the hind ones shorter than their tibiæ. Wings with an indistinct brown cloud along the front margin beginning beyond the end of the first vein and continuing to that of the second, reaching into the first posterior cell behind. The branch of the fourth vein makes an acute angle at its origin ; third vein not recurved forward at its tip. Posterior cross-vein a little oblique, somewhat bicurved, less than half its length from the margin.

♀. Front scarcely ciliated, black bands of abdomen slightly wider ; bristles of body shorter ; those of fore tibiæ the same as in the male. The middle tibiæ also have large bristles, arranged on the same plan. Fourth joint of middle tarsus black ; fore and middle tarsi rather darker than in the male.

Length 4 mm. ; of wing, the same.

Altitude 500 feet. May. Four males and six females.

In immature specimens the wings are hyaline.

4. *Psilopus insularis*, n. sp.

Wings hyaline, tegular cilia black, legs including fore coxæ yellow, middle metatarsus of male ciliated.

♂. Face wide bluish-green with silvery pollen. Palpi black, with black hairs ; proboscis yellow. Front wide and deeply excavated, bright blue or green. Antennæ black, the third joint rather long, rounded at the end. Arista dorsal, slender, rather long. In less mature specimens the third antennal joint is more or less shrivelled. Thorax bright blue-green, scutellum more violet. From above the root of the wing a distinct black stripe reaches the humerus, becoming attenuated anteriorly. Pleuræ green, white-dusted. Tegulæ and their cilia black. Halteres yellow. Bristles of moderate size, four large ones on the scutellum. Abdomen metallic-blue and green, with black bands nearly half the width of the segments. Hypopygium black, small, at the tip with a pair of small forcep-like organs of sordid grey colour. Bristles and hair of abdomen rather long, black, at the sides basally the hair is white. Legs wholly yellow, the tarsi but little darker. Front coxæ yellow with fine yellowish hair, and near the end two black bristles. Middle and hind coxæ black ; the former with white hairs and one or two black bristles, the latter on the outside with a single black bristle and a few white hairs. Front and middle metatarsi longer than their tibiæ, the middle one with a dense row of short, blunt, slightly curved cilia on the upper edge. On the front side is a row of five or six small erect bristles. Hind tibiæ unusually hairy. This peculiarity extends over the metatarsus and decreases on the following joints. Wings hyaline ; posterior cross-vein straight, not very oblique, distant two-thirds its length from the margin. The anterior branch of fourth vein makes an acute angle at its origin. Third vein not recurved forward at its tip.

♀ Colour less inclined to blue and violet; third joint of antennæ short : bristles shorter ; black bands of abdomen narrower, comprising about one-third the segment. Middle metatarsi not ciliated ; hind tibiæ and tarsi only a little hairy.

Length 4·5 mm.; of wing, the same.

Sea-level to 1000 feet. Nine males and numerous females.

LEPTORHETHUM.

Aldrich, Kans. Univ. Quart., July, 1893.

1. *Leptorhethum angustatum.* (Pl. XII., fig. 103, wing of ♂.)

Aldrich, *l. c.*

♂. Small, green, legs yellow, abdomen yellow with green spots above, wings narrowed at base, cilia of tegulæ yellow. Face narrow, wider above and below (the eyes almost contiguous in the middle), white pollinose, showing a little of the green ground colour below the antennæ. Antennæ small, yellow, arista dorsal. Front bright-green, not excavated (this may be owing to a little extent to the shrivelled condition of the eyes in my only specimen), the lateral bristles small. Proboscis and palpi yellow. Thorax bright-green, the bristles mostly small. Pleuræ green, white pollinose, the hind margin yellow, halteres, tegulæ and their cilia yellow. Abdomen yellow ; dorsum of first segment green except a line in front ; second segment green on the last two-thirds above ; third segment scarcely half green above, the colour not reaching the sides; fourth segment with only a small spot of green ; fifth and sixth except the base and venter of the former, wholly green ; hypopygium small, blackish, embedded, the small whitish lamellæ protruding. Legs, including coxæ, yellow ; tarsi but little infuscated ; front coxæ long, almost entirely bare ; front metatarsi longer than the tibia. Middle tibiæ rather stout, above the middle on the fore side with a rather prominent bristle. Metatarsi longer, on the hind side with a very sparse row of small bristles, more dense near the end, where they are quite brush-like. The following joints simple, but oddly drawn up in my specimen. No noticeable bristles on fore or hind legs. Wings hyaline, third vein recurved, as figured. Length 2 mm.; of wing, 2·2 mm.

May. A single male.

SYRPHIDÆ.*

MEROMACRUS.

Rondani, Esam. di var. sp. Ins. Bras., 10, 1848.

1. *Meromacrus pratorum.*

Syrphus pratorum, Fabricius, Syst. Ent., 765; Ent. Syst., iv., 286.
Eristalis pratorum, Fabricius, Syst. Antl., 236; Wiedemann, Auss. Zw. Ins., ii., 166.
Pteroptila pratorum, Osten Sacken, Catalogue, 113; Williston, Synopsis, 183.

Twelve specimens. Wiedemann's description applies well, save that it is not stated that the sutural thoracic band is interrupted. The species will be distinguished from *M. ruficrus* by the separated spots at the base of the abdomen; from all the other known species by the entirely yellowish red legs.

ERISTALIS.

Latreille, Hist. Nat. des Crust. et Ins., xiv., 363, 1804.

1. *Eristalis vinetorum.*

Syrphus vinetorum, Fabricius, Ent. Syst. Suppl., 562.
Eristalis vinetorum, Fabricius, Syst. Antl., 235; Wiedemann, Auss. Zw. Ins., ii., 163; Macquart, Dipt. Exot., ii., 2, 42; Williston, Synopsis North Amer. Syrphidæ, 171, pl. vii., fig. 8; Trans. Amer. Ent. Soc., xv., 280; Biologia Centr.-Amer. Dipt., iii., 63; F. Lynch, A. Dipt. Argentina, Syrphidæ, 116; Giglio-Tos, Dit. Messic., ii., 7.
Eristalis trifasciatus, Say, J. Acad. Sci. Phil., vi., 165; Compl. Wr., ii., 359.
Eristalis uvarum, Walker, List, iii., 623.

Hab. North, Central and South America, and the West Indies.

---

* By S. W. Williston.

VOLUCELLA.

1. *Volucella obesa.*

Syrphus obesus, Fabricius, Syst. Ent., 763. (For synonymy, see Williston, Biol. Centr.-Amer. Dipt., iii., 50.)

Six typical specimens of this cosmopolitan insect are in the collection.

Volucella, sp. n. ?

Three specimens belonging to the difficult group of *pallens, resinulosa,* etc. I cannot find any description that will apply well to the specimens. They differ from *V. pallens*, Wied., in the presence of a median and two lateral facial stripes, in the hair of the mesonotum being for the most part black, and in the presence of a large black spot on the scutellum. From both *V. caga*, Wied., and *V. hyaloptera*, Giglio-Tos, the facial stripe will distinguish the species, as well as other characters.

BACCHA.

Fabricius, Syst. Antl., 199, 1805.

1. *Baccha clavata.*

Syrphus clavatus, Fabricius, Ent. Syst., iv., 296.

Baccha clavata, Fabricius, Syst. Antl. 200; Wiedemann, Auss. Zw. Ins., ii., 94; Schiner, Nov. Exped., 344; Wulp, Tijdschr., v., Ent., xxvi., 10; Roeder, Stett. Ent. Zeit. 1885, 342; Williston, Trans. Amer. Ent. Soc., xv., 270; Biol. Centr.-Amer. Dipt., iii., 33; Giglio-Tos, Ditt. del Messic., ii., 57; Austen, Proc. Zool. Soc. Lond., 1893, 159; Hunter, Can. Ent., xxviii, 96.

Baccha babista, Walker, List, iii., 549; Williston, Synopsis N. A. Syrph. 117, pl. iv., fig. 9 (Williston, Austen).

Baccha caria, Walker, List., iii., 549 (Austen).

Paragus scutellatus, Walker, Trans. Linn. Soc. Lond., xvii., 342 (Austen).

Baccha facialis, Thomson, Eugenies Resa, 504 (Williston).

Spatigaster bacchoides, Bigot, Ann. Soc. Ent. Fr., 1883, 326 (Williston).

Numerous specimens. The most northern habitat so far given for this species is Nebraska, by Hunter ; the most southern one, Buenos Aires, by Lynch (Dipt. Argentina, Syrphidæ, 47). It is probably at home in all the intervening regions, as well as the adjoining islands.

OCYPTAMUS.

1. *Ocyptamus dimidiatus.*

Syrphus dimidiatus, Fabricius, Spec. Ins., ii., 434;
     Ent. Syst., 310 ; Wiedemann, Auss. Zw. Ins., ii.,
     140.
Scaeva dimidiata, Fabricius, Syst. Antl., 254.
Chrilosia dimidiata, Macquart, Dipt. Exot., ii., 2, 105.
Pipiza dolosa, Walker, Trans. Ent. Soc. New Ser., iv.,
     156 (Austen).
Pipiza divisa, Walker, *l. c.* (Austen).
Ocyptamus dimidiatus, Schiner, Nov. Exped., 346;
     Wulp, Tijdschr., v., Ent. xxvi., 10 ; Williston, Biol.
     Centr.-Amer. Dipt., iii., 30 ; Giglio-Tos, Ditt. del
     Messic., ii., 53 ; Austen, Proc. Zool. Soc. Lond.,
     1893, 134.
Baccha dimidiata, Williston, Synopsis N. A. Syrphidæ,
     120, pl. v., fig. 10.

Hab. Central and South America, and the West Indies.

ALLOGRAPTA.

Osten Sacken, Bull. Buff. Soc. Nat. Sc., iii., 49, 1876.

1. *Allograpta exotica.*

Allograpta exotica, Wulp (*nec* Wiedemann), Tijdschr.,
     v., Ent., xxvi., 2, pl. i., fig. 2, Guadeloupe.

A single female specimen, agreeing fully with the description of what Wulp thought was Weidemann's *Syrphus exoticus.* In the Biologia Centr.-Amer. I considered Wulp's species doubtfully identical with *A. fracta,* O. S. Osten Sacken's species, however, does not have the scutellum broadly black, as did the specimens Wulp described, and as does the specimen from St. Vincent now before me. Wiedemann does not mention the spot on the scutellum, and I doubt very much that it was present in his specimen, as he could hardly have failed to mention it, so conspicuous is it. If his "schwarzlich Erzfarbe" means bright metallic green, or green-black, then there can be but little doubt that Osten Sacken's *A. fracta* is the same as *A. exotica.* In the work cited I mentioned a species from Mexico having an opaque, dark green mesonotum, which I thought might be the true *A. exotica.* Lynch is wrong in uniting it with the species having a shining mesonotum.

MESOGRAMMA.

Loew, Centur., ii., 290, 1872.

I have refrained from naming any of the numerous species (with one exception) that have been described from North and South America, in this genus, convinced, as I am, that their great variability will require a thorough monographic treatment, with abundant material, to certainly distinguish them. Many of the species are very abundant in warm, sunny places.

1. *Mesogramma basilare,* var.?

Syrphus basilaris, Wiedemann, Auss. Zw. Ins., ii., 43.
Mesogramma soror, Schiner, Nov. Exped., 350.
Mesograpta basilaris, Wulp, Tijdschr., v., Ent., xxxvi., 40, pl. i., fig. 8.
Mesogramma ——?, Williston, Biol. Centr.-Amer. Dipt., iii., 25.
Mesogramma basilare, Giglio-Tos, Ditt. del Messic., ii., 45.

Hab. Mexico, Brazil, Argentine Republic.

Ten specimens, labelled "Fitzhugh Valley, 500 feet, Cacao orchard." They differ very materially from the typical forms, but I believe that they represent a variety only. The female described by me in the work above cited certainly belongs with the males, though Giglio-Tos thinks that they differ too much to belong with them. The scutellum in these specimens has a narrow yellow border, and the abdomen is wholly red and yellow, the first segment alone excepted. There is a narrow, blackish, pre-apical ring on the hind femora, and the hind metatarsi are brownish; otherwise the legs are wholly yellow. The female has a broad median black stripe on the face, and the abdomen has obscure blackish markings, in the shape of two slender, approximated, median stripes; the hind margin of the segments is brownish.

2. *Mesogramma laciniosa.*

Mesogramma laciniosa, Loew, Centur., vi., 50.—Cuba.

Several female specimens I refer doubtfully to this species. The third and fourth abdominal segments have each two oval, oblique, black spots, and the posterior bands with a geminate, anteriorly dilated, slender prolongation in the middle, their anterior margin on each side concave; the fifth segment has three anterior, oval, black spots.

3. *Mesogramma boscii.*

Syrphus bosci, Macquart, Dipt. Exot., ii., 2, pl. xvii., fig. 2.
Syrphus gurges, Walker, Dipt. Saund., 236 (Osten Sacken).

Hab.   Carolina, Alabama, Florida.

Several female specimens that agree with the description, save that the second abdominal segment is black, with a median, interrupted, yellow stripe. Mr. Hunter thinks that this species is identical with *M. parvula*, Loew, and he may be right.

4. *Mesogramma*, sp.

♂, ♀. Face yellow.   Antennæ reddish yellow. Frontal triangle and the lateral margin of the female front yellow; vertical triangle black. Mesonotum with an entire yellow, lateral stripe. Scutellum black, with a yellow border. First two abdominal segments black, the first with the anterior angles, the second with a broad median, band yellow; third and fourth segments each with a quadrangular spot posteriorly on each side, and a small spot on the front margin, together with a median, partly obsolete, geminate stripe. Fifth segment with three spots. Legs yellow; hind femora with a broad black ring; hind tibiæ and tarsi brown; middle femora with a partly obsolete spot on the upper side distally. Length, 7–8 mm.

Sixteen specimens. The hind femora are a little stouter than usual.

PIPUNCULIDÆ.

PIPUNCULUS.

Latreille, Hist. Nat. des Crust. et Ins., xiv., 1804.

1. *Pipunculus aculeatus.* (Pl. XI., figs. 87, wing ;
87*a*, antenna.)

Pipunculus aculeatus, Williston, Biol. Cent.-Amer.
Dipt., iii., 88.—Mexico.

Five specimens. Agreeing quite with the description.
I am not able to compare the type specimen, but I believe
the determination is pretty certain. In most of the
specimens, the middle of the hind femora is brown.

2. *Pipunculus politus*, n. sp. (Pl. XI., fig. 88, wing.)

♂, ♀. Small cross-vein situated at or beyond the tip of the
first longitudinal vein ; penultimate section of the fourth vein
scarcely longer than the antepenultimate section ; abdomen wholly
shining. Length 4 mm.

Face and front black, silvery pubescent. Antennæ black, the
third joint more or less yellowish at the tip, less produced than in
P. aculeatus. Mesonotum shining, scarcely pollinose. Abdomen
wholly shining black. Legs black ; the extreme tip of the femora,
the base of the tibiæ, and the first three or four joints of the tarsi
yellow. Femora stout, without distinct spines on the underside.
Wings hyaline ; no stigmatic spot ; small cross-vein opposite or a
little before the middle of the discal cell ; second longitudinal vein
short.

Five specimens. In one of the specimens the small
cross-vein is distinctly before the middle of the discal
cell, and opposite the termination of the first vein.

TACHINIDÆ.

CISTOGASTER.

Latreille, Cuvier's Regne Anim., v., 1829.

1. *Cistogaster insularis*, n. sp.

♂, ♀. First three segments of the abdomen shining; first
posterior cell petiolate. Length 5-6 mm.

♂. Front at the vertex about as wide as the length of the
antennæ ; bright golden yellow, with an opaque median black
stripe. Antennæ black, the third joint at the base red, the second

joint also, more or less reddish ; third joint a half longer than the second. Face ashy grey, somewhat yellowish in the middle below ; a slender black line on either side running from the root of the antennæ. Palpi reddish yellow. Dorsum of thorax opaque golden yellow, with two median slender stripes, and a lateral, broader one, anteriorly abbreviated, black. Abdomen wholly reddish-yellow, with black hairs ; fourth segment and the third, save an interrupted band, light golden opaque-yellow. Tegulæ light yellow. Legs black. Wings uniformly subhyaline ; first posterior cell closed at some distance from the margin.

♀. Sides of front and the face silvery grey, a little yellowish near the vertex. Mesonotum densely yellowish grey pollinose, with two median brown lines and a broad, shining, black stripe on each side. Abdomen shining black, the third and fourth segments opaque greyish white, save a posterior interrupted band on the third, and two small spots on the fourth. Tegulæ white.

Six males and two females. The species closely resembles some of the varieties of *C. occidua*, Walker, but seems sufficiently distinct in the pollinose markings of the abdomen and the petiolate first posterior cell, which is closed at some distance from the margin.

TRICHOPODA.

Latreille, in Cuvier's Regne Animal., v., 512, 1829.

1. *Trichopoda pennipes*.   (Pl. XI., fig. 100, wing.)

Musca pennipes, Fabricius, Ent. Syst., iv., 348.
Dictya pennipes, Fabricius, Syst. Antl., 327.
Trichopoda pennipes, Wiedemann, Auss. Zw. Ins., ii., 274 ; Desvoidy, Myodaires, 288 ; Wulp, Tijdschr., v., Ent., xxvi., 15 ; Biol. Centr.-Amer. Dipt., ii., 3 ; Brauer and Berg., Musc. Schiz., i., 79.
Phasia jugatoria, Say, Compl. Wr., ii., 64.

Hab.   United States ; West Indies ; Central and South America.

Five specimens.

ELACHIPALPUS.

Rondani, Esap. Ditt., Ann. di Bologna, 1850.

1. *Elachipalpus macrocerus*.   (Pl. XI., fig. 99, wing.)

Tachina macrocera, Wiedemann, Auss. Zw. Ins., ii., 290.

Cuphocera macrocera, Schiner, Nov. Exped., 330;
  v. d. Wulp, Tijdschr., v., Ent., xxvi., 22.
Elachipalpus macrocerus, Brauer and Berg., Musc.
  Schizometopa, ii., 102.
Hab. Brazil.

Five specimens, agreeing with others from Brazil in
my collection.

JURINIA.

Rob. Desvoidy, Myodaires, 34, 1830.

1. *Jurinia*, sp. (Pl. XI., fig. 88*a*, antenna.)

♂, ♀. In structure and size almost identical with *J. apicifera*,
Walk. Front shining black, through the rather thin pollen.
Mesonotum shining green-black, very thinly pollinose. Tegulæ
deep brown. Abdomen deep blue-black throughout. Otherwise
as in *J. apicifera*.

This species is different from any that I know, either
from North or South America, and may be new. Still,
the wide distribution of the species of this genus renders
it probable that it has been described from other regions
in America.

2. *Jurinia apicifera.* (Pl. XI., fig. 89, antenna.)

Jurinia apicifera, Walker, List, iv., 720; Williston,
  Trans. Amer. Ent. Soc., xiii., 300; Townsend,
  Trans. Amer. Ent. Soc., xix., 90, xxii., 70; Calif.
  Acad. Sci., iv., 618.

Hab. United States; Canada; San Domingo;
Mexico.

Numerous specimens which agree quite with others
from various localities in the United States, Canada, and
San Domingo.

GONIA.

Meigen, Illiger's Mag., ii., 1803.

1. *Gonia pallens.* (Pl. XI., fig. 90, antenna of ♂.)

Gonia pallens, Wiedemann, Auss. Zw. Ins., ii., 346;
  Macquart, Dipt. Exot., ii., 3, 50; E. Lynch, A.,
  An. Soc. Cient. Arg., x., p. viii.; v. d. Wulp,
  Tijdschr. voor Ent., xxvi., 23; Biologia Cent.-
  Amer. Dipt., ii., 39; Townsend, Trans. Amer. Ent.
  Soc., xix., 95.

Gonia chilensis, Macquart, Dipt. Exot., ii., 3, 51, pl. v.,
    fig. 4; Blanchard, Gay's Hist. Fis. y. Pol. de
    Chile, vii., 422, pl. iv., fig. 20; Roeder, Stett. Ent.
    Zeit., 1885, 345.
Gonia augusta, Macquart, Dipt. Exot., ii., 3, 51, pl. 5,
    fig. 5; Walker, List, iv., 798.
Gonia lineata, Macquart, Dipt. Exot. Suppl., iv., 178.

Hab.   South America; Mexico; West Indies.

One specimen, which with much probability is conspecific with those from Cuba, referred to *G. chilensis,*
by Macquart. That the species is the same as *G. pallens*
is, to me, somewhat doubtful. It therefore seems worth
while to give a better description of our specimen.

♂. Claws small: sides of the face with bristles; third joint of
the antennæ seven or eight times as long as the second joint. Front
and face light yellow, silvery white pollinose, the sides of the
front subtranslucent, as though oiled; sides of the face with
sparse, short, black bristles. Cheeks bare. Antennæ black.
Median depression of the face wider than the sides; no bristles on
its ridges. Dorsum of thorax grey pollinose, somewhat shining.
Scutellum largely yellow. Abdomen narrow; yellowish red; first
segment under the scutellum, second and third with a slender
median stripe, and the posterior part of the fourth black; pollen
inconspicuous, except posteriorly. Tegulæ white. Wings subhyaline; the costal, subcostal, and marginal cells markedly yellow;
veins elsewhere narrowly clouded with the same yellow colour or
a dark brown. Claws and pulvilli small, not as long as the last
joint of the tarsi. Length 11 mm.

PHOROCERA.

Rob. Desvoidy, Myodaires, 131, 1830.

1. *Phorocera* (*Prospherysa?*) *puer,* n. sp. (Pl. XI.,
    fig. 91, head of ♂.)

♂. Eyes very sparsely pilose, the scattered hairs visible only
under careful examination. Front about as wide as the eye, the
lateral, silver-grey margins narrower than the broad, brownish-red,
median stripe; the frontal bristles reach nearly to the base of the
third antennal joint. First and second joints of the antennæ red;
third joint black, four or five times as long as the second. Face
and cheeks silver-grey, the lower part of the face and the cheeks

yellowish in ground colour. Mesonotum thickly grey pollinose, with five black stripes, the lateral ones interrupted. Abdomen flattened ovate ; shining black, with the anterior part of the second and third segments opaque grey; first segment without median bristles ; second segment with a pair of marginal ones ; third segment with a posterior row ; fourth segment bristly on the posterior half. Legs black ; claws elongate. Calyptræ white. Wings cinereous hyaline. Length 4½ mm.

One specimen. *Prospherysa* seems to differ from *Phorocera* only in the bare eyes, and the eyes of this specimen are, practically bare, so that it is a question whether or not this species should not be located in that genus. The cross-veins on the outer side of the wing are more than usually oblique, still hardly as much so as in *Plagia*. The genus *Plagioprospherysa*, Towns., which is synonymous with *Prosopodes*, B. and B., was based upon this character alone, and is to me hardly entitled to acceptance.

EXORISTA.

Meigen, Illiger's Mag., iii., 1803.

1. *Exorista nobilis*, n. sp.   (Pl. XI., fig. 92, head of ♂.)

♂. Front somewhat prominent, only a little narrowed behind ; above, equal to about one-fourth of the width of the head ; light golden-yellow in colour, with an opaque black stripe, which is narrowed above ; vertical bristles strong ; ocellar bristles small, proclinate ; the single row of frontal bristles descends nearly to the base of the third antennal joint; the sides have only a few short weak hairs. Sides of the face yellow above, silvery below ; in width not equal to one-third of that of the median depression ; four or five bristles on the vibrissal ridges, extending, in some cases, nearly to the middle of the face ; median depression silvery-white. Cheeks narrow, bare, silvery. Proboscis black ; palpi and labella yellow. Antennæ nearly black, the first two joints and the base of the third rufous ; third joint five or six times as long as the second. Thorax densely grey pollinose ; mesonotum with two slender median stripes, reaching from the pronotum to beyond the suture ; and a broad shining stripe on each side, interrupted by the suture, and abbreviated in front and behind. Scutellum grey, with six bristles. Abdomen elongate and narrow, black throughout ; the second, third, and fourth segments broadly and densely grey pollinose in front ; first and second segments with a single pair of strong median bristles ; third segment with a posterior row ; fourth bristly on the posterior half. Legs black ; posterior surface of the front femora broadly grey pollinose ; claws and the yellowish-brown pulvilli nearly as long as the last two joints taken together ; hind tibiæ with strong, unequal bristles on the posterior side. Tegulæ white. Wings nearly hyaline, or with a light blackish tint ; small cross-vein a little before the middle of the discal cell.

♀. Front less yellowish, and with orbital bristles ; pulvilli and ungues not longer than the fifth tarsal joint.

Length 9–11 mm.

Five specimens. This species is, apparently, an *Exorista* in the sense of Brauer and Bergenstamm.

ATROPHOPODA.

Townsend, Trans. Amer. Ent. Soc., xix., 373, 1892 ; *Vanderwulpia*, Townsend, Trans. Amer. Ent. Soc., xix., 381, 1892 ; *Microchira*, Brauer and Bergenstamm, Musc. Schizometopa, iii., 138, 1893 ; *Wulpia*, Brauer and Bergenstamm, *l.c.*, 1893.

1. *Atrophopoda townsendii*, n. sp. (Pl. XI., figs. 93, head and part of antenna of ♂ ; 93*a*, tarsus of ♂ ; 93*b*, tarsus of ♀ ; 93*c*, wing.)

♂, ♀. Frontal row of bristles descending to the lower border of the eyes ; eyes bare ; costa with spine ; first posterior cell long petiolate. Male claws and pulvilli not enlarged. Length 4–5 mm.

Front shining bluish beneath the silvery pollen, the median stripe black. Face silvery ; sides narrow. Antennæ black ; second joint red ; third joint seven or eight times longer than the second in the male ; in the female more slender and a little shorter ; arista in the male bare, in the female with long pubescence, subplumose. Palpi yellow, a little dilated at the tip. Thorax bluish-grey, opaque ; mesonotum with two, rather broad, deep-brown stripes, extending from the front margin to the scutellum. Abdomen long-ovate in shape ; opaque bluish-grey ; the first segment and the posterior part of the second and third segments shining black, the black reaching well toward the front margin in the middle ; first, second, and third segments with a pair of erect marginal bristles ; third segment with a single lateral one ; fourth segment with a posterior row. Legs black ; pulvilli and ungues of the male small on all the feet ; of the female, rudimentary on the front pair, the terminal joints compressed. Wings brownish, deeper along the veins, hyaline on the posterior margin, first posterior cell closed and rather long petiolate, terminating in the margin a little distance before the tip ; costa with spine ; third vein bristly before the cross-vein, the first vein bare.

Southern end of the island. May. Open ground, near sea, on herbage. Six females and two males.

2. *Atrophopoda braueri*, n. sp. (Pl. XI., figs. 94, head of ♂ ; 94*a*, tarsus of ♀ ; 94*b*, tarsus of ♂ ; 94*c*, wing.)

♂, ♀. Frontal bristles descending to the border of the eyes ; eyes very sparsely hairy ; arista pubescent in the female ; costa with spine ; first posterior cell narrowly open at the tip ; all the claws and pulvilli of male much elongated. Length 5-6 mm.

Face a little less receding than in *A. townsendii*, narrower, and the front of more equal width. Third joint of antennæ not more than four times the length of the second joint. Sides of front light-yellow pollinose. Face silvery-white ; median frontal stripe black. Antennæ deep brown or black ; the second joint red ; arista in the male bare, or almost imperceptibly pubescent ; in the female distinctly pubescent. Thorax silvery-grey, with two broad, deep brown or black stripes extending the full length of the mesonotum. Abdomen long-ovate, shining black, the anterior portion of segments two, three, and four silvery-grey ; first segment with lateral, but no median bristles ; second segment with lateral and a pair of marginal bristles ; third and fourth segments with a posterior row. Legs black ; all the claws and pulvilli of the male much elongated ; those of the four posterior feet of the female small, on the front feet rudimentary, and their terminal tarsal joints compressed. Wings nearly uniformly brownish or sub-hyaline ; first vein with hairs throughout ; third vein with hairs as far as the small cross-vein ; first posterior cell terminating near the tip of the wing, narrowly open, its angle obtuse and without stump.

Twenty specimens.

It will be seen from the generic synonymy given above that I take a different view of the value of the characters in this genus, from that of Messrs. Townsend, Bergenstamm, and Brauer. I am opposed to the principle that a genus is necessary for every described species in this family, and refrain from here adding two more for the preceding species. It is with much regret that I reduce the above names to synonyms, for the worthy entomologist whose name they commemorate deserves better at the hands of his zealous confreres.

There are now seven known species :—*A. singularis*, Towns. ; *Vanderwulpia atrophopodoides*, Towns. ; *V. sequens*, Towns. ; *Microchira mexicana*, B. & B. ; *Wulpia aperta*, B. & B.; and the ones described above—all markedly characterized by the rudimentary front claws of the female, and having the general markings and structure all very similar. No two, however, save perhaps the two species of *Vanderwulpia*, agree in their structural characters. Townsend made the error, apparently, of mistaking females for males, describing the front claws as rudimentary in both sexes, while, without doubt, in all the species they are alone rudimentary in the female.* Perhaps a grouping of the described characters will bring out more clearly the value of those which have been used for distinguishing the genera.

Eyes hairy. *A. singularis, M. mexicana, A. Braueri.*

Frontal bristles descending to the cheeks. *A. singularis, A. Townsendi, A. Braueri.*

Frontal bristles not descending below antennæ. *V. atrophopodoides, V. sequens, M. mexicana, W. aperta.*

First posterior cell open. *A. Braueri, W. aperta.*

First posterior cell closed in the margin or short petiolate. *A. singularis, V. sequens.*

First posterior cell long petiolate. *V. atrophopodoides, A. Townsendi.*

Costal spine present. *A. singularis, M. mexicana, W. aperta, A. Townsendi, A. Braueri.*

Male claws normal. *A. Townsendi.*

Male claws elongate. *A. Braueri.* (Other males unknown.)

Undoubtedly other mutations of these characters will appear among species yet to be made known.

I will add, that, in the two males of *A. Townsendi*, there is a single, well-developed orbital bristle ; in the males of *A. Braueri*, there are none ; in all the females there are two.

---

* Townsend has since recognized the males, and suspects that *Lachnomura*, Towns., is also a synonym of this genus (Trans. Amer. Ent. Soc., xxxii., 77, 1895).

DIDYMA.

V. d. Wulp, Biologia Centrali-Amer., Diptera, ii., 156, 1890.

1. *Didyma calyptrata*, n. sp.   (Pl. XI., fig. 95, head of ♂.)

♂. Front above equal to about one-fourth of the width of the head, a little broader below ; silvery grey on the sides, the median stripe black, narrower above, and narrower than the sides. Sides of the face grey, the median depression darker. The frontal bristles descend as far as the base of the third antennal joint, and nearly as far as the uppermost of the vibrissal bristles. Eyes clothed thickly with dusky pile. Antennæ black, shorter than the face, the third joint four or five times longer than the second ; arista thickened at the base. Proboscis black, the palpi yellowish. Thorax black ; mesonotum shining, very thinly pollinose, and without distinct stripes. Scutellum black. Abdomen short-oval ; black, with thinly pollinose bands on the anterior part of the segments ; first and second segment with marginal bristles ; third with a posterior row ; fourth with the posterior part bristly. Legs black ; hind tibiæ with unequal bristles. Tegulæ large, yellowish-white. Wings greyish-hyaline ; small cross-vein at the middle of the discal cell ; angle of fourth vein broadly rounded ; first posterior cell terminating just before the tip, narrowly open. Length 4 mm.

Two specimens. The female specimen has the front broader, the eyes sparsely pilose, the mesonotum more distinctly pollinose, and with two narrow black stripes in front ; the abdomen broader, and the marginal bristles of the first and second segments possibly wanting. There is a pair of orbital bristles present in both sexes.

DEGEERIA.

Meigen, Syst. Beschr., vii., 249, 1838.

1. *Degeeria nigriventris*, n. sp.   (Pl. XI., fig. 96, head of ♂.)

♂. Abdomen shining black ; discal bristles present ; wings hyaline. Length 4 mm.

Front only a little narrower above, equal in width to about one-fourth of that of the head ; median stripe very broad, opaque-black ; sides grey, at the vertex shining black. Face opaque-grey, sides very narrow ; vibrissal row of bristles extending nearly to the base of the third joint, and nearly to the lowermost one of the frontal row. Antennæ black, reaching very nearly to the vibrissæ ; third joint six or seven times as long as the second. Mesonotum shining black, the sides in front pollinose. Abdomen shining black ; first segment with marginal bristles ; second and third segments with both marginal and discal ones, the latter with two additional posterior ones on each side ; fourth segment bristly on the posterior part. Legs black. Tegulæ nearly white. Wings hyaline ; posterior cross-vein straight, situated in the middle between the anterior cross-vein and the bend of the fourth vein, the angle obtuse and without stump ; last section of the fourth vein gently concave, terminating very near the tip of the wing. No costal spine.

Three specimens.

BESKIA.

Brauer and Bergenstamm, Denksch. K. Acad. Wissensch., lvi., 139, 1889 ; *Ocypterosipho,* Townsend, J. N. York Ent. Soc., ii., 79, 1894.

1. *Beskia cornuta.*   (Pl. XI., figs. 97, head of ♂ ; 97*a*, wing.)

Beskia cornuta, Brauer and Bergenstamm, Dencksch. K. Acad. Wissench., lvi., 139, fig. 276.

Ocypterosipho willistoni, Townsend, *l. c.*

Hab. San Domingo (Coll. Williston), Brazil (B. B.).

Several specimens ; agreeing well with the description.

DEXIIDÆ.

RHYNCHODEXIA.

Bigot, Bullet. Soc. Ent. Fr., 1885, p. xi.

1. *Rhynchodexia sororia,* n. sp.   (Pl. XI., fig. 98, head of ♂ .)

♂, ♀. Thorax and scutellum cinereous, with black stripes. Abdomen of male red, with a black stripe ; of the female, black ; palpi yellow, brown at the tip. Legs black. Length 9–13 mm.

♂. Head light opaque, golden-yellow, the cheeks more ashy ; ground-colour of the lower part of the face and the cheeks yellow. First two joints of the antennæ, and the base of the third, red ; third joint a little more than twice the length of the second ; arista thickened on the basal portion, plumose ; second antennal joint prominent, and with bristles. Proboscis black ; palpi slender, yellow, brownish at tip, a little broader on the distal portion. Mesonotum cinereous, with variable reflections, and with three broad black stripes, and on each side of the median stripe a narrow black line ; scutellum cinereous, its base black and tip red. Abdomen conical, yellowish red, with a broad black stripe, some-times interrupted at the sutures ; cinereous pollinose, variable in different reflections ; clothed with short black hairs and stout macrochætæ, as follows : three or four lateral ones on the first segment, as many lateral ones on the second segment, and three pairs of median ones; anterior, lateral ones, and a thick-set posterior row on the third segment ; the fourth segment covered. Legs black, the middle of all the tibiæ red or reddish ; front femora with a conspicuous row of long bristles on the under side ; middle femora with a fewer number forming a similar row ; hind tibiæ with about three pairs on the posterior side ; claws and the yellowish brown pulvilli somewhat longer than the last tarsal joint. Tegulæ yellow. Wings cinereous hyaline, the anterior cells yellowish ; small cross-vein at the middle of the discal cell ; angle of fourth vein rounded.

♀. Front above less than one-fourth the width of the head ; a pair of reclinate vertical, and two pairs of orbital bristles present. Abdomen black, with strong white reflections ; the fifth segment red ; first segment with a single lateral bristle ; second with one lateral and discal and marginal ; third segment with a discal pair and posterior row ; fourth segment wholly covered.

Numerous specimens. This species is apparently an *Eudexia*, B. & B., and seems nearest allied to *R. fraterna*, v. d. Wulp.

SARCOPHAGIDÆ.

SARCOPHILODES.

Brauer and Bergenstamm, Denkschr. der K. Acad. Wissensch., lvi., 164, 1889.

1. *Sarcophilodes puella*, n. sp. (Pl. XII., fig. 120*bis*, head of ♂.)

♂, ♀. Front broad, the median stripe scarcely one-third of its breadth ; at the upper corner of the eyes with two bristles, the inner longer one recurved, the outer one directed obliquely out-ward ; a pair of proclinate ocellar bristles ; and two orbital bristles, the upper one reclinate the lower one procliuate ; on either side of the median stripe with about four or five rather strong bristles ; front of the female of the same width as that of the male, but with two additional proclinate, orbital bristles. Third joint of the antennæ not more than three times the length of the second, the arista moderately plumose on the basal half. Sides of the face and the cheeks bare, the latter with bristles on the lower margin. Mesonotum with well-developed centro-dorsal bristles extending in front of the suture. Scutellum with two well-developed bristles on each lateral margin, but without a marginal apical pair. Abdomen short, oval ; second and third segments each with a pair of marginal bristles, the third with two additional lateral marginal ones, and the fourth with a posterior row ; hypopygium without bristles. Tibiæ without long hair, the bristles irregular. Third vein of the wings setulose at the proximal end, the distal section not sinuous : anterior cross-vein nearly opposite the end of the first vein and at the middle of the discal cell, the distance from the anterior cross-vein to the posterior cross-vein equal to the length from the latter to the angle ; posterior cross-vein much less oblique than the apical cross-vein ; angle of the fourth vein with a fold, but not distinctly appendiculated ; first posterior cell narrowly open before the border of the wing. Head yellowish-grey ; frontal stripe red or brownish-red : antennæ black. Mesonotum with three deep brown stripes, about as wide as the grey between them. Abdomen opaque yellowish-grey, changeable in different reflection, with a median stripe and a row of three rather small spots on each side ; hypopygium grey. Legs black. Wings hyaline. Length 4 mm.

Numerous specimens. St. Vincent. The present species does not wholly agree with the definition of the genus, as given by Brauer and Bergenstamm. It differs in having the first posterior cell open and inappendiculate, and in having the hypopygium rather small. It may be a *Sarcophagula*, Wulp.

SARCOPHAGA.

Meigen, Syst. Beschr., v., 14, 1826.

TABLE OF SPECIES.

1. Hypopygium or anal segments red 2
   Hypopygium or anal segments black or grey 5
2. Hypopygium large, with abundant black hair and without bristles ; scutellum with three pairs of stout bristles ; posterior tibiæ of males with long hair . . *otiosa*, n. sp.
   Tibiæ of male without long hair 3

3. First segment of the hypopygium with well-developed
   bristles on its posterior margin : first longitudinal vein
   with a few bristles at its proximal end ; scutellum
   without apical bristles. . . . . *chœtopygialis.*
   First segment of the hypopygium without bristles on its
   hind margin ; scutellum with a pair of apical bristles . 4
4. Hypopygium large, both segments red, black hair ; mesonotum without black bristles in front . *concinnata*, n. sp.
   Hypopygium small, its first segment black . . *pavida*, n. sp.
5. First longitudinal vein without bristles . . *micropygialis*, n. sp.
   First longitudinal vein with bristles . . . . sp.

1. *Sarcophaga micropygialis,* n. sp.

♂. Front above in width less than the length of the third
antennal joint ; vertex with two strong proclinate bristles, a little
in advance of the ocelli another, smaller, pair of reclinate bristles,
apparently the beginning of the rather long ones composing the
frontal rows ; ocelli with two proclinate bristles. Sides of the
face narrow, not more than one-half the width of the median flattened surface ; a row of minute bristles near the eyes, otherwise
bare. The bare, hair-like tip of the arista about as long as the
plumose portion. Cheeks with black hair, on the inferior
margin with black bristles, reaching to the stout vibrissæ,
which are situated only a little distance above the oral margin.
In colour, the sides of the front and face, the cheeks and the
posterior orbits are light golden yellow, opaque central portion
of the face grey ; frontal stripe and the antennæ black. Black
stripes of the mesonotum broad ; the mesonotum with black
hair and with four rows of well-developed bristles, reaching
to the front part. Scutellum with four stout bristles, and
in the middle of the apical border a pair of minute bristles,
closely approximated. Abdomen black, scarcely at all shining,
the second and third segments each with four oval spots, somewhat variable in different reflections ; third segment with a
pair of median marginal bristles ; fourth segment with a strong,
posterior row of bristles, and an oval black spot on each side
anteriorly ; hypopygium small, black, grey or yellowish-grey
pollinose, its first segment with a row of black bristles before its
posterior margin. Legs black ; middle tibiæ with a single stout
bristle on its posterior side near the middle; hind tibiæ with several
bristles and without long hair on the inner side ; pulvilli long.
Wings nearly hyaline ; first longitudinal vein without bristles ;
third vein with bristles for more than half the distance to the

anterior cross-vein, the latter situated at the middle of the discal cell; distance from the anterior cross-vein to the posterior cross-vein more than three times that from the latter to the angle of the fourth vein. Length 9 mm.

2. *Sarcophaga concinnata*, n. sp.

♂. Agrees with *S. otiosa* throughout, except that the middle and hind tibiæ are wholly without the thick long hair on the inner side, and the femora have less hair below. The specimens, moreover, seem to be less thickly hairy than in that species, and the size is less. Length 9–11 mm.

With the three specimens presenting the above characters, there are four females which may belong with them, but from their larger size, I suspect are *S. otiosa*. The front is broader than in the males; there are four well-developed bristles along the orbit and two orbital, proclinate bristles; the black stripes of the mesonotum seem a little narrower; the fifth abdominal segment is red, the legs are without the long hair, and the claws are a little shorter. It is possible that the species is identical with *S. chrysostoma*, Wied.

3. *Sarcophaga otiosa*, n. sp.

♂. Front narrow above, at the vertex the width is about equal to the length of the third antennal joint ; at each superior angle of the eyes there is a stout bristle directed backwards ; a little way in front of these there is a single, smaller bristle on each side ; along the edge of the frontal stripe, a row of thick-set bristles, short above, but becoming successively longer below. Sides of the face bare, except a row of minute bristles situated close to the eyes. The antennæ reach nearly to the stout vibrissæ ; arista long and densely plumose. Cheeks light-golden pilose, with a row of black bristles on the inferior margin, reaching to the vibrissæ ; vibrissæ situated at some distance above the oral margin. In colour, the sides of the front and of the face are opaque, light golden-yellow, the frontal stripe, the antennæ, and the vibrissal ridges black, the last greyish pollinose. Stripes of the mesonotum broad and deep black ; mesonotum with abundant black hair, but without bristles, except on the posterior part. Scutellum with three pairs of stout bristles, the apical pair approximated and cruciate. Abdomen marmorate, metallic-black and yellowish-grey, variable in different

reflections; third segment with two or four, median, marginal
bristles and two lateral ones; fourth segment with a row of strong
marginal ones; hypopygium large, reddish-yellow, thickly clothed
with black hair or pile, its first segment without bristles. Legs
stout, metallic-black; front femora pollinose behind; middle tibiæ,
except on the basal third, and the hind tibiæ throughout, with
abundant long black pile; all the femora have rather abundant
pile on the under-side; middle tibiæ with a single stout bristle on
the outer-side, near the middle, the hind tibiæ with four or five,
besides the terminal ones. Wings nearly hyaline; first longitudinal vein bare, the third with a few bristles at the extreme
base; outer cross-veins in nearly the same straight line, the
posterior cross-vein joining the fourth vein beyond the middle of
the distance between the anterior cross-vein and the angle. Claws
elongate. Length 12–13 mm.

Five specimens   There are no ocellar bristles. It is
not improbable that the female of this species is that
mentioned under the preceding.

4. *Sarcophaga pavida,* n. sp.

♂. Width of the front above greater than the length of the
third antennal joint; at the angle of the eyes above a strong
reclinate bristle; below the ocelli on either side, forming the
beginning of the frontal row (the bristles of which are distinctly
smaller) there are two, strong reclinate bristles; ocelli with two
small, proclinate bristles. A row of minute bristles on the sides of
the face near the eyes; otherwise bare. Cheeks with yellow hair
and with black bristles on its lower margin. In colour, the sides of
the front of the face, the cheeks, and the posterior orbits are light
golden-yellow, the median facial depression grey, the frontal
stripe and the antennæ black. Black stripes of the mesonotum
rather broader than the intervening grey stripes; bristles of
the mesonotum extending to the front. Scutellum with two stout
bristles on each lateral border, and a pair of smaller, approximated,
cruciate ones at the tip. Abdomen black, shining; the second,
third and fourth segments each with four oval, grey spots,
changeable in different reflections; third segment with median
marginal bristles; hypopygium small, its first segment yellowish-
grey, almost wholly concealed, the posterior segment shining-red,
with black hair. Legs black; middle tibiæ with two median
exterior bristles, the lower one stout; hind tibiæ without hair on
the inner side. Wings greyish-hyaline; first longitudinal vein
without bristles; outer cross-veins in nearly the same direction;

anterior cross-vein at the middle of the discal cell ; the distance between the cross-veins is less than three times that from the posterior one to the angle. Length 9 mm.

♀. A single strong reclinate bristle at the beginning of the frontal row ; two proclinate, orbital bristles on each side ; fifth abdominal segment very small, nearly concealed, red ; front a little broader above.

Four specimens. St. Vincent.

5. *Sarcophaga chætopygialis*, n. sp.

♂. Width of the front above less than the length of the third antennal joint ; a stout reclinate bristle at the angle of the eyes, another, less strong, forming the beginning of the frontal rows ; and a pair of small, proclinate ocellar bristles. Bristle of the antennæ plumose nearly to the extremity. Sides of the face bare ; cheeks with black hairs. The dorso-central bristles of the mesonotum extend to the front ; black stripes of the mesonotum much broader than the grey intervals. Scutellum with two stout bristles on each side, and without the apical pair. Abdomen shining black, with four rows of grey spots, only moderately changeable in different reflections. Hypopygium prominent, shining red, the first segment with well-developed bristles on its hind margin ; hair sparse, black. Wings distinctly greyish-hyaline ; first and third veins with bristles ; posterior cross-vein distinctly less oblique than the apical cross-vein ; anterior cross-vein at the middle of the discal cell. Length 7–8 mm.

♀. Front a little broader above ; aual segment red, small, nearly concealed ; front with orbital bristles.

Numerous specimens. St. Vincent.

MUSCIDÆ.

Musca.

Linné, Fauna Suecica, 1763.

1. *Musca domestica.*

Musca domestica, Linné, etc.—Cosmopolitan.
Musca harpyia, Harris, Ent. Correspond., 335.— North America.

Stomoxys.

Geoffroy, Hist. des Ins., i., 1764.

1. *Stomoxys calcitrans*, Linné, etc.—Cosmopolitan.

Lucilia.

Robineau Desvoidy, Myodaires, 452, 1830.

1. *Lucilia (Compsomyia) macellaria.*

Musca macellaria, Fabricius, Syst. Ent., 776 (for the extensive bibliography and synonymy, see Lynch A., An. Soc. Cient. Arg., x., 71, 233).— North and South America.

2. *Lucilia ruficornis.*

? *Lucilia ruficornis,* Macquart, Dipt. Exot. 1er Suppl., 198; Schiner, Reise der Novara, Dipt., 304; Roeder, Stett. Ent. Zeit., xiii., 347; Bigot, in Ramon de la Sagra. Nat. Hist., 821.—Colombia (Macq.), Chile (Schiner), Cuba (Bigot), Porto Rico (Roeder).

? *Lucilia cluvia,* Walker, List, iv., 885.—West Indies.

? *Musca insularis,* Walker, Dipt., Saund., 340.—West Indies.

I do not feel quite sure of the determination.

ANTHOMYIIDÆ.

Ophyra.

Robineau Desvoidy, Myodaires, 516, 1830.

1. *Ophyra ænescens.* (Pl. XII., figs. 120, head of ♂; 120*a*, wing.)

Anthomyia ænescens, Wiedemann, Auss. Zw. Ins., ii., 435.—New Orleans, West Indies.

Ophyra ænescens, Macquart, Dipt. Exot. 1er Suppl., 203; Roeder, Stett. Ent. Zeit., 1885.—Texas (Macq.), Porto Rico (Roeder).

♂. Deep shining green black, the face and legs black. Eyes nearly contiguous. Front below with short bristles. Antennæ dark-red; arista slender, bare. A small spot in the middle above the antennæ; the face and the cheeks light, silvery pollinose; oral and cheek bristles small. Proboscis short; palpi yellow. Abdomen ovate, with rather dense, erect, black hair; bristles at the tip slender and not long. Wings lightly tinged with brown. Hind tibiæ simple. Length 5 mm.

One specimen. St. Vincent.

LISPA.

Latreille, Precis, etc., 1796.

1. *Lispa uliginosa.*

Lispa uliginosa, Fallen, Dipt. Suec. Musc., 93 ; Loew, Stett. Ent. Zeit., viii., 24 ; Kowarz, Wien. Ent. Zeit., xi.—Europe, North America.

Six specimens. St. Vincent.

CYRTONEURA.

Macquart, Hist. Nat. Dipt., ii., 274, 1835.

1. *Cyrtoneura maculipennis,* n. sp. (Pl. XII., figs. 121, head of δ ; 121*a*, wing.)

δ. Eyes bare, separated at the vertex by a space not twice the width of the ocellar tubercle. Front with a median, narrow, black stripe, broader at the lower end; orbits silvery-grey, with a single row of bristles, descending as far as the proximal end of the second joint of the antennæ. Ocellar tubercle with two strong proclinate bristles. Antennæ black, the second joint and the immediate base of the third largely yellowish, the third joint reaching nearly to the strong oral bristles ; arista long plumose. Face light-grey pollinose. Proboscis and palpi black. Mesonotum lightly grey pollinose ; in some lights with two slender, interrupted stripes on each side, and the beginning of two median ones in front. Scutellum grey pollinose, large, triangular, with two approximated bristles at its apex. Pleuræ black, only slightly pollinose. Abdomen short and broad, greyish-yellow pollinose, somewhat variable in different reflections, the shining ground-colour showing through ; clothed with short bristly hairs and with moderately long bristles at the tip. Legs wholly black. Wings greyish-hyaline, or uniformly tinged with pale brownish ; a small blackish spot at the tip of the auxiliary vein, and one on the anterior cross-vein ; the posterior cross-vein, which is nearly straight and rectangular to the fifth vein, is lightly clouded ; first posterior cell slightly narrowed in the margin. Tegulæ nearly white, the upper one smaller than the under one. Halteres yellow. Length 4½–5½ mm.

♀. Front less than one-third of the width of the head, the median black stripe broad, and of equal width. Pulvilli a little smaller than in the male. Abdomen grey, with irregular light-brown markings.

Six specimens. St. Vincent.

Robineau Desvoidy, Essai sur les Myod., 517, 1830.

1. *Limnophora exilis*, n. sp.

♂. Front long, the eyes very nearly contiguous below the ocelli, leaving a very narrow space in which there are rows of long slender bristles ; below, the opaque black of this space broadens out into the frontal triangle, leaving the orbits narrowly silvery. Antennæ black, the third joint not reaching to the vibrissal bristles ; arista bare. Face lightly grey pollinose ; epistoma but very little projecting ; cheeks very narrow. Mesonotum shining black the lateral margins in front of the suture, the pleuræ and the abdomen, where not spotted, light-grey pollinose. Scutellum shining black. Abdomen ovate, the first segment in large part, the second and third each with three large, subconfluent, subopaque, black spots ; fourth segment for the most part shining. Legs black ; hind tibiæ with long black pile on the inner side ; pulvilli not elongated. Wings yellowish hyaline ; penultimate section of the fourth vein shorter than the posterior cross-vein, the latter rectangular. Palpi black. Length 3½ mm.

Two specimens. St. Vincent.

2. *Limnophora debilis*, n. sp.

♂. Eyes nearly contiguous below the ocelli. Front silvery white, with a large, opaque, black triangle below, with two rows of erect black bristles. Antennæ dark-brownish red ; arista bare. Face silvery grey. Thorax black ; mesonotum densely light yellowish-grey pollinose, with three complete and two incomplete, narrow, dark-brown stripes. Pleuræ densely light, grey pollinose. Scutellum of the same yellowish-grey colour as the dorsum of the thorax, with a discal, dark-brown spot; it is large and triangular, and has a pair of apical cruciate bristles, and one on each border. Abdomen ovate, opaque light yellow; first segment on the sides and the fourth segment for the greater part black, covered with light-yellowish pollen; second and third segments each with a pair of dark-brown, opaque spots. Legs black, the knees yellow; hind tibiæ not hairy. Tegulæ white, the under one projecting. Halteres yellow. Wings greyish hyaline. Length 5–6 mm.

Two specimens. St. Vincent. With these two male specimens, there is a large number of female specimens of smaller size, in which the abdomen is black in ground-colour, with two pairs of dark-brown spots on the second and third segments. The front is broad, with a black stripe. The wings show a noticeable difference in that the posterior cross-vein is at right-angles to the fourth vein, and is a little shorter than the penultimate section of the fourth vein. In the males described above the anterior angle of the discal cell is distinctly less than a right angle, and the posterior cross-vein is longer than the penultimate section of the fourth vein. The epistoma is but little prominent in either sex.

3. *Limnophora (Spilogaster?) exul,* n. sp.   (Pl. XII., figs. 122, head of ♂ ; 122a, wing.)

♂. Black. Eyes narrowly separated below the ocelli : median black stripe of the front expanded triangularly below ; orbital margins silvery pollinose. Antennæ black ; the third joint does not reach to the oral bristles ; arista short plumose. Face light-grey pollinose. Proboscis and palpi slender, black. Mesonotum light yellowish-grey, opaque, with three broad, black stripes, the lateral ones widened back of the suture to the root of the wings. Scutellum black, its margins grey with four bristles, the apical cruciate pair approximated. Pleuræ light-grey pollinose, the upper part black. Abdomen elongate ovate ; opaque light yellowish-grey; the first segment, except the posterior lateral margins and a pair of large triangles on the second and third segments, extending the whole length of each segment, and leaving a narrow stripe between them, black ; fourth segment with three black or brown spots, the median one elongate. Legs black ; pulvilli elongate ; none of the tibiæ hairy. Wings lightly tinged ; fourth vein sinuous near the extremity, narrowing the first posterior cell. Tegulæ white, the under one much larger than the upper one. Length 6–7 mm.

♀. Front less than one-third of the width of the head, with a broad black stripe. Abdomen broader and shorter, the deep-brown (not opaque black) markings more extensive, leaving a median stripe on the first three segments and the posterior angles of the first segment opaque grey.

Ten specimens. St. Vincent.

CŒNOSIA.

Meigen, Syst. Beschr. Europ. Dipt., v., 210, 1826.

1. *Cænosia flavipes,* n. sp.

♂. Front densely light-grey pollinose, the ground-colour showing through bluish ; in width about one-fourth that of the head.

Face, cheeks and occiput of the same colour or lighter. Antennæ pure light yellow ; arista bare, slender, yellow at its base. Thorax everywhere densely light-grey pollinose, but with a bluish tint as though from the black ground-colour ; mesonotum with a median brown stripe. Abdomen yellow, the distal segments brownish or blackish ; in shape elongate ovate and not flattened. Legs wholly yellow. Wings tinged with yellowish ; penultimate section of the fourth vein not longer than the posterior cross-vein. Length 6 mm.

♀. Mesonotum with three brown stripes. Antennæ darker, the third joint in part brownish. Abdomen darker, the second and following segments each with a pair of small rounded spots, and a median brownish stripe. Hind tarsi brownish.

Numerous specimens. St. Vincent.

2. *Cœnosia insularis*, n. sp. (Pl. XII., figs. 123, head of ♂ ; 123*a*, wing.)

♂. Front opaque golden yellow, a little less than one-third of the width of the head, and of nearly equal width. Antennæ black ; arista finely pubescent. Face yellowish-grey. Cheeks below the eyes rather narrower than the width of the third joint of the antennæ. Occiput swollen below ; greyish pollinose, the orbits yellow. Mesonotum densely light grey pollinose, with two broad, dark coffee-brown stripes extending on the sides of the scutellum, the latter with a median, light coloured stripe, extending from the mesonotum. Pleuræ greyish pollinose. Abdomen cylindrical, only a little broader at the base ; shining brownish-black with the anterior angles of the segments broadly grey pollinose ; covered with recumbent hairs, and with a slender lateral bristle on each segment. Legs black ; the knees and coxæ in front (beneath the pollen) yellowish. Wings tinged with pale-brown. Tegulæ nearly white, the under one projecting beyond the upper. Halteres yellow. Palpi black. Length 6-7 mm.

Numerous specimens. St. Vincent. The abdomen in the female is elliptical.

MICROPEZIDÆ.

TANYPEZA.

Fallen, Dipt. Suec. Opomyz., 4, 1820.

1. *Tanypeza claripennis*. (Pl. XII., figs. 124, head of ♂ ; 124*a*, wing.)

Tanypeza claripennis, Schiner, Reise der Novara, Dipt., 247.—Brazil.

A single specimen without abdomen and hind legs, but which, otherwise, agrees so well with the description of this species that I believe the determination is sufficiently certain.

CALOBATA.

Meigen, Illiger's Mag., 1803; *Ceyx*, Dumeril, 1801.

1. *Calobata angulata.*

Calobata angulata, Loew, Centur., vii., 87; Schiner,
  Reise der Novara, Dipt., 253, Brazil, Colombia
  (Schiner, Loew).

In the present collection there are about twenty specimens which were thought at first sight to be conspecific. A more careful examination, however, disclosed trustworthy specific differences. Both of the species are evidently closely allied to *C. lasciva,* Fabr., and it is not improbable that they have been confounded with that species. I do not know *C. lasciva,* but they differ, according to Schiner, in the light-coloured bands of the hind femora being oblique. Schiner thought that *C. angulata* might be identical with *C. annulata,* F., but, if my determinations are correct, he was in error. In the present species the front is very narrow and long, distinctly less than one-third of the width of the head. The front tarsi are white from near the middle of the metatarsi, the terminal joints scarcely perceptibly darker. The lighter-coloured portions of the wing are subhyaline, and the first posterior cell is narrowly open The head is reddish-yellow with a small dark-red or black spot in the middle of the front. The antennæ in all our specimens are more reddish than black. I have compared specimens from Brazil in my collection, and find no differences.

2. *Calobata annulata.*

Musca annulata, Fabricius, Syst., iv., 333; Syst. Antl.,
  262.
Calobata annulata, Wiedemann, Auss. Zw. Ins., ii.,
  531.—Cayenne.
Grallopoda annulata, Rondani, Esapoda Ditteri, 178.—
  Ins. St. Sebastian.

The species which I identify as this from both St. Vincent and Brazil, has a dark reddish-brown head, with a broad front, distinctly more than one-third of the width of the head, brownish-red antennæ, a rather narrow clypeus, stouter and rather longer front tarsi, with only the second, third, and fourth joints light-yellow, the lighter coloured parts of the wing more pure hyaline, and the first posterior cell closed.

The genus *Calobata* has been repeatedly subdivided by Macquart and Rondani, but their subdivisions have not been accepted by later writers. For *C. lasciva (C. albimana*, Macq.) Macquart proposed the genus *Tæniaptera*, but afterward withdrew it. For the same species Rondani proposed *Grallopoda.* For the species with open first posterior cell, bare arista and long anal cell, he proposed *Mimegralla* ; for those with closed first posterior cell, bare arista and long anal cell, *Grallomyia* ; while *Raineria*, which was afterwards changed to *Tanipoda*, was applied to species differing from *Grallomyia* in the short anal cell. *Calobata* he restricted to those species with plumose antennal arista.

3. *Calobata mellea*, n. sp. (Pl. XII., fig. 125, wing.)

♂, ♀. Reddish yellow ; abdomen black. Sides of the front shining ; in the middle a dark-red opaque stripe. Antennæ yellow, third joint not twice as long as wide ; arista short-plumose. Face yellow, silvery pollinose on the sides. Clypeus of moderate width, red or black, shining. Thorax reddish-yellow, shining, the pleuræ a little lighter coloured. Abdomen black, shining, slender ; male organs and the ovipositor, except its base, yellow. Legs yellow ; front tibiæ except the extreme tip black ; middle and hind tibiæ, middle tarsi, and the hind tarsi, except the greater portion of the metatarsi brownish ; front metatarsi light-yellow ; hind metatarsi yellow. Wings hyaline, with a large brown spot filling out the first posterior cell to beyond its middle, the outer half of the discal cell, and triangularly in the submarginal cell to near the tip of the second vein ; first posterior cell narrowly open ; anal cell not produced. Length 6-8 mm.

Nine specimens. St. Vincent.

NERIUS.

Fabricius, Syst. Antl., 1805.

1. *Nerius bistriatus*, n. sp. (Pl. XII., figs. 126, head of ♀ ; 126*a*, wing.)

♀. Front narrowly opaque yellow on the sides, in the middle with a broad opaque black stripe, broader in front, where it is reddish. Basal joints of the antennæ blackish; third joint brownish-red ; arista slender, black. Face yellow, somewhat blackish in the depression ; the sides above, running obliquely to the root of the antennæ, shining black. The yellow of the face continues back horizontally at the lower margin of the eye ; the occiput is black, except a yellow spot back of the middle of each eye. Mesonotum opaque black, with two light, greyish-yellowish, pollinose stripes. Scutellum opaque black, with a broad yellow stripe in the middle. Pleuræ opaque black, more or less yellowish-dusted ; along the dorsopleural suture a yellow stripe, as though continuous with the yellow spot of the sides of the occiput; lower portion of the pleuræ in front yellow ; a rounded process in front of the halteres yellow. Abdomen black, not at all shining; ovipositor cylindrical, yellowish. Coxæ and legs yellow, the tarsi somewhat infuscated ; front femora for the whole length below, and the four posterior femora distally, spinose. Wings strongly tinged with brownish-yellowish ; first posterior cell open. Length 6 mm,

One specimen. St. Vincent.

ORTALIDÆ.

EUXESTA.

Loew, Berl. Ent. Zeit., v., 385, 1867.

1. *Euxesta stigmatias.*   (Pl. XII., fig. 127, wing.)

Euxesta stigmatias, Loew, Berl. Ent. Zeit., xi., 310, pl. ii., fig. 18; Monogr., iii., 163, pl. ix., fig. 17.—Cuba, Brazil.

Numerous specimens agreeing with the description. The hind metatarsi are, for the most part, yellow.

2. *Euxesta annonæ.*

Musca annonæ, Fabricius, Ent. Syst., iv., 358.
Tephritis annonæ, Fabricius, Syst. Antl., 320.
Ortalis annonæ, Wiedemann, Auss. Zweifl. Ins., ii., 463.—South America.
Urophora quadrivittata, Macquart, Hist. Nat. Dipt., ii., 456.
Euxesta annonæ, Loew, Berl. Ent. Zeitschr., xi., 305, pl. ii., fig. 13 ; Monogr., iii., 162, pl. ix., fig. 13.—Cuba.
Amethysa annonæ, Schiner, Reise der Novara, Diptera, 283.—South America.

A single specimen which agrees with the description in everything save some of the wing-markings. The brown bands of the wings have blackish clouds continuing them to the hind margin, and there is a distinct hyaline interval in front of the second vein between the third and fourth bands.

3. *Euxesta*, n. sp.

A single specimen of a small species differs from all known to me of those having four bands, in the possession of a rounded hyaline spot in front of the second vein and beyond the third band. The purely hyaline interval is situated beyond this spot, and is narrow; the apical band is narrow, and the brown of the broad second band scarcely exceeds the third vein, but is filled out to the hind margin by a strong blackish cloud. The species is small, the front is brownish-red, the antennæ, front coxæ and metatarsi are yellowish. It is labelled "Southern end of the island. Open ground near sea, on herbage. May."

4. *Euxesta apicalis*, n. sp. (Pl. XII., fig. 128, wing.)

♂, ♀. Allied to *E. notata*, but the costal cell wholly brown. Steel-blue or green-blue, but little shining, the abdomen with blackish reflections. Front dark-red or reddish-brown, the orbits narrowly whitish; the vertex and the upper part of the orbits, blue; hair black. Antennæ brownish-yellow, the third joint oval. Face considerably excavated, and, together with the clypeus, steel-blue, shining, the upper part pollinose; cheeks reddish. An arcuate band extending across the middle of the mesonotum has a more blackish reflection. Coxæ and femora light yellow; front tibiæ and tarsi black; the four posterior tibiæ and the distal joints of their tarsi brown, their basal joints yellow or yellowish. Wings hyaline; the costal and subcostal cells throughout, a small spot in the extreme proximal end of the submarginal cell, and a small spot beginning at the extreme tip of the marginal and extending across the submarginal into the first basal cell, uniformly dark brown; fourth vein distinctly curved forward, narrowing the first posterior cell; the fifth vein reaches the margin of the wing; first section of the ovipositor a little longer than wide, distinctly longer than the last abdominal segment, yellowish at the base; abdomen for the most part black. Length 4-4½ mm

Six specimens. St. Vincent.

EPIPLATEA.

Loew, Berl. Ent. Zeit., 1867, 324.

1. *Epiplatea amabilis*, n. sp.

♀. Front moderately broad, slightly narrower above, opaque yellowish-red, with short black hairs. Face shining translucent reddish-yellow ; gently excavated under each antenna; nearly vertical and straight in profile. Frontal, facial and occipital orbits narrowly silvery-white. The clypeus forms a narrow, horse-shoe shaped body, not projecting in profile. Antennæ reddish-yellow ; third joint elongate oval, not reaching quite to the lower margin of the face ; arista black, bare. Proboscis stout ; palpi slender, yellowish, except at the base. Mesonotum uniformly yellowish-red (about the same colour as the front) ; scutellum somewhat brownish, with four bristles. Pleuræ shining, more brownish, in the middle below brown. The short hair of the mesonotum and the bristles are black. Abdomen wholly deep shining black, with short black hair ; ovipositor but little longer than the last abdominal segment, black. Legs deep brown, the knees and tarsi more yellowish ; middle tibiæ with a stout spur ; front femora with some bristles below. Wings nearly hyaline ; the costal and subcostal cells, reaching back through the beginning of the submarginal cell to the fourth vein, a band beginning at the outer part of the first vein and reaching over the anterior cross-vein, an elongate spot of about the same width covering the posterior cross-vein, and the apex of the wing, save a rounded interval at the very tip, brown ; third and fourth veins somewhat convergent at the tip ; anal cell rounded distally, not at all drawn out into a point. Length 4½–5 mm.

This species, it will be seen, does not agree in all its details with the characters given by Loew for the genus, but the discrepancies are trivial. In some specimens the brown spots of the wings are narrower, and that at the tip might be called an incomplete band. Four specimens.

TRYPETIDÆ.

TRYPETA.

Meigen, Illiger's Mag., ii., 1803.

1. *Trypeta (Aciura) phœnicura*.

Trypeta phœnicura, Loew, Monogr., iii., 269, pl. vi., fig. 12.—Brazil.

Four specimens, agreeing closely with Loew's description.

2. *Trypeta (Tephritis) fucata.* (Pl. XII., fig. 129, wing.)

Musca fucata, Fabricius, Ent. Syst., iv., 359.—West Indies.
Tephritis fucata, Fabricius, Syst. Antl., 321.
Trypeta fucata, Wiedemann, Auss. Zweifl. Ins., ii., 505.—South America.
Trypeta (Tephritis) fucata, Loew, Monogr., iii., 300.—Buenos Aires.

A female specimen agreeing well with Loew's description, which was drawn from one of Wiedemann's types.

3. *Trypeta (Ensina) peregrina.* (Pl. XIII., fig. 130, wing.)

Trypeta (Ensina) peregrina, Loew, Monogr., iii., 292, pl. x., fig. 30.—Brazil.

Two specimens, one of which is labelled "Leeward, near sea. By open stream. Sept."

4. *Trypeta (Evaresta) melanogastra.* (Pl. XIII., fig. 131, wing.)

Trypeta melanogastra, Loew, Monogr., i., 90, pl. ii., fig. 24; iii., 315, pl. x., fig. 24.—Cuba.

Five specimens. In several of the specimens the base of the abdomen is yellow; in all the metanotum is not shining, but pollinose.

5. *Trypeta (Urellia) solaris.* (Pl. XIII., fig. 132, wing.)

Trypeta (Urellia) solaris, Loew, Monogr., i., 84, pl. ii., fig. 19; iii., 325, pl. x., fig. 19.—United States.

Two specimens, which agree closely with the description and figures of this species. With them, however, are others which seem less certainly identical. They are smaller, and have in the wings a ninth ray, as is described for *U. polyclona*. The latter, however, is described as having four scutellar bristles.

6. *Trypeta* (*Plagiotoma*) *incompleta*, n. sp.

♂, ♀. Yellow, the mesonotum with two, the abdomen with eight black spots. Front rather narrow, especially below; on each side with three or four brownish bristles, and with two proclinate ocellar bristles. Antennæ light-yellow; arista bare, black on the distal half. Face vertical, the oral margin projecting a little. Proboscis short; palpi projecting slightly in front of the oral margin. Mesonotum light ochraceous yellow, with short yellow hairs and brownish bristles; just above and behind the root of the wing on each side, there is a small round black spot; scutellum with four bristles. Abdomen a little more reddish, with yellow hairs; on each side with four rounded black spots. Ovipositor yellow, as long or a little longer than the last two abdominal segments (in one specimen it is drawn out longer than the abdomen). Legs yellow. Wings very similar to those of *P. obliqua*, Say, except that the first oblique band back of the tip of the wing is represented only by the blackish spot at the tip of the fourth vein and a slight yellowish tinge in front of it. Length 3½-4 mm.

This species is closely allied to *P. obliqua*, Say, but differs in both sexes in the absence of the pleural spots (there is a blackish spot at the root of the halteres, and a small pair on the underside of the scutellum), and in the wing-markings.

SAPROMYZIDÆ.

Lonchæa.

Fallen, Ortalidæ, 1820.

1. *Lonchæa longicornis*, n. sp.

♂. Front narrow, with nearly parallel sides, about three times as long as wide; shining black. Antennæ brownish-black; third joint elongate, reaching to beyond the oral margin; arista bare. Eyes bare. Thorax and abdomen wholly deep shining black. Tegulæ white ciliate. Legs brownish-black, all the metatarsi light-yellow. Wings lightly tinged with brownish-yellowish. Length 4 mm.

One specimen.   St. Vincent.

2. Lonchæa brevicornis, n. sp.

♀ . Front and face shining greenish-black ; front about twice as long as wide. Antennæ black, the third joint oval, not twice as long as wide ; arista bare. Eyes bare. Thorax and abdomen deep metallic-green : ovipositor black. Legs brownish-black, the first two joints of all the tarsi light-yellow. Wings greyish hyaline. Length 4 mm.

One specimen. St. Vincent.

Physogenua.

Macquart, Dipt. Exot. Suppl., iii., 60, 1851 ; *Eupte-romyia*, Bigot. Rev. et Mag. Zool., 309, 1859.

1. *Physogenua nigra*, n. sp. (Pl. XIII., fig. 133, head of ♂ .)

♂ , ♀ . Deep shining black throughout, the third joint of the antennæ and the four posterior tarsi reddish-yellow. Face large, bare, smooth, evenly convex from side to side and from the antennæ to near the oral margin ; just above the oral margin a narrow horizontal groove ; the narrow orbits silvery ; clypeus slightly prominent ; the face on either side with three or four small bristles. Palpi slender, black. Third joint of the antennæ twice as long as wide ; arista black, plumose. Scutellum convex, subtri-angular, with four bristles. Halteres white. Abdomen short-oval. Wings tinged with brownish-yellow ; first posterior cell a little narrowed at the extremity ; anterior cross-vein nearly opposite the tip of the first vein. Length 4½ mm.

Six specimens. St. Vincent. From the two described species, *P. vittata*, Macq. (*Laurania variegata*, Loew), and *P. ferruginea*, Sch., the present is easily distinguished by its black colour.

Sapromyza.

Fallen, Dipt. Suec. Ortalid., 29, 1820.

1. Arista plumose 2
   Arista pubescent or bare 7
2. Mesonotum striped 3
   Mesonotum unicolorous ; wings without dark markings . 5
3. Pleuræ with stripes ; face with a small black spot in the middle below 4
   Pleuræ unicolorous . . . . *puella*, n. sp.

4. Wings with markings . . . . *octocittata*. n. sp.
   Wings unicolorous . . . . *macula*, Loew.
5. Shining black species . . . . (*Lauxania*), sp.
   Not shining black. 6
6. Third joint of the antennæ yellow . . . . . *sordida*, Med.
   Third joint in large part black . . . . . *vulgaris*, Fitch.
7. Mesonotum vittate 8
   Mesonotum not vittate 11
8. Wings for the most part dark-brown . . *angustipennis*, n. sp.
   Wings nearly hyaline 9
9. Mesonotum with four slender brown stripes ; third joint of
      the antennæ reddish-yellow . . . . . . *lineata*, n. sp.
   Mesonotum with broad stripes ; third joint of antennæ
      black 10
10. Mesonotum with broad ashy-grey and brown stripes *exul*, n. sp.
   Mesonotum with yellow and brown stripes . . *venusta*, n. sp.
11. Scutellum with two black spots on the margin *ingrata*, n. sp.
   Scutellum without spots . . . . *sororia* n. sp.

1. *Sapromyza macula.*

Sapromyza macula, Loew, Centur., x., 82.—Texas.

♂, ♀. Front opaque-yellow, with a median brown stripe ; ocelli with small proclinate bristles. Antennæ yellow, third joint twice as long as wide ; arista short-plumose. Face and cheeks light-yellow, the former with a round black spot above the oral margin in front, the latter with a small brown spot. Thorax ochraceous yellow, the mesonotum with four dark-brown stripes, the median pair extending on the scutellum. Pleuræ with two brown stripes, the upper one below the base of the wings ; the lower, shorter, one across the base of the middle coxæ. Abdomen yellow or luteous yellow, with three rows of black spots, the lateral ones more or less elongate and sometimes coalescent. Legs light-yellow, the tibiæ with a proximal, more or less indistinct (especially on the front pairs), narrow brown ring. Wings tinged with yellowish ; penultimate section of the fourth vein one-half the length of the ultimate section. Length 5–5½ mm.

Numerous specimens from St. Vincent and Chapada, Brazil. I have no North American specimens for comparison, but the description applies so well that I think the identification is probable. The West Indian specimens are lighter yellow, and the thoracic stripes are darker and are continued on the scutellum. Those from

Brazil agree more closely with Loew's description. In the West Indian specimens there is also a distinct frontal stripe, only slightly indicated in the South American ones.

2. *Sapromyza angustipennis,* n. sp.   (Pl. XIII., fig. 134, wing.)

♂, ♀.   Front broader above than below, its width at the anterior end equal to about one-half the length ; opaque reddish-brown with yellowish spots ; on either side with four small yellow tubercles, from the upper three of which the stout frontal bristles arise.   Antennæ brownish-yellow ; third joint a little longer than wide.   Face thickly greyish-pollinose, with two small, oval black spots.   Cheeks, proboscis, palpi, and the greater part of the occiput light-yellow.   Mesonotum and scutellum opaque reddish-brown, the former with the beginning of stripes and two or three minute spots on each side in front grey.   Pleuræ more yellowish-brown. Abdomen long ovate ; first three segments light-yellow ; the next three yellow with a narrow median stripe and an ill-defined spot, each side black.   Legs light-yellow ; hind tibiæ with a stout pre-apical bristle.   Wings elongate, deep brown in front, nearly hyaline on the posterior part ; in the outer part there are two or three small round hyaline spots, near which the brown is of a deeper colour.   Length 3½–4 mm.

Six specimens.   This species, in its front and elongated wings, is somewhat aberrant from most *Sapromyzæ.*

3. *Sapromyza puella,* n. sp.

♂, ♀.   Front only a little longer than wide ; reddish-yellow, brownish above and on the sides.   Antennæ black, the first two joints somewhat reddish ; third joint oval, more than twice as long as wide ; arista plumose on the upper side of the proximal part. Face, cheeks and lower part of the occiput light-yellow.   Thorax deep-brown or black, almost opaque, with two narrow greyish stripes.   Scutellum black.   Abdomen black, the terminal segments more or less reddish.   Legs light-yellow, the tarsi brownish ; hind tibiæ without a preapical bristle.   Wings yellowish ; ultimate section of the fourth vein rather more than twice the length of the penultimate section.   Length 2½–3 mm.

Twenty specimens.   St. Vincent.

4. *Sapromyza exul*, n. sp.

♂, ♀. Front about twice as long as wide, opaque yellowish-grey, with an opaque dark-brown median stripe, slightly narrowed anteriorly. Antennæ brownish-yellow, third joint in part blackish, rather narrow, about three times as long as wide ; arista pubescent. Face black in ground-colour, thickly silvery grey-pollinose. Occiput black, the narrow lateral orbits grey. Mesonotum densely yellowish grey-pollinose, with three broad, dark coffee-brown stripes, the middle stripe about equal in width to the adjacent light-coloured stripes. Scutellum with the yellowish-grey stripes of the meso-notum continued and uniting at the tip, leaving the middle as the continuation of the middle brown stripe. Pleuræ for the most part shining black, somewhat thinly pruinose above. Abdomen shining black, thinly greyish-pollinose in an oblique light. Legs deep-brown, the femora more black, the base of the tibiæ, the four posterior tarsi and the front metatarsi yellow ; hind tibiæ with a well-developed preapical bristle. Wings light brownish-yellowish ; penultimate second of the fourth vein more than one-half of the length of the ultimate section. Length 4–4½ mm.

Eight specimens. St. Vincent.

5. *Sapromyza octovittata*, n. sp.

♂, ♀. Front opaque yellow, rather longer than wide, with a median brown stripe, on either side of which there are three stout bristles ; ocelli with small proclinate bristles. Antennæ yellow, the third joint twice as long as wide ; arista short plumose. Face and cheeks light-yellow, the former with a rounded black spot above the oral margin in front. Thorax light opaque yellow, the mesonotum with light-brown stripes, the median pair extending on the sides of the scutellum. Pleuræ with two brown stripes, the one below the base of the wings, the other across the base of the middle coxæ. Abdomen yellow or brownish-yellow, with three rows of small, dark-brown spots, forming three interrupted stripes ; the spots are sometimes obscure, perhaps as the result of desic-cation. Legs light-yellow, the four posterior tibiæ with a proximal narrow brown ring. Wings clouded with dark-brown along the costa to the tip, on the cross-veins and on the base and outer part of the fourth vein ; penultimate section of the fourth vein not one-half the length of the ultimate section. Length 4–5 mm.

This species has its markings, aside from those of the wings, very much as they are in *S. macula*.

6. Sapromyza (*Lauxania* ?), sp.

♂. Shining black. Front with two bristles on each side below the vertical ones ; ocelli with small procliuate bristles. Face rather flat, wholly opaque light grey ; a transverse groove above the oral margin. Antennæ black, third joint oval, fully twice as long as wide ; arista moderately long plumose on the upper side, pubescent on the under side. Thorax and scutellum wholly shining, without stripes or spots. Abdomen shining brownish-black. Legs black or brownish-black, the four posterior tibiæ and tarsi more or less yellow. Wings hyaline, the penultimate section of the fourth vein about one-half the length of the ultimate section. Length 5 mm.

One specimen. St. Vincent. This species is allied to *S. longipennis*, but is distinct in the more shining colour and in the distinctly narrower front, which is perceptibly longer than wide. Possibly it is identical with *Lauxania muscaria*, Loew (Centur., i., 87; Schiner, Reise der Novara, Dipt., 282), but the face is not shining. As the shining black colour is the final difference between *Sapromyza* and *Lauxania*, this species would properly come under the latter. The difference from *S. longipennis* is, however, very slight.

7. Sapromyza sordida, n. sp.

? *Sapromyza sordida*, Wiedmann, Auss. Zw. Ins., ii., 456.—West Indies.

♂, ♀. Head and antennæ yellow. Front as broad as long shining ; ocellæ bristles wanting or rudimentary. Third joint of the antennæ twice as long as wide ; arista black, long plumose on the upper side. Face rather flat, lightly silvery-pollinose. Mesonotum shining reddish-yellow, the pleuræ a little more yellowish. Abdomen yellowish-brown, moderately shining. Legs yellow. Wings lightly tinged with yellowish ; penultimate section of the fourth vein more than half the length of the ultimate section. Scutellum unicolorous, large, with four strong bristles. Palpi wholly yellow. Length 5 mm.

Twenty-four specimens.

8. *Sapromyza vulgaris.*

Chlorops vulgaris, Fitch, Reports, vol. i., 300, pl. i., fig. 4.

Sapromyza plumata, Van der Wulp, Tijdschr., v., Entom. (2), 159.—Atlantic States.

Sapromyza ocellaris, Townsend, Can. Entom., 1893, 303; F. Lynch, A., An. Soc. Cient. Arg., xxxiv., 283, 1893.—New Mexico.

♂, ♀. Front reddish-yellow, broad, a minute spot at the ocelli ; ocelli with two well-developed ocellar bristles. Antennæ yellow, the third joint black at the tip, and along the under side, more than twice as long as wide ; arista plumose on the upper side. Face and cheeks light-yellow. Thorax shining ; mesonotum reddish-yellow, the pleuræ more yellowish. Scutellum large, with four bristles on its margin. Abdomen yellow, brownish-yellow or brown ; in some specimens reddish-yellow with a narrow, but distinct, brown band on the posterior part of each segment. Legs smoky hyaline ; penultimate section of the fourth vein not more than one-half the length of the ultimate section. Palpi black at tip. Length 4–5 mm.

Numerous specimens. St. Vincent. *S. cincta,* Loew, from Cuba and Porto Rico (Roeder), must be very closely allied, probably identical with this species.

9. *Sapromyza venusta,* n. sp.

♂, ♀. Front rather narrow, nearly twice as long as wide, opaque brownish-yellow, with three pairs of recurved bristles. First two joints of the antennæ yellow ; third joint black, oval, about twice as long as wide ; arista black, short pubescent. Face and cheeks light-yellow ; palpi for the most part black. Thorax shining yellow, with three broad, brown or brownish stripes, the middle one obsoletely geminate. Abdomen brown, at the base yellow. Legs yellow. Wings smoky hyaline ; penultimate section of the fourth vein but little more than one-third of the length of the ultimate section. Length 4 mm.

Six specimens. In some of the specimens, the abdomen has a median series of black spots, with the sides of the segments blackish. Like most specimens in this genus the abdomen has seemed to suffer in its coloration in drying, and fresh specimens are needed to determine the markings with clearness.

10. *Sapromyza lineata,* n. sp.

♂. Shining yellow. Front as long as broad. Third joint of the antennæ a little brownish at the tip, twice as long as broad ; arista black, long pubescent. Mesonotum somewhat reddish-yellow, with four slender brown stripes. Abdomen in the dried specimens light brownish-yellow, immaculate. Legs light-yellow ; the distal joints of the front tarsi brown. Wings yellowish hyaline; penultimate section of the fourth vein not more than one-half the length of the ultimate section. Length 4 mm.

Four specimens. St. Vincent. The colour in some of the specimens is light reddish-yellow throughout. The terminal joints of all the tarsi are somewhat brownish. The palpi are wholly yellow.

11. *Sapromyza sororia,* n. sp.

♂, ♀. Front yellow or brownish-yellow, narrow, less than one-third the width of the head, with the usual three pairs of bristles and a small proclinate ocellar pair. Face and antennæ yellow, the third joint of the latter oval, its length only a little greater than its width. Palpi black at the tip. Mesonotum reddish or brownish-yellow, pleuræ more yellow, both shining but little. Abdomen yellow or brownish-yellow, with a median row of rounded black spots. Wings greyish hyaline ; the penultimate section of the fourth vein but little more than one-third the length of the ultimate section. Length 4–5 mm.

Numerous specimens. St. Vincent. In some specimens the abdomen is brown or black, probably due to the effects of drying ; allied to *S. rotundicornis,* Loew.

12. *Sapromyza ingrata,* n. sp.

♂, ♀. Front rather narrow, yellow, or brownish-yellow, but little shining. Antennæ reddish-yellow ; third joint oval, not twice as long as wide ; arista black, short-pubescent. Face and cheeks yellow, opaque, the former with a minute spot near the oral margin in front. Mesonotum reddish-yellow, with short black bristly hairs ; the two median rows of bristles do not extend in front of the middle. Scutellum yellow, with a round, deep black spot on each side between the origin of the bristles. Pleuræ yellow. Abdomen yellow or brown, apparently in life with series of median and lateral black spots. Legs yellow. Wings smoky hyaline ; veins black ; penultimate section of the fourth vein rather less than half of the length of the ultimate section. Length 5 mm.

Numerous specimens. St. Vincent. I was at first

inclined to identify this species with *S. grata* from Brazil, but the brief description shows such discrepancies that it is hardly possible that the species are identical. Possibly it is *S. octopuncta*.

HETERONEURIDÆ.

HETERONEURA.

Fallen, Agromyzidæ, 1823.

1. Thorax black 2
   Thorax in large part yellow 3
2. Tip of antennæ black . . . . *flavipes*, n. sp.
   Antennæ wholly yellow . . . . *concinna*, n. sp.
3. Wings cinereous hyaline 4
   Wings in large part brown 5
4. Mesonotum wholly yellow in front . . . . . *lumbalis*, n. sp.
   Mesonotum black on the sides in front . . . . *valida*, n. sp.
5. Mesonotum and scutellum black . . . . . . *pleuralis*, n. sp.
   Mesonotum and scutellum in large part yellow *xanthops*, n. sp.

1. *Heteroneura xanthops*, n. sp.

♂, ♀. Head, including the proboscis, wholly yellow ; front and face of equal width, the former widened near the vertex only ; arista black, long pubescent or short-plumose. Mesonotum shining black on the sides, a broad stripe, about one-third of the whole length, beginning at the neck and running to the tip of the scutellum, light-yellow, the sides of the scutellum brown or brownish. Pleuræ, pectus, and coxæ pure light-yellow, lighter than the yellow of the mesonotum. Abdomen black or dark-brown, the basal segments yellowish, the thickened under portion of the hypopygium yellow. Legs yellow, the tarsi slightly brownish ; middle tibiæ with a stout spur and a preapical bristle. Wings clouded with brown on the distal half, less strongly so on the proximal portion ; penultimate section of the fourth vein one-fourth or one-fifth the length of the ultimate section, and shorter than the last section of the fifth vein. Length 3-3½ mm.

Five specimens. St. Vincent. A single female specimen has the mesonotum black, except an elongate yellow triangle reaching nearly to the scutellum, the metanotum black, and the abdomen black. Several males have the black of the mesonotum beginning further back, and the whole hypopygium yellow. It is not improbable that there are two distinct species here.

2. *Heteroneura flavipes*, n. sp. (Pl. XIII., fig. 135, wing.)

♂, ♀. Front gently convex on the sides, the eyes most approximated immediately below the antennæ, and then immediately receding, Front brown, below red, the narrow orbits more yellowish. Antennæ yellow, the third joint brown or blackish at the tip ; arista black, finely pubescent. Face, cheeks, and lower portion of the occiput light-yellow. Thorax black, but little shining, the pleuræ somewhat pitchy-black ; mesonotum covered with light-coloured pubescence. Abdomen black, with black hairs. Halteres nearly white. Legs pure light-yellow ; middle femora with a row of short bristles below ; middle tibiæ with a strong spur ; all the tibiæ without distinct preapical bristle. Wings brown, at the immediate base hyaline, and across the middle subhyaline ; penultimate section of the fourth vein but little longer than the posterior cross-vein. Length 3 mm.

Six specimens. St. Vincent. The front is comparatively narrow, distinctly less than one-third of the width of the head.

3. *Heteroneura concinna*, n. sp.

♂, ♀. Very much like *H. flavipes*, from which it differs in the antennæ being wholly light-yellow, in the wings being nearly uniformly blackish, except the immediate base, and especially in the presence of distinct preapical bristles on the middle and hind tibiæ. It is also a little smaller.

Four specimens. St. Vincent.

4. *Heteroneura pleuralis*, n. sp.

♂. Head, including the antennæ and proboscis, wholly light-yellow, except a minute spot near the vertex, and the upper part of the occiput. Arista black, yellow at the base, very finely pubescent. Mesonotum shining brownish-black, the fine pubescence in an oblique light appearing yellow ; pleuræ light-yellow with a spot of the same colour as the dorsum reaching down in front of the wings ; metanotum dark-brown. Abdomen opaque black, with black hair, the immediate base yellow. Legs light-yellow ; hind and middle tibiæ with a distinct preapical bristle. Wings smoky hyaline ; the distal third, as far as the fourth vein, and a spot covering the cross-veins brown ; penultimate section of the fourth vein about one-third of the length of the ultimate section of the fifth vein, and only a little longer than the posterior cross-vein. Length 2½ mm.

One specimen. St. Vincent.

5. *Heteroneura valida,* n. sp. (Pl. XIII., fig. 136, wing.)

♂, ♀. Head, including the antennæ, proboscis, and occiput, light-yellow. Arista black, pubescent. Thorax light-yellow, mesonotum on the sides and behind, and the scutellum, brown or black, shining ; the yellow extends as a broad stripe to or beyond the suture. Abdomen black or dark-brown, its base, the ovipositor, and the hypopygium yellow. Legs yellow ; middle tibiæ with a stout spur and a preapical bristle. Wings cinereous hyaline ; penultimate section of the fourth vein as long as the last section of the fifth vein. Length 2½ mm.

Numerous specimens. St. Vincent.

6. *Heteroneura lumbalis,* n. sp.

♂, ♀. Differs from *H. valida* in the mesonotum being wholly yellow before the middle, the scutellum and posterior part wholly black. The arista is distinctly longer pubescent, almost short plumose. The wings are a little more darkly tinged. Length 2¼ mm.

Numerous specimens. St. Vincent.

TRIGONOMETOPUS.

Macquart, Hist. Nat. Dipt., ii., 419, 1835.

1. *Trigonometopus rotundicornis,* n. sp. (Pl. XIII., fig. 137, head of ♂.)

♂. Head triangular, the face very much receding ; front plane, horizontal, with three pairs of bristles reaching two-thirds of the distance to the root of the antennæ. Eyes longitudinally oval. Antennæ porrect, the first two joints short, the third rounded, not longer than broad. Face on either side with a slender groove, running from the root of the antennæ to the back part of the check. Proboscis with large labella ; palpi slender. Thorax elongate ; mesonotum flattened, with bristles in the middle nearly to the anterior margin ; scutellum flattened, semi-oval, with four bristles. Abdomen oval, depressed, composed of six segments. Legs rather stout ; front femora with a row of bristles below ; hind tibiæ with a preapical bristle. Auxiliary and basal cells distinct. Arista bare. Sides of the checks with a row of long bristles. Yellow, opaque. Front a little darker coloured, with black hair. Antennæ reddish-yellow. Face light-yellow. Sides of the frontal projection somewhat brownish. Mesonotum ferruginous, darker towards the sides, and forming a sharply-limited brown stripe on the dorso pleural suture; in the middle a more or less feebly indicated slender light-coloured line extending on the scutellum. Abdomen in large part brown, perhaps of post-mortem origin. Legs light yellow. Wings cinereous hyaline, the narrow costal margin, extending to the tip of the fourth vein, brown; on the cross-veins slight indications of clouds. Posterior cross-vein less than its own length on the fifth vein from the margin of the wing. Length 4½ mm.

Two specimens. This species will be best distinguished from *T. vittatus* by the brown costal margin of the wings.

EPHYDRIDÆ.

NOTIPHILA.

Fallen, Hydromyzidæ, 1823.

Mesonotum not vittate; abdomen coffee-brown and grey, opaque.
   Mesonotum with numerous small brown dots; grey spots
      of the abdomen irregular . . . . *bellula*, n. sp.
   Mesonotum not with numerous small brown dots; grey
      spots of the abdomen regular . . . . *decorata*, n. sp.

1. *Notiphila decorata*, n. sp.

♂, ♀. Front opaque grey, the triangle and the narrow orbits a little lighter coloured. Antennæ black, the third joint at the base somewhat yellowish. Face, cheeks, and occiput densely light-grey, opaque. Palpi brownish. Mesonotum and scutellum densely light-grey, opaque; the bristles of the mesonotum and scutellum arise from small black spots, but the hair is shorter than in *N. bellula* and does not arise from small brown dots. Abdomen opaque dark coffee-brown, with a narrow, complete, median stripe, and interrupted posterior bands to the second and following segments nearly white, opaque; the spots are separated in all save the last segment from the median stripe by a narrow brown space. Femora, except the immediate tip, the tibiæ in large part, and the terminal joints of the tarsi, black; the legs elsewhere yellow. Wings brownish-hyaline. Length 4 mm.

Two specimens. St. Vincent.

2. *Notiphila bellula*, n. sp.

♂, ♀. Front opaque brownish, the large vertical triangle more yellowish-grey, the narrow orbits grey. Antennæ red, the upper border of the second and third joints brown or blackish. Face, cheeks, and occiput, for the greater part, densely grey-pollinose. Palpi light-yellow. Mesonotum densely brownish grey-pollinose, with numerous small rounded points where the bristles and hairs arise; scutellum like the mesonotum. Pleuræ and metanotum densely grey-pollinose; a small brown spot on the upper part of the mesopleuræ. Abdomen light coffee-brown; the first segment and a narrow median stripe, and irregular spots on the sides of the other segments posteriorly opaque grey; the median stripe is narrow and of equal width throughout. Femora black, with the tip yellow; front tibiæ, except the base and immediate tip, and the front tarsi black; middle and posterior tibiæ and tarsi yellow, the tibiæ more or less brownish in the middle, the tarsi blackish at the tip. Wings nearly uniformly tinged with brownish-yellowish. Length 4 mm.

Ten specimens. St. Vincent. A closely allied species in the writer's collection, from San Domingo, differs in the presence of distinct stripes on the mesonotum. In some specimens the irregular grey spots of the abdomen, nearly subdivide the brown into four series of spots or stripes.

PARALIMNA.

Loew, Monogr., i., 138, 1862.

Mesonotum with numerous small brown spots; abdomen con-
        spicuously banded . . . . *multipunctata*, n. sp.
Mesonotum not spotted; bands of the abdomen inconspicuous
                                 obscura, n. sp.

1. *Paralimna multipunctata*, n. sp.

? ? *Paralimna secunda*, Schiner, Reise der Novara, Dipt., 241.—South America.

♂, ♀. Face and cheeks densely greyish white-pollinose, with a slight shade of yellowish. Clypeus very prominent, of the same colour as the face; palpi slender, brown. Antennæ black, the third joint in an oblique light with a whitish reflection, the pile on its upper side long. Front opaque brown; anteriorly with minute blackish dots and of a more greyish colour ; on the upper side, near the eyes, with an elongated, more blackish triangle. Meso-notum and scutellum greyish-yellowish, with numerous, in part coalescent, small, dark-brown dots, giving the mesonotum a brown appearance ; in the middle may be distinguished two entire, narrow, brown stripes. Pleuræ and metanotum densely light-grey, without the dots of the mesonotum. Abdomen opaque, light yellowish-grey ; second segment with a small, semi-oval, coffee-brown spot on each side anteriorly, and in the middle a slender incomplete stripe ; third and fourth segments each with a continuous narrow stripe and on each side a large semi-oval anterior spot united with it, of the same coffee-brown colour ; the grey thus forms interrupted cross-bands, broader on the outer ends ; fifth segment with the spots on the side small, and the median stripe narrow ; in the female marked like the fourth ; fifth segment of the male a little shorter than the pre-ceding. Legs black, greyish-pollinose ; front metatarsi at the base and the basal portion of the four posterior tarsi yellow. Wings lightly tinged ; second section of the costal vein more than twice as long as the third. Length 3–4 mm.

Numerous specimens. St. Vincent. This species must be closely allied to *P. appendiculata,* Loew, but differs in lacking the stump of a vein on the fourth vein of the wing.

2. *Paralimna obscura,* n. sp.

♂, ♀. Front opaque dark-brown. Antennæ black, the third joint somewhat yellowish at the base. Face, cheeks and the lower part of the occiput opaque brownish-grey ; proboscis and palpi black or dark-brown. Thorax throughout nearly uniform deep brown, moderately shining. Abdomen rather broad, brownish-black, moderately shining ; the second, third, and fourth segments with a complete posterior greyish band ; fifth segment in the male a little longer than the preceding segment ; fifth and sixth seg-ments in the female successively shorter, with an obscure band as in the preceding segments. Legs deep black throughout. Wings nearly hyaline ; second section of the costal vein nearly three times the length of the third section ; ultimate and penultimate sections of the fourth vein of nearly equal length. Length 4 mm.

Numerous specimens. St. Vincent.

Discomyza.

Meigen, System. Beschr., vi., 76, 1830.

1. *Discomyza dubia*, n. sp.   (Pl. XIII., figs. 138, wing ;
138*a*, head of ♂.)

♀. Black, shining. Front, broad above, narrowed below; smooth,
the elongated vertical triangle metallic-green and finely punctulate ;
the anterior part of the front flattened. Antennæ black, the third
joint rounded, and with rather long whitish pile on its upper side ;
arista with seven rays ; spine of the second joint moderately strong.
Face much narrowed a little above its middle, gently convex from
side to side and vertically, the lower part much receding, and the
oral opening small ; in the middle finely punctulate ; on the sides
with coarse wrinkles for its whole length ; moderately shining, not
dusted, its bristles short and small. Clypeus large, much receding,
cheeks narrow. Abdomen flattened, ovate ; fourth segment much
longer than the preceding. Halteres nearly white. Legs black,
the posterior tibiæ and all the tarsi, save the distal two joints, yellow.
Wings tinged with brownish ; third section of the costal vein
short, not more than one-third of the length of the second section ;
penultimate section of the fourth vein not one-half the length of
the ultimate section. Length 2 mm.

Numerous specimens. St. Vincent. This species, in
its small oral opening and large clypeus, is rather
aberrant.

Psilopa.

Fallen, Hydromyzidæ, 1820.

1. Face shining black or metallic-green 4
   Face pollinose 2
2. A minute blackish spot at the tip of the third vein,
   nigropuncta, n. sp.
   No spot at the tip of the third vein 3
3. Antennæ red . . . . *desmata*, n. sp.
   Antennæ black . . . . *nigra*, n. sp.
4. Front tarsi deep black ; face shining black . , *nigrimana*, n. sp.
   Front tarsi yellow ; face shining green . . . *aciculata*, Loew.

1. *Psilopa nigra*, n. sp. (Pl. XIII., fig. 139, head of ♀.)

♀. Front and face deep black, the former broader than long, a
little shining ; the latter lightly-dusted, gently and evenly convex
in the middle above, the convexity not reaching to the margin of
the eye, thus forming a concavity for each antenna ; face on the
sides below with two stout bristles, the upper one arising very
close to the eye. Antennæ black, the third joint oblong ; bristle of
the second joint stout and long ; arista with ten or twelve rays.
Clypeus moderately projecting ; proboscis and palpi black. Thorax
and abdomen black, moderately shining, in an oblique light lightly
yellowish greyish-dusted ; second, third, and fourth segments of
the abdomen of nearly equal length, the fifth a third longer
than the preceding ; in the female the fifth segment of the same
length as the preceding ; the sixth less than half the length of the
fifth. Legs black; all the tarsi yellow, with the distal joints blackish.
Wings greyish or brownish hyaline ; second section of the costal
vein about one-third longer than the third section ; ultimate
section of the fourth vein only a little longer than the penultimate
section. Length 3 mm.

Two specimens. St. Vincent.

2. *Psilopa nigropuncta.*

♂. Front black, moderately shining, much broader than long.
Antennæ black ; third joint oblong ; bristle of the second joint of
moderate size ; arista with five rays above. Face densely light
grey-pollinose ; the structure of the upper part as in *P. nigra*, but
the face narrower ; on the lower part with two stout bristles on
each side, the upper one more remote from the eye than in *P. nigra*.
Thorax and abdomen deep shining black, the scutellum opaque.
Abdomen broad, the fifth segment a little shorter than the fourth.
Legs deep black ; all the tarsi yellow, with the terminal joints
blackish. Wings greyish ; third section of the costal vein a little
more than half the length of the second section; penultimate
section of the fourth vein about one-half the length of the ultimate section ; a minute black spot at the tip of the third vein.
Length 2 mm.

One specimen. St. Vincent.

3. *Psilopa nigrimana*, n. sp.

♂. Shining black. Front, with a light depression on each side
above the root of the antennæ. First two joints of the antennæ
black, the third brown, on the inner underside reddish ; spine of

the second joint stout; third joint oblong; arista with seven or eight rays. Face convex above, gently convex from very near the margin of the eye, the orbital margin being exceedingly narrow ; on the lower part the face has very fine grooves. Mesonotum and scutellum thinly yellowish-dusted in an oblique light. Abdomen deep shining metallic-green ; fourth segment longer than the third, the fifth about half the length of the third. Legs black ; the front coxæ, the base of the front femora, the tip of the four posterior femora, the four posterior tibiæ wholly, and the four posterior tarsi, except the distal joint, yellow ; front tarsi stout and deep black, like their tibiæ. Wings greyish hyaline ; third section of the costa as long as the second. Length 2 mm.

One specimen. St. Vincent.

4. *Psilopa aciculata.*

Psilopa aciculata, Loew, Monogr., i., 142.—Cuba. (Pl. XIII., fig. 140, wing.)

♂, ♀. Head shining metallic-green. Vertical border very sharp. The bristles of the front are confined to the vertex, two on the ocellar tubercle and two on each side. The vertical triangle is bounded by a well-marked groove, its anterior angle truncated below, just above the base of the antennæ, and continuous to the eyes on the side of the face below. The face is narrower than the front, the eyes approaching each most at a little distance above the oral margin ; the face is smooth, gently convex transversely, and with parallel sides from the grooves, which are continuous from the front; nearly opposite the narrowest portion there is a single black bristle on each side. Antennæ yellow ; the second joint above and the third in front, reddish; arista black, with about six rays. Mesonotum and scutellum bronze-black, but little shining, finely aciculate ; pleuræ more shining green-black. Abdomen brilliant metallic-green, with coppery reflections ; first segment very short, the second, third, and fourth successively longer, the fifth again short. Legs black, the knees, tip of tibiæ and all the tarsi yellow. Wings with a distinct yellowish tinge, the basal portion obliquely across to about the middle of the anal cell, blackish; second and third sections of the costal vein of nearly equal length. Length 2 mm.

Five specimens. St. Vincent. This species is rather aberrant from other members of this genus in its colour and structure of the head.

5. *Psilopa desmata*, n. sp.

♂. Face not broad, a little wider below ; gently convex in the middle above, with a depression below each antennæ ; opaque yellowish-grey ; on either side below with four or five strong bristles, convergent above. Front broader than the face, opaque black, thinly brownish-dusted below. Antennæ yellowish-red, the second joint somewhat blackish in front, and with a moderately strong bristle at its tip ; arista with five rays. Cheeks narrow, with a row of strong bristles continuous with those of the sides of the face. Proboscis yellow. Mesonotum deep brown, moderately shining. Pleuræ whitish-pollinose. Abdomen black, moderately shining ; first segment short, the others successively increasing in length. Femora black, the immediate tip yellow ; tibiæ and tarsi light yellow, the hind tibiæ with a blackish ring in the middle. Halteres yellow. Wings nearly hyaline ; second section of the costal vein of nearly the same length as the third, or slightly longer. Length 2 mm.

One specimen. St. Vincent. " Near the sea by open stream." It is possible that this species were better located under *Discocerina*. The third joint of the antennæ is rounded, but the face can not be said to be carinate, though the convexity of the upper part is confined to the middle part.

DISCOCERINA.

Macquart, Hist. Nat. Dipt., Suites a Buffon, ii., 527, 1835 ; *Clasiopa*, Stenhammer, Monogr. der Ephydr., 251, 1844.

1. Face silvery-grey with a median black stripe . . *nana*, n. sp.
   Face uniform in colour 2
2. Face vaulted, oral opening very large . . . . *facialis*, n. sp.
   Oral opening of moderate size 3
3. Last abdominal segment largely or wholly silvery-grey
   leucoprocta, Loew.
   Last abdominal segment not unlike the preceding *obscura*, n. sp.

1. *Discocerina leucoprocta*.

? *Discocerina leucoprocta*, Loew, Berl. Ent. Zeit., 1861, 255 ; Monogr., North Amer. Dipt., i., 148.— Maryland.

♂, ♀. Front opaque yellowish-brown, narrowly whitish on the lower orbital margins. Antennæ reddish-yellow, the third joint orbicular, and blackish on the upper distal part. Face narrowest a little distance below the eyes ; opaque greyish-yellow, the orbits silvery-grey, becoming broader below ; distinctly keeled on the upper portion, arched below ; on either side, near the silvery orbit with two or three stout bristles : cheeks and inferior occipital orbits silvery-grey. Thorax in ground-colour black, opaque greyish-pollinose, the mesonotum somewhat yellowish or brownish. Abdomen opaque black, the anterior segments lightly greyish-pollinose in well-preserved specimens ; the fifth segment silvery-grey, except the tip ; sometimes the grey is confined to the sides and may also appear on the sides of the preceding segment, especially in the female ; in the male the abdomen is elongate conical ; in the female more oval. Femora for the most part black ; tibiæ yellow with the middle portion more or less brown ; tarsi yellow, the distal joints brownish or brown. Wings cinereous hyaline; second section of the costa less than twice the length of the third. Length 1½ mm.

Twenty specimens. St. Vincent. The identity of this species with that which Loew described is somewhat doubtful. The tibiæ in most of the specimens are yellow, with the hind pair blackish in the middle. In none of the specimens is the last abdominal segment wholly silvery-white.

2. *Discocerina nana*, n. sp.

♂. Face considerably narrower than the front, much receding on the lower half, moderately carinate above ; densely silvery-white-pollinose on the sides, leaving a deep black, shining, median stripe ; the two bristles of the sides not strong. Antennæ yellow, the third joint rounded, blackish on its margin ; arista with five rays. Front opaque greyish-black, with an elongate median triangle below the ocelli, and the lateral margins on the lower half opaque black. Thorax deep shining steel-blue or green. Abdomen shining black, with slightly coppery reflections. Legs black, the knees, tips of the tibiæ, and all the tarsi light-yellow. Wings greyish-hyaline ; second section of the costa a half longer than the third. Length 2 mm.

Numerous specimens. St. Vincent. The cheeks are narrow.

3. *Discocerina facialis*, n. sp. (Pl. XIII., fig. 141, head of ♂.)

♂, ♀. Front dark-brown, opaque, the sides gently convex, except near the vertex. Antennæ reddish-yellow, the third joint orbicular, brownish on the upper margin. Face broadly arched,

moderately carinate on the upper part, with the cheeks and
occiput silvery-grey ; two moderately strong bristles on each side ;
oral cavity very large. Mesonotum opaque dark-brown : pleuræ
opaque grey. Abdomen, like the rest of the body, black in
ground-colour, greyish-pollinose ; second, third and fourth segments of nearly equal length. Legs black : the knees, base and
tip of the front and hind tibiæ, the middle tibiæ wholly, and all
the tarsi, save the terminal joint, yellow. Wings cinereous
hyaline; third section of the costa two-thirds the length of the
second section. Length 1½–2 mm.

Five specimens. St. Vincent. This species is peculiar in the very large oral opening, resembling the forms
placed in the vicinity of *Ephydra*, from which, however,
it is distinctly separated by the presence of a spinous
bristle at the tip of the second antennal joint.

4. *Discocerina obscura*, n. sp.

♂. ♀. Antennæ reddish-yellow ; third joint only a little longer
than wide, its upper margin, as also that of the second joint, sometimes narrowly blackish; arista with five pectinations. Face black,
covered with fine white pubescence or dust, which does not wholly
obscure the ground-colour save in an oblique light. Front black,
but mostly concealed beneath fine yellow or brownish-yellow
pubescence. Thorax black, shining through the thin brownish
dust ; pleuræ thinly greyish-dusted. Abdomen black, moderately
shining ; oval, the fifth segment of the male much longer than the
preceding one. Legs black, the tip of the tibiæ, the knees and the
tarsi light-yellow, the distal joints of the last brownish. Wings
greyish-hyaline ; second section of the costal vein a half longer than
the third. Length 2–2½ mm.

Numerous specimens. St. Vincent. ♀ ♀ *c.*. . . . .

ARTHYROGLOSSA.

Loew, Neue Beitr., vii., 12, 1860.

1. *Arthyroglossa nitida*, n. sp. (Pl. XIII., fig. 142,
head of ♂.)

♂. ♀. Front wholly shining black, flattened or depressed on
the anterior portion. Antennæ black, the third joint somewhat
reddish and pubescent ; arista with six rays. Face deep shining
black, gently convex transversely ; clypeus large, prominent, oval,
convex, shining black like the face. Face on the sides near the

lower margin of the eye with wrinkles or rugosities. Thorax deep
shining black, smooth ; scutellum concolorous. Abdomen black,
less shining than the thorax, finely scrobiculate under high magnification ; first and fifth segments very short, scarcely visible, the
second and third of nearly equal length, the fourth longer than the
third ; the abdomen is elongate, oval in shape, and is much
flattened. Legs black ; the tip of the four posterior tibiæ, the
first two joints of the front tarsi, and the first three joints of the
other tarsi light-yellow. Wings tinged with brown ; third section
of the costal vein less than half the length of the second section.
Length 2½ mm.

Two specimens. St. Vincent. The species seems to
be a typical *Arthyroglossa*.

HECAMEDE.

Haliday, Annals Nat. Hist., iii., 224, 1839.

1. *Hecamede abdominalis*, n. sp.

♂. Front opaque brown, the frontal lunule whitish. Antennæ
black, the first two joints whitish above ; third joint orbicular.
Face brown on the upper part, the lower portion, the cheeks and
the posterior orbits silvery-grey ; the orbital space, bounded by
the curved line, exceedingly narrow above, becoming broad below
the eyes ; near this line on either side below there are two moderately strong bristles ; face in the middle strongly carinate, or sub-
tuberculate ; clypeus projecting, of the colour of the lower part of
the face. Mesonotum, scutellum, and upper part of the plenræ
opaque dark-brown ; a narrow stripe just above the dorso-pleural
suture, to the root of the wings, silvery-grey ; lower part of the
pleuræ and the metanotum grey, all opaque. Abdomen broadly
oval, the first and fifth segments concealed, the fourth long ;
opaque silvery grey, the second segment more or less brownish-
grey. Legs black ; all the tarsi, except the terminal joint, yellow.
Wings whitish ; third section of the costa about half the length of
the second section. Length 1½ mm.

Five specimens. St. Vincent. Because of the narrow-
ness of the first and fifth segments, the abdomen appears
to be composed of but three segments, the chief characteristic of *Trimerina*. However, the same character
appears in some of the species placed under *Hecamede*,
and while the colorational differences from the known
species of *Trimerina* are marked, they very closely

resemble those of *II. lateralis*, Loew, from Europe. I doubt not that the species belongs wherever *II. lateralis* does; in fact, I am not quite sure that the species may not be identical, for the deeper colour of the present species seems to be the chief difference between them. The cheeks cannot be called broad, nor the median carina " warzenformig."

HYDRELLIA.

Rob. Desvoidy, Myodaires, 790, 1830.

1. *Hydrellia parva*, n. sp.   (Pl. XIII., fig. 143, wing.)

♂. Front broad, distinctly broader than long, somewhat flattened above the antennæ ; opaque brownish-black. Antennæ short, the first two joints blackish, the third blackish above, somewhat reddish below. Arista with six long pectinations on the upper side, and two or three short ones distally below. Eyes very closely pubescent. Face opaque, a little more greyish than the front; in the middle below with a moderate convexity ; on the sides below with two or three bristles. Clypeus narrow. Cheeks narrow ; below the eyes with a long, stout bristle, and a smaller one further back. Thorax short, rounded ; black, but thickly covered like the front with brownish-greyish dust ; on the pleuræ more greyish. Halteres light-yellow. Abdomen black, but little shining, thinly greyish-dusted. Legs black ; all the tarsi, except the terminal joint or joints, yellow. Wings greyish hyaline, with stout black veins ; neuration as in the figure. Length 1 mm , or less.

One specimen. St. Vincent. This species belongs doubtfully in this genus. The pubescence of the eyes is exceedingly short and erect, visible only under the highest magnification.

2. *Hydrellia pulchra*, n. sp.   (Pl. XIII., fig. 144, wing.)

♂. Front opaque black, the narrow orbits and the margins of the large vertical triangle grey. Antennæ yellow ; third joint large, longer than wide, convex on its lower border, nearly straight above, its upper half black ; arista with seven or eight pectinations. Face opaque yellowish-grey ; much narrowed a little above its middle, with a slender groove running downward from each antenna on the cheek ; between the grooves the narrow space is convex ; below on the sides with two or three fine bristles. Eyes rather long silvery pubescent. Mesonotum opaque dark-brown or black, with six series of yellowish-grey, more or less irregular yellowish-grey spots, forming stripes ; scutellum opaque black ; pleuræ grey-pollinose. Abdomen shining black ; a narrow, yellow pubescent, interrupted, posterior band on the second and third, perhaps also on the fourth and fifth segments. Legs yellow ; the femora except the immediate tip and the last joint of all the tarsi black ; hind tibiæ with a brown ring before its middle. Wings yellowish hyaline ; an arcuate black band beginning at the tip of the first vein, which is thickened and deep black, and extending to the posterior edge of the wing ; third section of the costal vein a little longer than the second. Length 1½ mm.

One specimen. St. Vincent.

HYDRINA.

Rob. Desvoidy, Myod., 1830 ; *Philygria*, Stenhammer, Monogr. der Ephydr., 238, 1844.

1. *Hydrina nitida*, n. sp. (Pl. XIII., figs. 145, wing ; 145*a*, head of ♂.)

♂. Front composed almost wholly of the shining black vertical triangle, leaving only a narrow margin opaque black and silvery. Antennæ black ; third joint light-yellow on the lower half, much longer than broad ; arista short pectinate. Face very narrow, gently convex from side to side, without grooves, receding below, in colour silver-white ; bristles of the sides below weak ; inferiorly the sides and the cheeks are shining black. Clypeus concealed. Eyes very sparsely pubescent. Thorax deep black : mesonotum much shining ; scutellum opaque ; the pleuræ whitish dusted. Abdomen shining black ; fourth segment about as long as the two preceding together. Legs wholly light-yellow as are also the coxæ. Wings yellowish or brownish hyaline : third section of the costal vein longer than the second ; penultimate section of the fourth vein very short, the posterior cross-vein remote from the border of the wing. Length 1 mm.

One specimen. St. Vincent. Notwithstanding the pectination of the arista I locate this species under *Hydrina*, by reason of the comparative bareness of the eyes, the structure of the face, and the position of the posterior cross-vein. According to the canons of zoological nomenclature the genus *Hydra* and its family termination *Hydrinæ* do not conflict with the name *Hydrina*, and it should have priority over *Philygria*.

Philygria

2. *Hydrina nitifrons*, n. sp.

♂. Front broad and short, wholly shining black. Antennæ yellow : all the joints blackish on the upper margin ; third joint more than twice as long as broad, hairy on the upper border; arista pubescent. Face black, lightly silvery dusted ; convex from side to side and gently receding below ; bristles of the sides small and short. Cheeks very narrow. Eyes very sparsely pubescent. Thorax deep black ; mesonotum and scutellum shining, the pleuræ whitish dusted ; the mesonotum has two strong bristles near the middle, and the scutellum two equally strong ones on its margin. Abdomen shining black. Legs light yellow, the last two joints of the tarsi black ; coxæ black. Wings nearly hyaline ; third section of the costa two-thirds the length of the second section ; penultimate section of the fourth vein short. Length 1 mm.

One specimen. St. Vincent. In the structure and markings of the head, except the arista, this species agrees closely with *H. nitida* ; the face is somewhat broader. The second section of the costal vein and the penultimate section of the fourth vein are longer.

Ochtheroidea, n. g.

Small, black species. Eyes bare. Front broad, slightly narrower in front. Face narrowest a little distance below the antennæ, lightly concave above, and with a shallow depression under each antenna. Face on each side below slightly wrinkled. Cheeks broad, the oral cavity rather small. Clypeus projecting. Face and cheeks wholly without bristles save two or three small ones on the sides of the former. Second joint of the antennæ with a small, short bristle at its tip : third joint oval, with a pectinate arista. Bristles of the vertex and the thorax very short and thin. Abdomen much flattened, elongate oval ; first and fifth segments short, the others successively increasing in length. Front femora incrassate, and with a row of short spines on the under distal third ; claws and pulvilli normal; all the tarsi slender. The costa reaches to the fourth vein ; third and fourth veins parallel. Middle tibiæ without bristles on the outer side.

1. *Ochtheroidea atra*, n. sp. (Pl. XIII., figs. 146, wing ; 146*a*, front leg of ♂.)

♂. Front and face shining, submetallic black. Antennæ black, the third joint whitish pubescent, the arista with five or six rays. Thorax and abdomen deep opaque, the pleuræ moderately shining.

Wings smoky hyaline, distinctly clouded at the tip. Legs black ; the first two joints of the front tarsi and the four posterior tibiæ and tarsi, except the terminal joints of the latter, light-yellow. Length 3 mm.

Twelve specimens.   St. Vincent.

OCHTHERA.

Latreille, Hist. Nat. Crust. et Ins. xiv., 1804.

1. *Ochthera cuprilineata*, n. sp. (Pl. XIII., fig. 148, wing.)

♂, ♀. Front with a large shining black spot, leaving the lateral and front margins opaque brown. Antennæ black. Face opaque, light-yellow, with a median, shining black spot. Palpi light yellow.   Cheeks and posterior orbits opaque light-yellow. Mesonotum and scutellum sub-shining, lightly bronze or brassy, the former with three dark purple and coppery stripes. Pleuræ lighter, on the lower part shining black. Abdomen metallic-bronze colour ; in some specimens the second and third segments with a narrow shining black posterior band, apparently due to the detrition of the metallic covering. Legs black ; the femora with more or less of the metallic covering, like that of the mesonotum. Front coxæ white dusted, with a shining black spot on the outer side ; front tibiæ in part, and all the tarsi, save the distal joints and the swollen hind metatarsi, red. Wings lightly clouded ; somewhat yellowish on the costa in front. Length 5 mm.

Eight specimens.   St. Vincent.

EPHYDRA.

Fallen, Hydromyzidæ, 1820.

1. *Ephydra pygmæa*, n. sp. (Pl. XIII., figs. 147, wing ;
147a, head.)

♂, ♀. Front opaque velvety black, the large ocellar triangle shining. Antennæ black, the third joint rounded ; arista bare or very short pubescent. The vaulted portion of the face shining metallic-green, very lightly yellowish dusted ; border of the mouth with a number of hairs on each side; otherwise the face is bare, except some weak bristles on the sides inferiorly. Wings clouded with blackish grey. Legs black, not at all shining, the tarsi and portions of the tibiæ more brownish. Halteres yellow. Hypopygium very small ; fifth segment longer than the fourth. Length 2¼ mm.

Fifteen specimens.   Perseverance Valley, St. Vincent.

SCATELLA.

Rob. Desvoidy, Myod., 801, 1830.

1. Scatella obscura, n. sp.

♂, ♀. Black. Face with brownish dust, opaque, the bristles in
front and on the margin moderately long. Bristle of antennæ with
long pubescence. Front, thorax, and abdomen (in unrubbed specimens) only a little shining, with brownish dust. Legs black. Wings
smoky, with five small, uniform, rounded, hyaline drops, the first
in the submarginal cell, two in the first posterior cell, and one on
each side of the posterior cross-vein. The costal vein attains the
tip of the fourth vein. Second, third, fourth, and fifth (♀) segments of the abdomen of nearly equal length. Length 2 mm.

Eight specimens.   St. Vincent.

ILYTHEA.

Haliday, Annals Nat. Hist., iii., 408, 1839.

1. ? Ilythea flavipes, n. sp.

♂. Front short and broad, opaque brown, the black ground-
colour somewhat shining through the dust. Face opaque grey;
very broad and arched below; on the upper part gently carinate
in the middle, the carina ending in an angle whence the face
recedes markedly to the oral margin; orbital ridges very narrow;
across the narrowest part of the face brownish; on the sides near
the most prominent part of the face with a row of rather weak
bristles; a single small bristle near the lower border of the eyes;
otherwise the face is entirely bare. Thorax deep black, shining,
with some metallic reflections; when seen obliquely, with a fine
yellowish pubescence, which is more apparent on the pleuræ;
metanotum greyish dusted. Abdomen deep shining black, somewhat metallescent; broadly oval in shape, the second, third, and
fourth segments of nearly equal length, the fifth longer. Legs yellow,
the tip of the tarsi brownish. Wings nearly hyaline, with narrow
brown spots forming incomplete bands; the first begins at the end
of the first vein, and reaches to the fourth, and is curved; the
next spot is in the middle of the submarginal cell; another between this and the tip of the cell, two others in the first posterior
cell, and the posterior cross-vein is clouded; second and third
section of the costal vein of nearly equal length. Antennæ black,
the third joint on the under-half reddish-yellow; arista with
eight rays. Length 2 mm.

Two specimens. St. Vincent. Sea-level. This species does not fully agree with the characters of *Ilythea* in the structure of the face, but the differences are not sufficient to establish a new genus, which would otherwise be required.

DROSOPHILIDÆ.

STEGANA.

Meigen, Syst. Beschr., vi., 79, 1830.

Front uniformly reddish or yellowish ; legs yellow . *tarsalis*, n. sp.
Front with a broad, black hour-glass-shaped stripe ; legs for the
    most part blackish . . . . *horæ*, n. sp.

1. *Stegana tarsalis*, n. sp. (Pl. XIII., figs. 149, front leg
    of ♂ ; 149*a*, middle tarsus of ♂ ; 149*b*, palpus;
    149*c*, wing.)

♂. Front at the anterior end about one-fourth of the width of the head, at the vertex about one-third ; reddish-yellow, shining. Antennæ yellow, the third joint on the distal half or two-thirds black ; about three times as long as wide, gradually tapering ; arista long-plumose. Face, cheeks and occiput, except at the upper part, light-yellow ; palpi yellow, the tip brownish. Mesonotum and scutellum brownish-red, shining ; scutellum flattened, with a sharp border; pleuræ with a horizontal, deep brown or black stripe, above which the colour is more like that of the mesonotum, below which the colour is light-yellow. Abdomen elongate ovate, brownish-black in colour. Legs light-yellow, all the femora brownish near the extremity ; second, third, and fourth joints of the front tarsi much dilated transversely and deep black in colour; middle and hind tarsi short and strong, compressed ; hind tibiæ dilated ; front femora with some bristles at the outer part. Wings deep brown anteriorly, becoming less strong posteriorly ; second vein nearly parallel with costa for a large part of its length ; third strongly convex anteriorly; first posterior cell very narrowly open; ultimate section of the fourth vein not twice the length of the penultimate section. Length 3 mm.

♀. Third joint of the antennæ a little larger ; front tarsi not dilated and wholly yellow.

So far as I am able to learn from the literature at my command, but two species of this genus have been hitherto made known, *S. curvipennis*, Fallen, and *S. coleo-*

ptrata, Scop., both European, and both said to occur in North America, by Loew. In the descriptions of *S. coleoptrata,* to which species the above seems closely allied, no mention is made of the peculiar male tarsi.

2. *Stegana horæ,* n. sp. (Pl. XIII., fig. 150, antenna of ♀.)

♀. Front narrower above than in *S. tarsalis*; yellow, with a broad, black, hour-glass-shaped stripe reaching nearly to the root of the antennæ. Antennæ yellow; third joint except the upper basal portion, black, rather longer than in *S. tarsalis.* Face yellow; cheeks black below the eyes. Proboscis yellow; palpi black. Occiput on the lower portion, yellow. Mesonotum and scutellum deep brown, almost black; a large spot on the humeri light-yellow. Pleuræ light-yellow with a horizontal black stripe, connected with the black of the mesonotum near the root of the wings; below this stripe there is a narrow yellow one above the black or dark-brown coxæ. Abdomen black. Legs deep brown, the knees, the tip of all the tarsi, the basal portion of the four posterior tibiæ, and all the tarsi light-yellow; tarsi less compressed than in *S. tarsalis*; middle tibiæ with a row of bristles on the outer side; front femora with a few long bristles near the outer end. Wings as in *S. tarsalis.* Length 3 mm.

Two specimens. St. Vincent.

DROSOPHILA.

Fallen, Dipt. Suec., Geomyzid., 4, 1823.

The present collection includes, as is seen, a very large number of species belonging to this genus. I have scrutinized them with the utmost care, and have given, I trust, descriptions which will enable them to be recognized again. I have been able to recognize but a single species previously described, though it is possible that there may be others which have been already named. The difficulty in the determination of the obscurer coloured species from remote localities, is, however, so great that only a direct comparison of specimens from different habitats will settle the question of their identity. Two species are included in the list (Nos. 17 and 18) which may not properly belong to the genus, but which would in all probability be sought for here.

Table of Species.

1. Wings distinctly spotted 2
   Wings not spotted 5
2. Front vittate 3
   Front not vittate 4
3. Wings with a blackish spot at the tip . . 2 *vittatifrons*, n. sp.
   Wings with the cross-veins clouded . . . . 4 *annulata*, n. sp.
4. Wings variegated . . . . 1 *ornatipennis*, n. sp.
   Wings with clouds on the cross-veins . . . 3 *sororia*, n. sp.
5. Mesonotum vittate 6
   Mesonotum not vittate 9
6. Mesonotum deep brown with two narrow brownish stripes,
      as though continuous with the narrow frontal orbits;
      pleuræ light-yellow . . . . 5 *bilineata*, n. sp.
   Not such marked species. 7
7. Tip of the first section of the costal vein black, 8 *fasciola*, n. sp.
   Tip of the costal vein not black 8
8. Larger species ; thorax deep brown . . . 6 *coffeata*, n. sp.
   Smaller species, thorax yellowish . . . . . 7 *bellula*, n. sp.
9. Mesonotum deep black ; legs light-yellow 10
   Mesonotum not deep black. 13
10. Head and thorax deep shining-black . . . . . 17 n. sp.
    Pleuræ in part at least light-yellow 11
11. Head, mesonotum, scutellum and the upper part of the
       pleuræ opaque velvety black . . . . . 9 *opaca*, n. sp.
    Mesonotum and scutellum shining 12
12. Abdomen black. . . . . 11 *pleuralis*, n. sp.
    Abdomen with yellow and black markings . 10 *thoracis*, n. sp.
13. Mesonotum brilliant blue or purple. . . 12 *splendida*, n. sp.
    Mesonotum not shining blue 14
14 Mesonotum grey, with numerous small, rounded, dark
       brown spots. . . . . 13 *punctulata*, Loew
    Mesonotum not spotted 15
15. Front legs black, with the four distal joints of the front
       tarsi light-yellow . . . . 14 *procnemis*, n. sp.
    Front legs not black, with the distal joints of the tarsi
       yellow 16
16. Front and face narrow ; the costal vein terminates at the
       tip of the third longitudinal vein. . 15 *frontalis*, n. sp.
    Front and face of the usual width ; the costal vein reaches
       the tip of the fourth longitudinal vein 17
17. Mesonotum in ground-colour black, opaque brownish-
       greyish pollinose . . . . 18 *pollinosa*, n. sp.
    Mesonotum shining, reddish or yellowish. 18

18. Third section of the costal vein nearly as long as the
second ; front metallic-blue at the vertex

16 *verticis*, n. sp.

Third section of the costal vein not more than one-half of
the length of the second section ; front not at all
blue 19

19. Wings distinctly clouded along the anterior part

19 *limbata*, n. sp.

Wings uniformly yellowish or brownish hyaline 20

20. Third section of the costal vein short, not longer than the
penultimate section of the fourth vein, the second
and third veins nearly parallel 21

Third section of the costal vein distinctly longer than the
penultimate section of the fourth vein, the second
and third veins not at all parallel 22

21. Small, more yellowish species. . . . . . 21 *similis*, n. sp.

Larger, more brownish species . . . . . . 22 *illota*, n. sp.

22. Light-yellow species, the abdomen with brownish bands

20 *pallida*, n. sp.

Reddish-brown, the abdomen black . . . . 23 *nana*, n. sp.

1. *Drosophila ornatipennis*, n. sp.   (Pl. XIII., fig. 151,
wing.)

♂, ♀. Front broad, light-yellow above, somewhat orange-
yellow below.   Remainder of head yellow.   Third joint of the
antennæ oval ; face carinate.   Mesonotum opaque-yellow, with six
narrow dark-brown stripes, the middle pair coalescent, and the
outermost ones connected at the suture with the adjacent ones.
Abdomen opaque, deep brown, with interrupted grey cross-bands.
Legs yellow ; femora sometimes infuscated.   Wings variegated ; a
blackish spot at the proximal end of the submarginal and the first
basal cells, including also the outer part of the costal cell ; one on
the anterior cross-vein ; a narrow one on the posterior cross-vein
and outer part of the fifth vein ; a larger one about the middle of
the second section of the costal vein, reaching to the third vein,
and continues less deeply coloured in the anterior portion of the
first basal cell with that on the posterior cross-vein, and more
or less completely with ones on the outer ends of the second, third
and fourth veins, the colour surrounding these spots is more purely
hyaline, in the posterior cells and anal angle, subhyaline.   Length
2 mm.

Numerous specimens.   St. Vincent.

2. *Drosophila vittatifrons*, n. sp.   (Pl. XIII., fig. 152, wing.)

♂, ♀. Front about one-third of the width of the head, a little broader above ; yellow, the slender shining median triangle reaching two-thirds of the distance to the root of the antennæ, on either side of which there is a deep brown or black stripe, the two convergent anteriorly. Antennæ yellow, third joint somewhat brownish, and elongate oval in shape. Face pallid-yellow, in the middle with a very prominent carina ; cheeks with a brownish spot below the eyes. Palpi blackish at the tip; proboscis and the lower portion of the occiput, yellow. Mesonotum shining yellow with six slender brown stripes, the median pair separated by a line, the outer ones not continued in front of the suture ; more outwardly in front, on either side there is a slender strigula reaching as far as the suture. Pleuræ and legs wholly yellow. Abdomen black, the immediate base yellowish ; the narrow lateral margin of the second and third segments, and the fourth and fifth except a median triangle, yellow. Wings nearly hyaline ; a blackish subquadrate spot at the tip of the wing, in the submarginal and first posterior cell, reaching from the tip of the second to the tip of the fourth vein ; second section of the costal vein more than twice the length of the third section. Length 1¾-2 mm.

Numerous specimens. With these specimens there are several in which the front is yellow or brownish-yellow, and the spot at the tip of the wing is apparent only as a blackish cloud. They appear to be immature specimens.

3. *Drosophila sororia*, n. sp.

♂, ♀. Head and antennæ yellow, opaque : front rather more than one-third of the width of the head, a little broader above ; arista with only a few rays. Thorax light reddish-yellow, opaque. Abdomen reddish-brown or blackish, probably in life with black hind margins to the segments. Legs wholly yellow. Wings lightly tinged with blackish, more noticeable along the costa and at the tip ; a rather broad, dark cloud on the cross-veins, and indistinct clouds on the veins at the tip of the wing, that of the second vein, however, distinct ; third section of the costal vein short; posterior cross-vein straight. Length 1¼ mm.

Four specimens. St. Vincent.

4. *Drosophila annulata*, n. sp.

♂, ♀. Front less than one-third of the width of the head; silvery-grey and opaque black. Antennæ reddish-yellow, the first joint above, and the third at the base, blackish. Face blackish, greyish dusted; median carina yellowish, nose-like, subsulcate. Mesonotum opaque coffee-brown, with narrow, irregular, yellowish-grey markings. Scutellum darker brown, its basal angles and the apex greyish. Abdomen black, the narrow angles of the segments yellow, forming more or less complete bands, and a narrow yellow stripe in the middle of the posterior segments. Femora, except the yellow tip, dark brown; tibiæ yellow, with a basal and terminal brown ring; tarsi yellow. Wings subhyaline, with blackish clouds on the cross-veins, and a black spot at the tip of the first section of the costal vein. Length 2½ mm.

Fifteen specimens. St. Vincent.

5. *Drosophila bilineata*, n. sp.

♂. Front of equal width, not widened above; opaque velvety black, the orbits and a slender median line opaque yellowish-grey. Face light yellow, on the sides above dusted like the frontal orbits. Cheeks and the dilated palpi black, the cheeks yellow behind. Face distinctly receding, carinate in the middle. Antennæ brownish-yellow or brown, the third joint more than twice as long as wide; arista with about five rays above and three below. Occiput black above. Mesonotum and scutellum opaque deep brown, the former with two narrow stripes, not reaching the hind margin, and appearing like continuations of the frontal orbits. Pleuræ light-yellow. Abdomen oval, not elongate; opaque deep brown or black, the fifth segment, except sometimes a small spot in the middle, the remainder of the abdomen, and the narrow lateral margin of all the segments yellow. Legs light-yellow. Wings greyish hyaline; ultimate section of the fourth vein not twice the length of the penultimate section. Length 1¾ mm.

Three specimens. St. Vincent.

6. *Drosophila coffeata*, n. sp.

♂, ♀. Dark coffee-brown. Front at the lower part a little less than one-third of the width of the head, with two opaque, anteriorly convergent, velvety black stripes. Basal joints of the antennæ yellowish, the third joint brownish on its margin, only a little longer than broad; arista with four rays above. Face yellow, brown in the middle ; strongly carinate. Mesonotum with three inconspicuous whitish stripes in front. Scutellum black, brownish pollinose in an oblique light. Pleuræ nearly black. Abdomen black or brownish-black. Legs luteous. Wings tinged with brownish; ultimate section of the fourth vein not twice the length of the penultimate section ; third section of the costal vein less than half the length of the second section. Length 3–4 mm.

Numerous specimens. St. Vincent.

7. *Drosophila bellula,* n. sp.

♂, ♀. Front broader above ; the orbits yellowish, in the middle a large truncated triangle brown, the inner portion of which—the vertical triangle—lighter coloured, or yellow. Antennæ yellow, the base in the larger part of the short third joint blackish; arista pectinate above and below. Face and cheeks yellow, the former carinate. Mesonotum brown, with three greyish-yellowish stripes, the middle one broader and more diffuse in front, narrow behind. Scutellum brownish, yellowish on the borders. Pleuræ brown, with two slender yellowish stripes. Abdomen black or dark brown, the segments with a more or less narrow yellowish anterior border. Legs yellow. Wings yellowish hyaline ; second section of the costa about three times the length of the third section. Length 2 mm.

Eight specimens. St. Vincent.

8. *Drosophila fasciola,* n. sp.

♂, ♀. Front broader above ; the orbital margins yellowish (at their lower part a brownish spot); two convergent brown stripes, within which the vertical triangle is lighter coloured ; the front is wholly opaque. Antennæ yellowish ; the short third joint brown at the base. Face yellowish, the thin median carina nose-like, not appreciably sulcate. Cheeks brown. Mesonotum opaque greyish-yellowish, with incomplete brown stripes and irregular spots ; in the middle behind, the brown forms a large triangle, bisected by a slender yellowish line. Scutellum opaque yellowish, brownish towards its base ; the four bristles each arise from a small blackish spot. Pleuræ brown, yellowish vittate. Abdomen brown, the segments yellow or yellowish in front. Wings yellowish hyaline ; tip of the first section of the costa black ; third section of the costa not one-half the length of the second section. Legs yellow ; base of all the femora brown or blackish ; all the tibiæ with a proximal and distal brown ring. Length 2 mm.

Five specimens.

9. *Drosophila opaca*, n. sp.

♂, ♀. Front broad, more than one-third of the width of the head, considerably broader above ; deep opaque black. Antennæ reddish-brown or blackish, the third joint more or less blackish on the upper margin ; second joint tumid, with two or three bristles; third joint about twice as long as wide : arista with long rays, about eight in number, on the upper side. Face black, lightly dusted ; cheeks narrow. Palpi black. Mesonotum and scutellum wholly deep opaque, velvety black. Pleuræ opaque black, yellow below, a slender yellow line along the dorso-pleural suture. Halteres yellow. Abdomen opaque black and light-yellow; the first segment yellow ; the next three segments yellow, with the sides black, extending more or less across the hind margin, and leaving the yellow as a semi-oval space; fifth segment yellow, with a posterior band ; sixth segment yellow. Legs, including the coxæ, wholly light-yellow. Wings with a distinct brownish tinge ; penultimate section of the fourth vein about one-half the length of the ultimate section ; the third vein terminates at the extreme tip of the wing ; third section of the costal vein more than one-half the length of the second section. Length 1½ mm.

Numerous specimens. St. Vincent.

10. *Drosophila thoracis*, n. sp.

♀. Front a third of the width of the head, broader above ; opaque or brown or black, the narrow orbits and median triangle shining. Antennæ lutescent yellow, the third joint a little blackish and rather elongate. Face luteous yellow, distinctly carinate above, the oral margin narrowly blackish. Cheeks yellow behind. Proboscis yellow. Mesonotum shining deep brown or nearly black. Scutellum black, shining. Uppermost part of the pleuræ, near the dorso-pleural suture, black, below light-yellow ; metanotum nearly black. Abdomen shining black, the middle of the first and second segments, anterior border of the fourth and fifth segments and the ovipositor, yellow; third segment yellow with a narrow, interrupted black band. Venter and legs light yellow. Wings yellowish hyaline ; the third costal section two-thirds of the length of the second section. Length 2 mm.

Two specimens. St. Vincent. "In fungi."

11. *Drosophila pleuralis*, n. sp.

♀. Front yellow below, on the upper part blackish. Antennæ reddish or yellowish, the third joint more or less infuscated and rather long ; arista with five rays above. Face,

cheeks, and the lower part of the occiput light-yellow ; facial
carina small.   Mesonotum and scutellum deep shining black or
nearly black.   Pleuræ and legs wholly light-yellow.   Abdomen
black, moderately shining, the fifth segment on the sides and the
venter yellow.   Wings nearly hyaline, the third section of the
costal vein little more than one-half the length of the second
section ; penultimate section of the fourth vein about one-third
the length of the ultimate section.   Length 2 mm.

One specimen.   St. Vincent.

12. *Drosophila splendida*, n. sp.

♂, ♀ .   The large frontal triangle metallic-blue, the sides more
brownish and the frontal lunile yellow.   Antennæ yellow, the
third joint somewhat brownish ; arista thickly and long plumose.
Face opaque yellow, somewhat blackish in the concavities, with a
slight median carina.   Mesonotum brilliant deep metallic-blue ;
scutellum deep opaque black ; pleuræ black but little shining.
Abdomen black, the basal segments more or less yellow, apparently
in life with distinct markings.   Legs yellow ; all the femora more
or less black.   Wings greyish or yellowish hyaline ; third section
of the costal vein two-thirds the length of the second section.
Anal cell incomplete.   Length 2 mm.

Four specimens.   St. Vincent.

13. *Drosophila punctulata.*

Drosophila punctulata, Loew, Centur., ii., 100.—Cuba.

Four specimens.   St. Vincent.

14. *Drosophila procnemis*, n. sp.

♂ .   Front broad, broader above; opaque yellow, the narrow
orbits greyish.   Antennæ yellow, the third joint brownish ; arista
with three or four rays above and two below.   Face and cheeks
yellow, the former not carinate, the latter narrow.   Thorax shining
reddish-yellow, with black hair.   Abdomen rather elongate, deep
shining black.   Legs yellow, the front femora for the most
part, the front tibiæ and the front metatarsi deep brown
or black, the remaining joints of the front tarsi light-yellow.
Wings tinged with greyish ; the third and fourth veins are gently
convergent, the former terminating at the tip of the wing : the

third section of the costal vein is about three-fourths the length of the second section, and the penultimate section of the fourth vein about one-third the length of the ultimate section ; costal cell infuscated ; anal cell complete. Length 2 mm.

Four specimens. The wings are whitish at the tip.

15. *Drosophila frontalis*, n. sp.

♂, ♀. Front narrow, more than twice as long as wide, less than one-third of the width of the face, of equal width above and below, and not wider than the face ; opaque light-yellow, in some specimens with a shade of brown above. Third joint of the antennæ fully twice as long as wide. Antennæ, face, and lower part of the occiput light-yellow, the occiput elsewhere blackish ; cheeks linear ; face not carinate. Mesonotum and scutellum light reddish-yellow, moderately shining. Pleuræ light-yellow. Abdomen yellow or light reddish-yellow, rather elongate ; the second segment, except the narrow front margin, the third and fourth segments each with three spots, of which the median one is the larger, black ; fifth segment of the female small, with a black spot on each side. Legs wholly light-yellow. Wings yellowish or greyish hyaline ; third section of the costal vein less than half the length of the second section ; penultimate section of the fourth vein less than half the length of the ultimate section ; the costal vein terminates at the tip of the third vein. Length 2½ mm.

Eight specimens. St. Vincent.

16. *Drosophila verticis*, n. sp.

♀. Front very broad above ; yellow, the vertical stripes and a stripe or spot near the orbits, metallic-blue ; lower part of the front wholly yellowish. Antennæ yellow, the third joint brown ; arista with long rays above and below. Face yellow, flat, not carinate. Mesonotum shining reddish-yellow ; scutellum opaque brown on its upper surface. Pleuræ more brown. Abdomen apparently yellow, with brown posterior bands to the segments. Legs yellow. Wings nearly hyaline ; third section of the costal vein two-thirds or more the length of the second section ; anal cell incomplete, the vein closing the cell outwardly indistinct or wanting. Length 2 mm.

Two specimens. St. Vincent.

17. *Drosophila*, sp. ?. (Pl. XIV., fig. 153, wing.)

♂. Deep shining black. Front very broad, broader than long. Antennæ blackish; third joint narrow and pointed. Face not more than half the width of the front, gently convex in the middle, the narrow orbits, the inferior margin and the cheeks greyish dusted. Legs, including the front coxæ, wholly light-yellow. Wings nearly hyaline; third costal section a little longer than the second. Length 2 mm.

One specimen. "Union Is., Oct."

18. *Drosophila pollinosa*, n. sp.

♂. Black in ground-colour, thickly pollinose. Front longer than broad, only a little broader above; densely yellowish-grey pollinose, with four rows of bristles, the median ones not extending quite as far as the orbital ones. Antennæ reddish-yellow, the third joint rounded, the arista with but few rays on the upper side. Face greyish-pollinose, like the front, flat or with a slight carina above; vibrissæ present; cheeks not broad. Thorax densely pollinose, the mesonotum and scutellum yellowish-grey, the pleuræ more grey; apex of the scutellum reddish. Abdomen black, yellowish-grey dusted. Legs reddish-yellow. Wings nearly hyaline; anterior cross-vein situated before the insertion of the first vein; third section of the costal vein only a little shorter than the second section. Halteres yellow. Length 2 mm.

Two specimens. St. Vincent. In all probability the present species belongs among the *Ephydridæ*, but the very flat face and the presence of vibrissæ will lead one to search for the species in this genus. The presence of the additional row of frontal bristles, the few rays to the antennal arista, the small carina, and the partial absence of the anal cell are all characters out of accordance with those of this genus, as well as the general colouring of the species.

19. *Drosophila limbata*, n. sp.

♂, ♀. Head, thorax and legs yellow or reddish-yellow, but little or not at all shining; third joint of the antennæ brownish; face carinate. Abdomen yellow, with a posterior black band to the segments, the bands broader in the middle and narrow at the sides. Wings distinctly clouded with blackish along the front border, filling out the costa, marginal and submarginal cells, and reaching

the middle of the first posterior cell : behind, the wing is distinctly lighter coloured, but not hyaline; on the posterior cross-
vein there is an indistinct cloud ; third section of the costal vein
about one-third the length of the second section. Length 2 mm.

Twelve specimens.   St. Vincent.

20. *Drosophila pallida*, n. sp.

♂, ♀. Yellow, not shining, the mesonotum light reddish-
yellow and a little shining ; face obtusely carinate above, not
nose-like.   Abdomen reddish-yellow, with a narrow brownish
posterior border to the segments. Front broad, broader above.
Wings distinctly yellowish ; second section of the costal vein fully
twice the length of the third section. Length 1½ mm.

Twelve specimens.   St. Vincent.   In most of the
specimens the narrow brown bands of the abdomen are
visible, but in some the whole abdomen is brown. The
penultimate section of the fourth vein is very nearly equal
to one-half the length of the ultimate section. A single
female specimen agrees in other respects but has the
third costal section about three-fourths the length of the
second section and the penultimate section of the fourth
vein not more than one-third the length of the ultimate
section.

21. *Drosophila similis*, n. sp.

♂, ♀. Very much like *D. pallida*, but is larger, and the
third section of the costal vein is very short, not longer than the
penultimate section of the fourth vein.   The second and third
veins are parallel through nearly their whole length, and the second
vein is unusually long.   In most of the specimens the abdomen is
brown, but in some there are black or brown bands as in *D. pallida*.
The colour is reddish-yellow, sometimes more purely yellow.
Length 2–2⅔ mm.

Numerous specimens.   St. Vincent.

22. *Drosophila illota*, n. sp.

♀. Yellowish or brownish-red, the abdomen brown or blackish,
the legs yellow. Front as broad or broader than long, a little
wider above, opaque brownish or ochraceous yellow, the ocellar
tubercle blackish.   Third joint of the antennæ twice as broad as
long, blackish ; arista with two or three rays on the under side.

Face more yellowish, in the middle with a strong, obtuse carina, leaving a deep depression on each side in which is lodged the antenna. Palpi and proboscis yellowish. Mesonotum a little shining. Abdomen more reddish toward the base. Wings with a brownish tinge ; penultimate section of the fourth vein about one-half as long as the ultimate section ; posterior cross-vein nearly as long as the ultimate section of the fifth vein ; third section of the costa not half the length of the second section. Length 2½ mm.

Two specimens. St. Vincent.

23. *Drosophila nana*, n. sp.

♂, ♀. Front a little broader above ; brown, somewhat yellowish below. Antennæ yellow, the third joint oval, brownish. Face obscure yellowish-brown ; carina small, low, confined to the upper part of the face. Arista with four or five rays above and two long ones below. Mesonotum yellowish-brown, shining ; pleuræ more blackish. Abdomen oval, black, shining. Legs lutescent yellow. Wings yellowish hyaline ; third section of the costal vein more than one-half the length of the second section ; anal cell incomplete, its outer cross-vein indistinct. Length 1¾ mm.

Six specimens. St. Vincent.

PHORTICA.

Schiner, Wien. ent. Monatschr., vi., 1862. *Amiota*, Loew, Centur., ii., 93, 1862.

1. *Phortica scutellaris*, n. sp.

♀. Front opaque black, brownish pollinose, a little wider posteriorly, less than one-third the width of the head. Antennæ brownish-yellow or yellow, the first two joints brownish ; arista long plumose. Face flattened, grey pollinose. Thorax black, thinly greyish-yellowish pollinose and but little shining ; scutellum flattened, opaque-black. Abdomen black or brownish-black, more or less yellowish in the middle and at the tip ; venter yellow. Legs wholly light-yellow. Wings greyish hyaline, distinctly pubescent ; cross-veins approximated, the penultimate section of the fourth vein scarcely as long as the first section of the third vein ; second and third veins nearly parallel, the distance between

their tips not twice as great as that between the tips of the fourth
and third veins.

♂. Second, third, and fourth joints of the front tarsi dilated,
the first joint stout ; the whole tarsi and the tip of the tibiæ
blackish.

Length 2 mm.

Five specimens. St. Vincent. I refer this species
with some doubt to the present genus, as it does not
have the typical markings of *Phortica*. There is a complete posterior basal cell ; otherwise the species resemble
those of *Drosophila*. The oral vibrissæ are weak.
The bristles of the front are strong and reach nearly
to the oral margin ; there is no preapical bristle to the
hind tibiæ.

OSCINIDÆ.

ELACHIPTERA.

Macquart, Hist. Nat. Dipt. Suites a Buffon, ii., 621,
1835 ; *Crassiseta*, Von Roser, Verh. Wurtt. Dipt.
Nachtrag, 1840.

1. *Elachiptera flavida*, n. sp.

♂, ♀. Light reddish colour, the arista black, and the legs
more purely yellow. Vertical triangle large, reaching nearly to
the root of the antennæ, shining. Head usually a purer yellow
than the mesonotum and abdomen. Mesonotum shining. Scutellum trapezoidal, with two moderate-sized bristles on the angles.
Abdomen of some specimens brownish, probably from desiccation.
Wings hyaline, with a slight yellowish tinge ; third section of
the costal vein only a little shorter than the second. Length
2-2½ mm.

Ten specimens. St. Vincent.

HIPPELATES.

Loew, Centur., iii., 67, 1863.

1. Proboscis elongate, folding backwards (*Siphomyia*) . . . 2
   Proboscis not elongate 3
2. Thorax black, thinly greyish dusted . . . *proboscideus*, n. sp.
   Thorax yellow, the mesonotum, except on the sides and
      behind, black, thickly yellowish dusted . *dorsatus*, n. sp.

3. Thorax shining black 5
Thorax not wholly black 4
4. Thorax reddish-yellow; front black; second and third
sections of the costal vein of nearly equal length

equalis, n. sp.

Mesonotum brown or blackish; front yellow, with a
moderate-sized brown triangle; second section of
the costal vein much longer than the third

dorsalis, Loew.

5. Scutellum black; third section of the costal vein much
shorter than the second . . . . *flaripes*, Loew.

Scutellum reddish; second and third sections of the costa
of nearly equal length . . . . *scutellaris*, n. sp.

1. *Hippelates* (n. subg., *Siphomyia*) *proboscideus*, n. sp.

♂. Front opaque yellow, the vertical triangle black, but
covered with light greyish dust, leaving a small, rounded, shining
spot near the ocelli. The triangle reaches to about the middle of
the front, and its sides are nearly equilateral; a row of small
bristles on either side reaches to below the middle of the front.
Antennæ, face, cheeks and palpi wholly yellow; on either side of
the oral margin in front a small vibrissal bristle. Proboscis slender,
elongate, bent near its middle and turned back, its slender proximal
portion a little shorter than the length of the head. Cheeks rather
broad. Palpi cylindrical, a little broader toward the end. Thorax
black, thickly greyish dusted, the mesonotum with three, slender,
indistinct lines; the pleuræ shining black on the lower portion.
Scutellum oval, with two bristles on its border. Abdomen red or
brownish-red; in some specimens reddish-brown with yellowish
incisures. Legs wholly light-yellow; spur of the hind tibiæ long
and stout. Wings cinereous hyaline; third section of the costa
short. Length 2 mm.

Ten specimens. St. Vincent. This and the following
species, while agreeing sufficiently well in the other
characters with the genus *Hippelates*, I have thought
well to distinguish subgenerically from the other species
by the name *Siphomyia*, on account of the elongate
proboscis. Others of the previously described species
evidently belong to the same subdivision.

2. Hippelates (Siphomyia) dorsatus, n. sp.

♀. Front opaque yellow, the minute ocellar spot brownish.
Antennæ yellow, the third joint a little brownish in front; arista
brown, slender, bare. Face, cheeks, proboscis and palpi yellow;
proboscis elongate, the labella slender and turned backward.
Mesonotum, except on the sides and posterior margin, black, but
largely concealed beneath light-yellow dust; thorax elsewhere
yellow, opaque. Scutellum convex, yellow, with two small,
approximated bristles at the tip. Abdomen yellow, the second,
third and fourth segments with three series of black, subconfluent
spots, of which the middle ones extend furthest back. Legs light-
yellow; spur of the hind tibiæ very long, curved and black.
Wings nearly hyaline; second section of the costal vein nearly
twice the length of the third section. Length $2\frac{1}{3}$ mm.

One specimen. St. Vincent.

3. Hippelates equalis, n. sp.

♂, ♀. Front broad; the very large shining black triangle
extends to near the root of the antennæ; remainder of the front
opaque black. Antennæ, face, and the very narrow cheeks yellow.
Occiput black. Thorax light reddish-yellow, the mesonotum
shining. Scutellum flattened subquadrate, the marginal bristles
remote from each other on the angles. Abdomen reddish-yellow,
the distal segments somewhat obscure. Legs wholly light-yellow;
spur of the hind tibiæ long, curved and black. Wings greyish
hyaline; second and third sections of the costa of nearly equal
length. Length 2 mm.

Four specimens. St. Vincent. This species is
related to *H. pallidus*, Loew, but will be distinguished
by the colour of the front.

4. Hippelates dorsalis.

Hippelates dorsalis, Loew, Centur., viii., 75.—Cuba.

♂, ♀. Front broad, light-yellow opaque; vertical triangle
reaches to about midway, and is shining black or dark red, sometimes partially concealed beneath greyish dust. Third joint of the
antennæ large, rounded; on its upper part black, below yellow
The face, the moderately broad cheeks, and the palpi yellow, the
proboscis black. Thorax reddish-yellow, the mesonotum black or

brown, moderately shining and with feebly marked linear stripes. Scutellum reddish-yellowish; oval, convex, and with approximated apical bristles. Abdomen reddish or yellowish at the base, becoming brownish distally. Legs reddish or lutescent yellow, the tarsi brownish distally. Wings nearly hyaline; third section of the costa but little more than half the length of the second section. Length 2 mm.

Four specimens. St. Vincent.

5. *Hippelates flavipes.*

Hippelates flavipes, Loew, Centur., vi., 95.—Cuba.

A large series of specimens from St. Vincent agree with the description of this species so closely that there can be no question of their identity. With them, however, there is yet a larger number which show such discrepancies that their specific identity is somewhat doubtful. I give herewith a description of the variety or species, whichever it may be.

♂, ♀. Front opaque black or dark brown on the sides; on the lower third, from the tip of the very large shining black triangle, opaque yellow. Antennæ yellow, the upper part of the third joint blackish; arista black, bare. Face and cheeks yellow, the former with a large notch in front, which is margined with brown. Mesonotum shining black, with black pubescence; scutellum opaque, convex, and with a pair of approximated bristles at the apex. Pleuræ shining black. Abdomen black; the base, the venter, and the ovipositor yellow or yellowish. Halteres light-yellow. Legs, including the front coxæ, light-yellow; hind femora for the greater part black, the middle femora and hind tibiæ sometimes blackish in the middle. Length 1¾–2 mm.

In yet another large series the legs are almost wholly black, save the tarsi, and the antennæ are wholly black.

6. *Hippelates scutellaris*, n. sp.

♂. Front yellow, including the lower part of the very large, shining black triangle, which reaches very nearly to the base of the antennæ. Antennæ reddish-yellow; the arista black and very finely pubescent. Eyes sparsely, but distinctly, pubescent. Face yellow, somewhat blackish in the middle. Cheeks very narrow. Palpi yellow. Mesonotum wholly shining black, not pollinose.

Scutellum reddish, blackish at the base, its straight distal margin with two rather remote bristles. Pleuræ reddish-yellow. Abdomen elongate; shining black, at its base obscurely reddish. Legs yellow, the hind tibiæ somewhat, and the last two joints of the tarsi, brown. Wings nearly hyaline; third section of the costa as long as the second section. Length $2\frac{3}{4}$ mm.

One specimen. St. Vincent.

OSCINIS.

Latreille, Nouv. Dict. d'Hist. Nat., xxiv., 196, 1804.

1. Scutellum elongated, triangular, pointed 2
   Scutellum oval, convex 3
2. Scutellum wholly light-yellow; mesonotum black in the
      middle, yellow on the sides . . . . *triangularis*, n. sp.
   Scutellum black, yellow at the tip; mesonotum wholly
      black . . . . *apicalis*, n. sp.
3. Second section of the costal vein not twice the length of
      the third 6
   Second section of the costal vein fully twice the length of
      the third 4
4. Antennæ yellow 5
   Antennæ black . . . . *fur*, n. sp.
5. Mesonotum black, greyish-yellowish dusted . . *incipiens*, n. sp.
   Mesonotum yellow, with four narrow brown stripes,
                                        quadrilineata, n. sp.
6. Thorax yellow, shining . . . . *nitis*, n. sp.
   Thorax not shining, yellow 7
7. Thorax shining black, front mostly shining black 8
   Thorax opaque, vittate; front opaque . . . . . *nana*, n. sp.
8. Front tarsi yellow; scutellar bristles approximated, third
      joint of the antennæ largely yellow . . . *concinna*, n. sp.
   Front tarsi black; antennæ black . . . . *anonyma*.

1. *Oscinis triangularis*, n. sp. (Pl. XIV., fig. 153a, wing.)

♂, ♀. Eyes densely pubescent. Front narrow, not one-third of the width of the head; opaque yellow, a minute black spot at the ocelli; the small frontal triangle shining. Antennæ yellow. Face, the narrow cheeks, the palpi, and the proboscis light-yellow. Thorax light-yellow, with light-yellow hair; mesonotum with three broad, coalesced or coalescent black stripes, the middle one of which extends further forward than the others. Pleuræ with a small, round, black spot above the middle coxæ. Scutellum large, nearly equilaterally triangular, with its apex rounded and provided with two approximated bristles : wholly light-yellow. Metanotum and the abdomen, except the immediate base, shining black ; venter yellow. Legs yellow ; front tibiæ and tarsi brown or brownish ; the distal two joints of the hind tarsi in the ♂ black. Wings greyish hyaline ; third section of the costa about two-thirds the length of the second section ; third and fourth veins parallel. Length 2¼ mm.

Five specimens. St. Vincent, Leeward side, 500–1000 feet.

2. *Oscinis apicalis*, n. sp.

Eyes distinctly pubescent. Front opaque reddish-yellow, the large vertical triangle deep shining black, its anterior point reaching about two-thirds of the distance to the root of the antennæ. Antennæ reddish-yellow, the upper margin of the third joint brownish ; arista black, finely pubescent. Face, cheeks, and clypeus black. Palpi reddish-yellow. Mesonotum deep black, moderately shining, finely punctulate. Scutellum elongate, triangular, pointed ; black, its apical one-third light-yellow ; there are two upright, small bristles at the tip, and on either side a minute tubercle. Pleuræ shining black. Abdomen shining black, the venter yellowish. Halteres nearly white. Legs, not including the coxæ, wholly light-yellow. Wings greyish hyaline ; third section of the costa not more than one-half the length of the second section ; second, third, and fourth veins parallel. Length 2 mm.

One specimen. St. Vincent. "Forest, 1800 feet, W. slope of Sonfriere, Sept. 23."

3. *Oscinis quadrilineata*, n. sp.

♂, ♀. Eyes pubescent. Front opaque yellow, with a small brown spot between the ocelli ; vertical triangle small, but little shining. Antennæ yellow, the third joint brown on its front margin. Face, cheeks, and palpi yellow. Thorax yellow, the mesonotum with four narrow brown stripes, not shining, the median pair more narrowly separated. Scutellum light-yellow. Metanotum and abdomen black, the latter at its immediate base yellow ; venter yellow. Legs yellow. Wings nearly hyaline ; third section of the costa scarcely one-half the length of the second section. Length 2 mm.

Four specimens. St. Vincent. The abdomen varies much in colour, from reddish-yellow to black, and the antennæ may be wholly yellow. There are numerous rather short stubbly bristles on the lateral and posterior margins of the mesonotum and on the margin of the scutellum, which are highly characteristic of the species.

4. *Oscinis anonyma*, n. sp.

♂, ♀. Front opaque black on the side, with a large shining black triangle, reaching nearly to the root of the antennæ. Antennæ wholly black, the arista very finely pubescent. Face black ; cheeks yellow. Thorax deep shining black. Scutellum convex, black, with two strong, rather remote bristles. Abdomen black, moderately shining. Halteres yellow. Legs yellow, the hind tibiæ in part and all the tarsi brown ; the tip of the front tibiæ and their tarsi were blackish. Wings greyish hyaline ; second section of the costa slightly longer than the third. Length 1¼ mm.

Two specimens. St. Vincent.

5. *Oscinis nana*, n. sp.

♂, ♀. Front opaque, black in ground-colour, but covered with a thin brownish dust ; the large vertical triangle is somewhat elevated, its sides nearly equilateral, and separated by a distinct groove from the rest of the front ; it reaches about midway of the front. Face brown or blackish ; cheeks yellowish. Antennæ black, the third joint in large part yellow. Thorax black ; the mesonotum with four broad, greyish-yellowish, not conspicuous stripes, leaving three narrow, more blackish intervals. Scutellum black, the bristles of its apex not remote from each other. Pleuræ greyish dusted. Abdomen black, not shining. Legs yellow, the femora for the greatest part, and the last two joints of the tarsi black. Wings nearly hyaline ; second and third sections of the costa of nearly equal length. Length 1-1¼ mm.

Four specimens. St. Vincent. The bristles are everywhere short and inconspicuous.

6. *Oscinis concinna*, n. sp.

♂. The very large, shining black vertical triangle reaches nearly to the root of the antennæ, leaving the sides below opaque-brown. Antennæ reddish-yellow, the front margin of the third joint black ; arista pubescent. Eyes distinctly pubescent. Face black in the middle. Cheeks yellow, somewhat silvery. · Thorax and scutellum deep shining black, with black hair ; bristles of the scutellum approximated. Abdomen shining black. Legs yellow, the femora for the most part pitchy black ; front tibiæ in part brown. Wings nearly hyaline ; second section of the costa scarcely longer than the third. Length 1¼ mm.

Three specimens. St. Vincent. This species closely resembles *O. anonyma*, but differs in the yellow antennæ, the black femora, the approximated bristles at the tip of the scutellum, the shorter, more slender and yellow front tarsi, and the rather longer second section of the costal vein.

7. *Oscinis mitis*, n. sp.

♂, ♀. Yellow, the head with a minute black spot at the ocelli, and the abdomen for the larger part brown. The very large, shining vertical triangle reaches to the antennæ and nearly from eye to eye at the vertex. Scutellum rather large, subquadrate, the bristles of its apex not approximated. Mesonotum shining, with yellow hairs. Legs lighter yellow. Wings greyish-hyaline ; second section of the costa only a little longer than the third ; third and fourth veins parallel. Length 2 mm.

Four specimens. St. Vincent, " Windward side."

8. *Oscinis incipiens*, n. sp.

♂, ♀. Front opaque light-yellow, the opaque, whitish-dusted vertical triangle scarcely reaching the middle of the front. Antennæ, face, cheeks and palpi light-yellow, the third joint of the antennæ somewhat brownish above. Thorax and the oval scutellum deep black, but little shining, covered with greyish-yellowish dust or pubescence, the scutellum somewhat yellowish at the apex. Abdomen brownish-black, opaque. Legs yellow, the hind femora, and the hind tibiæ in the middle somewhat brownish. Wings nearly hyaline; second section of the costa more than twice the length of the third. Length 1¾ mm.

Thirty specimens. St. Vincent.

9. *Oscinis fur*, n. sp.

♂, ♀. Front light-yellow, opaque, with a V-shaped impressed line, back of which the vertical triangle is more or less black or brown and greyish-dusted. Face, cheeks and palpi yellow. Antennæ black, the basal joints yellow. Thorax black, only a little shining, covered with thin greyish dust or pubescence. Scutellum oval. Abdomen black, moderately shining. Legs black or dark brown, the trochanters, knees, more or less of the anterior tibiæ and the base of the middle tarsi yellow. Wings greyish-hyaline; third section of the costal vein about half the length of the second section. Length 2 mm.

Ten specimens. St. Vincent. This species is closely allied to the foregoing, *O. incipiens*, but differs in the colour of the antennæ and legs, especially.

CHLOROPS.

Meigen, Illiger's Magazin, ii., 278, 1803.

1. *Chlorops trivittata*, n. sp.

♂, ♀. Front reddish-yellow, mostly shining, with a small black spot between the ocelli. Basal joints of the antennæ yellowish-red; third joint black. The face, the broad cheeks, palpi and broad margins of the occiput yellow. Thorax light-yellow; the broad median black stripe begins at the neck and reaches two-thirds of the way to the scutellum; the lateral stripes begin a little way back of the front margin and reach further toward the scutellum; in addition there is a black strigula above the root of each wing, and a minute black spot on each humerus. Scutellum light-yellow, semicircular in shape. Metanotum black. Abdomen brownish-yellow; venter yellow. Legs yellow; the distal joints of the tarsi brownish. Wings nearly hyaline; the third section of the costal vein only a little more than half the length of the second section; third and fourth longitudinal veins gently divergent; last section of the fifth vein more than twice the length of the penultimate section of the fourth. Length 2 mm.

Fifteen specimens. St. Vincent.

AGROMYZIDÆ.

PLATOPHRYMYIA, n. g.

Allied to *Agromyza*, but the front very long, plane, and the epistoma projecting, the proboscis long and slender, folding backward near the middle. Front long, descending, plane or gently concave longitudinally, with moderately strong bristles reaching nearly to the root of the antennæ. Antennæ short, third joint large, rounded, arista bare. Face excavated in profile, short, the epistoma projecting as far forward as the antennal projection ; oral margin of cheeks long, horizontal, straight ; well developed vibrissal bristles present. Oral margin in front notched. Palpi large, projecting, a little thickened at the extremity. Thorax moderately arched in front, flattened behind, with bristles on the sides and in front of the scutellum. Scutellum large, with four bristles. Abdomen oval, depressed, composed apparently of five visible segments, genitalia not prominent. Legs short and rather strong, not at all bristly. Auxiliary vein rudimentary ; first longitudinal vein short ; basal cells small but distinct ; cross-veins approximated, the posterior one situated before the middle of the wing.

1. *Platophrymyia nigra*, n. sp.

Black. Frontal triangle prominent, with a depression on either side, which extends in the middle in front to the antennæ shallowly. Face with a distinct median keel. Palpi black. Thorax lightly greyish-dusted. Scutellum oval, with four bristles, the median pair decussate. Abdomen pruinose. Halteres yellow. Metatarsi yellowish. Wings whitish-hyaline ; penultimate section of the fourth vein about as long as the ultimate section of the fifth vein ; the third vein terminates a very little beyond the apex of the wing, and is curved a little toward the fourth vein towards its extremity. Length 2 mm.

One specimen. St. Vincent.

OPHTHALMOMYIA, n. g.

Auxiliary vein feebly distinct at its beginning, continuing as an indistinct line and then uniting with the first vein. First vein short, extending little more than one-third of the length of the wing, with an incision in the costa before its tip. Cross-veins not approximated, the ultimate section of the fourth vein scarcely twice the length of the penultimate section; anterior cross-vein situated a little before the termination of the first vein ; basal cells small, but complete. Face narrow, feebly carinate on the upper part, broader in the female than in the male, with a row of rather long bristles on each side extending nearly to the antennæ, but without true vibrissæ. The face is plane, not projecting in profile ; in the middle, not reaching much more than three-fourths the distance from the root of the antennæ to the lower border of the eyes ; epistoma not at all projecting ; clypeus projecting lappet-like ; cheeks linear, with bristles along the oral margin. Eyes forming nearly the entire head in profile, with a distinct excision on the occipital border near the middle. Occiput concave. Antennæ short, third joint rounded, arista bare. Proboscis slender, when folded enclosed within the oral cavity, the labella slender and turned backward. Legs moderately slender, with bristles on the under side of the femora, but no preapical bristles and no spurs, save on the middle tibiæ. Mesonotum with bristles on the sides and before the scutellum, the latter oval, with four bristles. Abdomen ovate, composed of five segments ; ovipositor of female telescopic, cylindrical, when extended about as long as the fifth segment ; male genitalia not exserted. Eyes bare. First posterior cell nearly closed.

1. *Ophthalmomyia lacteipennis.* (Pl. XIV., figs. 154, wing ; 154a, b, head of ♂.)

Lobioptera lacteipennis, Loew, Centur., vi., 97.—Cuba.

♂, ♀. Deep shining metallic black ; the front and face more opaque; legs brownish-black. Abdomen opaque, somewhat bronze-black, the margins and the fifth segment shining metallic ; palpi reddish ; wings whitish. Length 2–3 mm.

Numerous specimens.

CERATOMYZA.

Schiner, Wien. Ent. Monatschr., vi., 1862; *Odontocera*, Macquart, Hist. Nat. Dipt., ii., 1835 (preoc.).

1. *Ceratomyza dorsalis.* (Pl. XIV., figs. 155, wing ; 155a, head.)

? *Odontocera dorsalis*, Loew, Centur., iii, 98.—District Columbia.

♂, ♀. Front opaque dusky-yellow, with a rounded black spot about the ocelli. Face and cheeks yellow. First two joints and the under basal portion of the third joint of the antennæ yellow the third joint otherwise black. Mesonotum light-yellow, with three broad, opaque black stripes confluent in front, the median stripe reaching but little past the middle ; in addition, a slender strigula above the root of each wing. Scutellum blackish on the lateral margins; with two erect bristles at the apex. Pleuræ light-yellow. Metanotum black, except on its uppermost part. Abdomen black, but whitish pruinose ; the fifth segment with a yellowish hind margin ; venter yellow. Legs yellow ; coxæ and femora light-yellow, the tibiæ brown, the tarsi black or blackish. Length 2½ mm.

Two specimens. This species, the only one that has been recognized in the western continent, appears to resemble the European *C. acuticornis*. As in that species, the fourth vein terminates at the extreme tip of the wing, the distance between the two cross-veins is less than half of the length of the last section of the fifth vein. The wings are nearly hyaline.

AGROMYZA.

Fallen, *Agromyzidæ*, 1823.

1. *Agromyza lateralis*, n. sp. (Pl. XIV., fig. 156, head.)

♂, ♀. Front of equal width throughout, less than one-third the width of the head, wholly light-yellow opaque, except a minute black spot between the ocelli. Antennæ black, the second joint and the third at its base somewhat yellowish. Face and cheeks yellow like the front, the latter narrow, and with a row of small bristles along the oral margin, the anterior one of which forms a moderately stout vibrissa. Palpi black. Occipital orbits yellow, obsolete above. Occiput concave, opaque black. Thorax black ; mesonotum moderately shining, the lateral margins light-yellow, broader in front of the wings, and extending over their root, and sometimes including the postalar callosities. The mesonotum has short black hair, and the median rows of bristles extend as far forwards as the middle. Abdomen black, a little shining, clothed with black hair. Halteres light-yellow. Legs black or brownish-black, the tarsi brown or brownish-yellow. Wings hyaline ; penultimate section of the fourth vein not longer than the posterior cross-vein ; first and second basal cells united. Length 2–3 mm.

Numerous specimens.

2. *Agromyza xanthophora.* (Pl. XIV., fig. 157, wing.)

? *Agromyza xanthophora,* Schiner, Reise der Novara, Diptera, 291.—S. America.

♂. Front opaque black, lightly whitish dusted when seen from the side; above about one-third of the width of the head, moderately narrowed below; immediately above the root of the antennæ an oval yellow spot. Antennæ wholly black, the arista bare. Face black, lightly whitish dusted like the front. Cheeks narrow, hairy behind, but apparently without a row of bristles along the oral margin. Cheeks very narrow. Palpi black. Posterior orbits very narrow through it. Mesonotum opaque black, with black hair; the lateral margins, except a small spot on the humeri, the hind margin laterally, and a large confluent, quadrilateral spot behind, sulphur-yellow. Scutellum wholly yellow. Pleuræ black below; on the upper part confluent with the yellow of the sides of the mesonotum; the yellow is broadest below the root of the wings. Abdomen yellow; third, fourth and fifth segments each with a median black spot, partly confluent with each other and becoming successively larger posteriorly. Ovipositor black, cylindrical, gently tapering, about twice as long as broad, and about as long as the fifth segment. Wings hyaline; auxiliary vein distinct, except at its tip, where it is so slender and so closely approximated to the first vein that it is scarcely to be distinguished; penultimate section of the fourth vein scarcely longer than the posterior cross-vein and about half the length of the ultimate section of the fifth vein. Length 4 mm.

One specimen. Schiner's rather brief description applies well to this specimen, except in the size, which is given at 1–1½ lines. I believe, notwithstanding, the species are identical.

3. *Agromyza sorosis,* n. sp.

♂, ♀. Head, including the antennæ, yellow, a minute spot at the ocelli and the upper part of the occiput black. Front about one-third of the width of the head, a little broader on the upper part. Cheeks moderately broad, with bristles along the oral margin. Thorax light-yellow, with three broad, black stripes, separated by linear intervals or wholly confluent; the middle stripe begins at the collar and extends to back of the middle; the lateral portions behind, near the humeri, and reach nearly to the scutellum, with an angular incision at the hind end and at the suture. The scutellum has a small blackish spot on each margin and its dorsum is sometimes brownish. The ovipositor is about as long as broad, and about as long as the fifth segment. Metanotum black. Halteres light yellow. Abdomen yellow, the dorsum brownish or reddish-yellow. Wings hyaline ; penultimate section of the fourth vein a little longer than the posterior cross-vein and not more than a fourth or a fifth of the length of the last section of the fifth vein. Length $1\frac{3}{4}$-2 mm.

Numerous specimens. St. Vincent. There is some variation among the specimens, which possibly may indicate specific differences. ♀. Wings as described ; black of the mesonotum extending furthest back in the middle, nearly to the scutellum ; abdomen brownish-yellow, the first three segments with a brown cross-band, the last two with a small brown spot in the middle. ♂. Like the typical specimens, but the penultimate section of the fourth vein not one-third the length of the last section of the fifth vein. One of the typical specimens is labelled : " Mt. St. Andreas at Cavalries Forest, 1200 feet, Oct. 16."

4. *Agromyza anthrax*, n. sp.

♂. Black, but little shining. Front very broad, nearly square, its width rather exceeding its length ; opaque black, on its lower margin yellowish. Antennæ black, third joint rounded, large, pubescent ; arista very short pubescent. Face receding, excavated, not at all visible from the sides ; cheeks linear, with black bristles along the oral margin and a rather stout vibrissal bristle in front. Palpi projecting beyond the oral margin, yellow. Mesonotum and scutellum a little shining. Abdomen opaque, oval. Halteres yellow. Knees and tarsi yellow, the distal joints of the latter brownish. Wings lightly tinged ; the third vein terminates in the apex of the wing ; penultimate section of the fourth vein about one-third as long as the ultimate section of the fifth. Length $1\frac{1}{2}$ mm.

One specimen. St. Vincent.

LOBIOPTERA.

Wahlberg, Œfvers. af K.Ventenska Acad. Forh.,1847, 259.

1. *Lobioptera leucogastra.*

Milichia leucogastra, Loew, Wien. Entom. Monatschr.,
v., 43, 20.—Cuba.

Lobioptera leucogastra, Loew, Centur., viii., 95.

A single specimen from St. Vincent, agreeing well
with the description.

SEPSIDÆ.

SEPSIS.

Fallen, *Ortalidæ,* 20, 1820.

1. *Sepsis insularis,* n. sp.   (Pl. XIV., figs. 159, wing;
159*a*, front leg of ♂.)

♂, ♀. Front shining black, somewhat reddish below, with a
median longitudinal depression on the lower part. Antennæ
yellowish-red, the third joint sometimes a little brownish ; third
joint comparatively large. Face and cheeks yellowish-red. Thorax
shining black throughout. Abdomen deep shining black, with
coppery and purple reflections. Legs yellow or lutescent yellow,
the distal joints of all the tarsi and the hind tibiæ brown or blackish ; front femora in the male dilated for the basal two-thirds, as
far as a bifid tubercle, in which is inserted a short bristle ; beyond
the tubercle the femur is immediately narrowed, and a little
distance before it there is a bristle near the middle of the femur ;
tibiæ with a small tubercle corresponding to that of the femur.
Wings hyaline, the immediate base in the costal cells blackish.
Length 4 mm.

Numerous specimens. St. Vincent.

BORBORIDÆ.

LIMOSINA.

Macquart, Hist. Nat. Dipt., ii., 571, 1835.

TABLE OF SPECIES.

1. Third section of the costal vein longer than the second . .   2
    Third section shorter than the second   3
2. Distal section of the second vein distinctly longer than the
        first section of the third vein   .   .   .   . *perparva,* n. sp.

Distal section of the second vein not longer than the first
     section of the third vein . . . . *lugubris*, n. sp.
3. Scutellum deep opaque-black, noticeably different from the
     mesonotum . . . . *scutellaris*, n. sp.
Scutellum not noticeably different in colour from the
     mesonotum 4
4. Third vein beyond the cross-vein nearly straight, terminat-
     ing at the tip of the wing . . . . . . *pumila*, n. sp.
Third vein with a marked anterior curvature, terminating
     at some distance before the tip of the wing . *dolorosa*, n. sp.

1. *Limosina scutellaris*, n. sp.

♂, ♀. Front black, moderately shining, the lower portion and
the face, and the antennæ red. Mesonotum yellowish-red. Scutellum deep velvety black. Abdomen deep black, slightly metallescent, and thinly greyish-pollinose. Legs yellow, hind femora
blackish ; middle tibæ with spinous bristles. Length 2-2½ mm.

Numerous specimens. St. Vincent, etc.

2. *Limosina pumila*, n. sp. (Pl. XIV., fig. 160, wing.)

♂, ♀. Front opaque black, a median stripe or slender triangle
shining, below red or pitchy. Antennæ black ; arista finely
pubescent. Face black, obscurely red or pitchy across the middle.
Thorax black, moderately shining ; scutellum opaque, flattened,
with four strong bristles. Abdomen black, but little shining. Legs
luteous or brown, the femora and tibiæ more or less blackish, the
tarsi for the larger part yellowish ; middle tibiæ with strong bristles
on the outer side ; hind metatarsi but little longer than broad,
moderately dilated, scarcely more than half the length of the
slender second joint. Wings smoky hyaline ; the three sections
of the costa of nearly equal length, the first section with longer
bristles. Length 2-2½ mm.

Six specimens. St. Vincent.

3. *Limosina dolorosa*, n. sp.

♂, ♀. Black, thinly greyish-dusted, opaque. Antennæ black,
arista pubescent ; third joint transversely oval. Face and cheeks
black, but little shining. Scutellum coloured like mesonotum, its
margin reddish. Legs dark-brown ; middle tibiæ with stout
bristles on the outer side ; hind tibiæ and tarsi of nearly equal
length, the metatarsi about half the length of the second joint.

Wings lightly tinged with brownish ; first section of the costa with
bristles ; second section a fourth or a third longer than the third
section ; the third vein is conspicuously curved forward and
terminates distinctly before the tip of the wing ; fourth vein
beyond the discal cell feebly represented, gently curved. Length
2½–3 mm.

Numerous specimens. St. Vincent.

4. *Limosina perparva*, n. sp.   (Pl. XIV., figs. 161,
    wing ; 161a, antenna.)

♂. Front and face opaque-black. Antennæ obscurely yellow,
the third joint whitish pubescent, heart-shaped, with a terminal
arista ; arista black, pubescent. Thorax and scutellum deeply
black, the former shining, the latter opaque. Abdomen black.
Legs black ; the tip of the tibiæ and the tarsi yellowish ; hind
metatarsi nearly as long as the second joint. Wings nearly
hyaline : the second vein joins the costa in a very acute angle, and
is concave on the posterior side throughout ; costa with longer
bristles on its first section. Length 0·9 mm.

One specimen.

5. *Limosina lugubris*, n. sp.   (Pl. XIV., fig. 162, wing.)

♂, ♀. Face and cheeks yellow or brownish-yellow. Antennæ
yellow, the third joint brownish at the tip, whitish pubescent,
heart-shaped, the finely-pubescent arista terminal ; second joint
with a coronet of strong bristles. Front opaque-reddish or
brownish-yellow. Thorax, scutellum, and abdomen black shining :
scutellum flattened. Legs yellow, middle tibiæ with bristles on
the under side. Wings tinged with brownish, with a narrow
cross-band and the tip more nearly hyaline ; the third vein takes
its origin beyond the insertion of the first ; the first section of the
third vein is a little shorter than the terminal section of the
second vein, and the third section of the costa is nearly three
times the length of the second section ; posterior cross-vein but
little longer than the anterior cross-vein. Length 1½ mm.

One specimen. With this specimen there is another,
which has the front brown above, the pleuræ brownish-
yellow, the wings rather narrower, not clouded,
and with the distal section of the third vein more
nearly straight, and terminating exactly at the tip of
the wing. It undoubtedly belongs to a different
species.

BORBORUS.

Meigen, Illiger's Mag., ii., 276, 1803.

1. *Borborus venalicus.*   (Pl. XIV., fig. 163, wing.)

Borborus venalicus, Osten Sacken, Catalogue of Diptera, 2nd ed., 263. — Africa, Cuba, Brazil (Col. Williston).

♂, ♀. Front deep red, blackish above; opaque, with about ten small silvery spots. Antennæ brownish-red; arista bare. Cheeks and face yellow, the latter shining. Thorax black or nearly black, moderately shining, the dorsum with two pollinose stripes and about twenty small, white-pollinose partially confluent spots. Scutellum large, subtriangular, opaque-black, the base and small spots at the tip white. Abdomen black, the narrow hind-margin of the segments whitish. Femora black or deep brown, with the tip yellowish; tibiæ brown, the front pair with one, the middle and hind pairs with two dark-brown rings. Tarsi yellow, with the two distal joints black and the moderately thickened hind metatarsi partly brown. Wings nearly hyaline, with a small brown cloud at the angulated tip of the second vein and at the origin of the third. Third vein gently curved; front border of the wings without spinous bristles. Length 2–3 mm.

Twelve specimens. "Dr. Loew (*in litt.*) informs me that this is an African species; and as I have found it abundantly in Cuba, it seems probable it was brought over in slave-ships." Sacken, *l. c.* I have the species from Brazil.

2. *Borborus illotus*, n. sp.   (Pl. XIV., fig. 164, wing.)

♀. Front opaque-black, on the lower part red. Antennæ red, the third joint rounded; arista finely pubescent. Face reddish-brown. Thorax dark yellowish-red, opaque; mesonotum with abundant and rather long black hair; pleuræ black near the root of the wing. Abdomen opaque-black. Legs brown or brownish-yellow, the femora for the most part blackish; middle and hind tibiæ with stout bristles on the outer side; hind metatarsi moderately dilated, but little more than half the length of the slender second joint. Wings yellowish-hyaline; third section of the costal vein not more than two-thirds the length of the second section;

second vein sinuous, the third terminates before the tip of the wing ; fourth vein thin, but distinct. Length 2½ mm.

One specimen. St. Vincent.

SPHÆROCERA.

Latreille, Hist. Nat. Ins. et Crust., xiv., 1804.

1. *Sphærocera bimaculata,* n. sp. (Pl. XIV., fig. 165, wing.)

♂, ♀. Front and face black, opaque, sometimes in part yellowish, finely roughened. Antennæ brownish-red or reddish-brown, the third joint whitish at the tip : arista bare. Thorax brownish-black, the dorsum slightly shining, with four punctulate lines. Scutellum subtriangular, rounded and convex, bare (a minute point on either margin). Abdomen broadly oval, flat, bare, opaque-black, with two large, yellow spots, the anterior one more rounded or sub-quadrangular, the posterior one oval and smaller. Venter largely yellow. Legs, including the coxæ, light-yellow, without distinct bristles ; front femora thickened ; hind legs elongate ; hind metatarsi about as long as the three following joints together, much thickened ; second joint a little thickened. Wings nearly hyaline ; last sections of the third and fourth veins nearly parallel ; fifth vein complete. Length 3 mm.

Six specimens. St. Vincent.

PHORIDÆ.*

PHORA.

Latreille, Hist. Nat. Crust., etc., xiv., 1804.

1. *Phora fungicola.*

Coquillett, Canadian Entomologist, xxvii., 106, 1895.

One specimen, seemingly a male. 1500 feet. The lower part of the pleuræ is yellowish.

2. *Phora interrupta.*

Zetterstedt, Insecta lapponica, 797, 12, 1840.
Coquillett, Canadian Entomologist, xxvii., 103, 1895.

Eight specimens. Sea level to 1500 feet.

° By J. M. Aldrich.

3. *Phora fasciata.*

Fallen, Diptera suecica, Phytomyz., 7, 9, 1823.

Coquillett, Canadian Entomologist, xxvii., 103, 1895.

Fourteen specimens. Sea level to 1500 feet. They are but little different from *Phora interrupta*, but average larger, less dark on abdomen, wings clearer, and first light vein less curved. Both species have the hind femora tipped with brown.

4. *Phora venata,* n. sp.

♂. Head and abdomen black, thorax brownish-black, legs including tarsi yellow, femora a little darker. Palpi brown, antennæ blackish. Legs destitute of setæ, second heavy vein not forked. Anterior frontal bristles proclinate. Bristles of the front small, except the verticals. Halteres brown. Under surface of fore femora with a row of delicate curved hairs. Pleuræ yellowish below. Hypopygium yellow, rather large, with two black projecting claspers below and a brownish lamellar portion, bristly below, projecting backward ; also a slender yellow styliform organ (penis ?) in the centre below. Length 1·3 mm.

The most noticeable peculiarity of the species is the venation. The heavy veins reach beyond the middle. The so-called light veins are much heavier than in any other known North American species, comparatively straight, and have the appearance of making a complete union with the heavy veins, instead of stopping a little short and then running parallel with them.

One male. 1000 feet.

5. *Phora furtiva,* n. sp.

♀. Third vein forked, anterior frontal bristles proclinate, tibiæ destitute of large bristles on the outer side ; head, thorax and abdomen black, legs brownish, the tarsi and anterior tibiæ yellow. Front black, the bristles rather below medium size, the fine hairs somewhat conspicuous, antennæ blackish, more or less yellowish at base, palpi yellow. Thorax sub-shining, pleuræ shining black, halteres black. Femora in fully coloured specimens dark brown, in less mature ones yellowish-brown, the tibiæ lighter. Hind tarsi almost twice the length of the tibiæ.

Hind tibiæ on the posterior edge with longer hairs, on the inner side of this a row of about twelve small bristles. Wings slightly yellow, heavy veins reaching but little past the middle, second vein reaching barely more than half-way from the humeral vein to the fork of the third, on the costa. First and second light veins ending about equally far from the apex, the cell before the first as wide as the narrowest part of the one behind it. Length 1·5 mm.

Two females. 1000 feet.

6. *Phora divaricata*, n. sp.

♂,♀. Antennæ, palpi, pleuræ, halteres and legs deep yellow, anterior frontal setæ reclinate and divaricate : second heavy vein forked, the first attaining three-fourths of the distance from the humeral to the second, the first light vein moderately arcuated, the fourth scarcely visible, very slender. Front dark brown or black, the lower edge yellowish ; thorax above varying from yellow to black, frequently yellow with indistinct darker markings longitudinally. Abdomen black or brown, the posterior margin of each segment with a narrow band of light-yellow, which continues more or less as a stripe down the middle of the dorsal surface. Venter yellow. Anterior tibiæ on the front side with a row of four setæ, middle tibiæ with two together a trifle below the knee, hind tibiæ with a minute row of fine hairs down the posterior edge, but no setæ except at apex. Hind femora considerably thickened. Wings tinged with yellow, costa reaching a little past the middle, with two rows of fine setæ, which are more divaricate at the base. The two branches of the second vein are very close together, yet distinct. In the males the genitalia are bent up under the venter, giving the abdomen a knobbed appearance. Length 1·4 to 1·8 mm.

Two males, five females. Sea level to 1000 feet. May.

7. *Phora aurea*, n. sp.

♂, ♀. Yellow, lower frontal bristles proclinate, second vein forked, the abdomen, or at least the dorsal part, reddish-orange in colour. Front, antennæ and palpi yellow, arista yellow at base ; thorax wholly yellow, halteres yellow, in some cases brownish about the apex ; legs wholly yellow, the tarsi scarcely darker, middle and hind tibiæ with a row of nearly a dozen small bristles running down the posterior edge ; hind femora moderately thickened, with a few little bristles below near the tip ; abdomen bright reddish-orange in colour, toward the tip and below irregularly blackened. In one specimen, a male, the reddish colour is confined to the base, and there is a well-defined black spot on each side of the middle of the dorsum. Wings quite deeply tinged with yellow, the heavy veins reaching far beyond the middle, the first light vein but little curved, ending at or but little before the apex. The first heavy vein ends just perceptibly past the middle of the distance between the humeral vein and the tip of the branch of the second vein. The fourth light vein is distinct to the border. Length 1·3 to 1·7 mm.

Two males, seven females. 500 to 1500 feet.

8. *Phora magnipalpis*, n. sp.

♂. Second vein forked, anterior frontal bristles proclinate, legs yellow, the hind femora a little brownish, head, antennæ, thorax, and abdomen black ; palpi, halteres and pleuræ brownish-black. The palpi in the male are enlarged, divaricate, destitute of the usual strong setæ. Wings hyaline, the light veins very slender, tip of second vein just midway between the humeral and the fork of the second, on the costa ; second light vein with a greater curvature than usual, almost parallel with the vein before it, ending but little behind the apex. The heavy veins reach but little beyond the middle of the wing. Length 1·2 to 1·4 mm.

Four males. Sea level to 1000 feet. May.

I have also four females, same size and locality, which differ in having a lighter but variable coloration. The halteres and palpi vary from yellow to brown ; dorsum of thorax brown. The wings are as in the preceding males. I regard them as the same species, although there is not usually such a range of variation, especially between the two sexes.

In addition to the species described above, the collection contained two specimens of somewhat different coloration from any described species, and different from each other, which, on account of the absence of any striking characters, I leave undetermined for the present.

HIPPOBOSCIDÆ.*

ORNITHOMYIA.

Latreille, Hist. Nat. Crust. et Ins., xiv., 1804.

1. *Ornithomyia erythrocephala.*

? *Ornithomyia erythrocephala*, Leach, Eprob. Ins., 13, pl. xxvii., figs. 4, 5.

Four specimens which probably belong to this species. I have only Wiedemann's quotation of Leach's description for comparison, which does not give the length. The specimens are from nine to ten millimetres in length, the costal border of the submarginal cell is about two-thirds the length of that of the marginal cell, the second posterior cell is only a little longer than the first, etc.

SUPPLEMENT.

EMPIDIDÆ. (See p. 307.)

HEMERODROMIA.

Meigen, Syst. Beschr., ii., 1822.

1. *Hemerodromia defessa*, n. sp.   (Pl. XIV., fig. 166, wing.)

♂. Head and thorax shining, deep pitchy black or black, the lower part of the face and the occipital orbits grey pollinose. Eyes broadly contiguous on the face. Antennæ light yellow, the third joint as long as the first two together. Bristles of thorax and scutellum wholly inconspicuous. Abdomen opaque black, the venter yellow. Legs light-yellow; front femora much thickened, a little longer than the coxa, not emarginate for the reception of the tibial spine. Wings nearly hyaline; anal cell and discal cell wanting; anterior cross-vein situated a little beyond the middle of the basal cell; second posterior cell and its petiole of nearly equal length; no stigma. Proboscis light yellow, shorter than the height of the head.

Four specimens. The present species is related to *H. captus*, Coq., but differs in the shining colour of the head and thorax.

° By S. W. Williston.

2. *Hemerodromia*, sp.

♀. Head black, thickly grey pollinose. Eyes narrowly separated in the middle of the face. Antennæ and proboscis light yellow. Thorax reddish yellow, the mesonotum somewhat greyish pollinose, and with feeble indications of longitudinal stripes. Legs light yellow; front femora greatly thickened, and with a distinct emargination for the reception of the tip of the tibiæ. Wings as in *II. defessa*.

One specimen. In the absence of specimens for comparison, it is hazardous to say that this is the same as *II. oratorio*, Fall., but I can find no important differences from Loew's description. I suspect that *II. empiformis*, Say, may also be the same species (Coquillett has wrongly identified it). Coquillett makes no mention of the contiguity of the eye in his *II. rogatoris*, and leaves it to be inferred that the bristles of the thorax are microscopic. If such be the case, the two species are distinct.

For those species of *Hemerodromia*, in the sense of Loew, in which the neuration is normal, Coquillett has recently resuscitated the table name *Mantipeza*, Rondani, referring all the others to *Hemerodromia*, with the exception of *II. scapularis*, Loew, for which he creates the genus *Neoplasta*. *Hemerodromia precatoria*, Fall. (*II. monostigma*, Meigen), is a true *Mantipeza*, in Coquillett's sense, but he leaves it in *Hemerodromia*, so that it is difficult to say just what his conception of *Mantipeza* really is. In the examination of the descriptions and specimens of most of the known species of *Hemerodromia*, in the sense of Loew, I find the following different combinations of characters :—

> 1. Anal cell present, discal and second posterior cells also present.—*Mantipeza* of Coquillett.

This is *Hemerodromia* of Bigot, and it should be considered that of Meigen also.

> 2. Anal cell present, second basal cell present, discal cell wanting.—*Mantipeza* of Bigot.

This includes *II. nigriventris*, *II. defecta*, etc. Mr. Coquillett also includes in this group *II. albipes*, Walker. Mr. Coquillett's acumen in the detection of so many of Walker's defectively described species is to be commended. In the present case, however, has he some special information concerning the type of *II. albipes*? Mr. Walker

located *albipes* with *precatoria*, in which there is a " dis-
coidal areolet," and which should, therefore, belong in
Coquillett's *Mantipeza*.   He also describes the body as
being "fulvo-canis" in colour, with a "slight tawny
tinge," while Coquillett calls the "thorax and abdomen
black."   If Mr. Coquillett has information concerning the
type, then Walker's description should be cancelled *in
toto*, and the species rest upon Coquillett's diagnosis.

  3. Anal cell present, second basal and discal cells
     united ; second posterior cell sessile.—*Neoplasta* of
     Coquillett.
  4. Anal cell wanting ; second basal cell present and
     elongated ; discal cell wanting.—*Microdromia* of
     Bigot.

This includes the species described above, and a number of others.
  If Thomson is correct in his reference of *H. analis*,
then there is yet another group, differing from *Neoplasta*
in the second posterior cell being complete.

DRAPETIS.

(See page 308.)

TABLE OF SPECIES.

3. *Drapetis apicis*, n. sp.   (Pl. XIV., figs. 167, wing;
167*a*, antenna.)

♂, ♀. Front black, of moderate width, narrowed below, not at
all shining. Antennæ brown or reddish brown ; third joint very
small, onion-shaped. Eyes contiguous on the face. Thorax black;
mesonotum moderately shining, lightly pruinose in some reflections.
Scutellum with two bristles. Abdomen black, nearly opaque ;
hypopygium shining. Legs brown or blackish brown; front coxæ,
basal portion of all the femora, the hind tibiæ in part, and the
proximal portion of the four posterior tarsi yellow or yellowish ;
front femora considerably thickened on the proximal portion, its
under border straight ; middle femora less thickened, the hind
femora rather slender. Wings nearly uniformly tinged with brown ;
second and third sections of the costa of nearly equal length ; third
and fourth veins nearly parallel, the third terminating at the
extreme tip ; penultimate section of the fourth vein about twice
the length of the posterior cross-vein. Palpi, proboscis, and halteres brown. Front and hind tibiæ without spurs.

Three specimens.

4. *Drapetis minuta*, n. sp.   (Pl. XIV., figs. 168, wing;
168*a*, antenna.)

♂. Eyes closely contiguous above and below the antennæ.
Vertical triangle and occiput black, whitish pruinose. Antennæ
light yellow ; third joint as long as the first two together, a half
longer than wide. Thorax black ; mesonotum shining, clothed with
black hair. Scutellum with two bristles. Abdomen black, moderately shining. Legs light yellow ; all the femora moderately
thickened, the front pair more so than the others. Wings nearly
hyaline ; second vein deeply concave anteriorly ; third vein widely
divergent from the fourth, the first posterior cell widely open.

The hair of the mesonotum in some lights has a yellowish cast. A closely related species from Grenada has the
antennæ darker coloured, the third joint smaller, the
second vein of the wing less concave, etc. Two specimens.

5. *Drapetis*, n. sp.

♂. Very much like *D. flavipes*, but smaller, the second longitudinal vein shorter and more concave, the third vein straighter, the fourth terminating at the extreme tip of the wing, instead of a little beyond it, etc. Length 1 mm.

One specimen.

AGROMYZIDÆ. (See p. 426.)

PHYLLOMYZA.

Fallen, Diptera Suec., Ocht., 8, 1823.

1. *Phyllomyza megnipalpis*, n. sp. (Pl. XIV. fig. 169, head of ♀.)

♀. Head deep black. Front broad, large, the narrow orbits, on which are placed the lateral row of bristles, subshining. Third antennal joint very large, the arista, which springs from its superior angle, finely pubescent. Face excavated, retreating in profile. Palpi very large, projecting; proboscis small, rather slender. Thorax deep black; mesonotum shining, with black hair. Scutellum large, trapezoidal, with a stout bristle on each apical angle. Abdomen black, with black hair, not shining; in shape, short ovate, the five segments of nearly equal length. Legs black, the immediate tip of femora, the front tibiæ, the middle tibiæ in part and all the tarsi yellow. Wings nearly hyaline; basal cells small, but complete; submarginal cell narrowed at the extremity, its costal margin only about half the length of that of the first posterior cell; the third vein terminates at the extreme tip of the wing; penultimate section of the fourth vein less than one-third the length of the ultimate section. Length 1½ mm.

One specimen.

AGROMYZA. (See p. 428.)

5. *Agromyza innominata*, n. sp. (Pl. XIV., fig. 153, head of ♂.)

♂. Head yellow, a blackish spot at the ocelli; front broad. Antennæ yellow; third joint longer than broad; arista finely pubescent. Face short, gently excavated in profile; cheeks rather broad. Palpi elongate, dilated. Thorax obscurely reddish-yellow;

mesonotum with black hairs. Scutellum large, with two stout, remote, black bristles. Abdomen brown or blackish, yellowish at base. Legs light yellow ; hind femora black at the immediate tip. Wings cinereous hyaline ; basal cells complete ; penultimate section of the fourth vein a little longer than the posterior cross-vein, or the last section of the fifth vein. Length 1¼ mm.

One specimen.

GEOMYZIDÆ.

ANTHOMYZA.

Fallen, Spec. Entom., 1810; *Leptomyza*, Macquart, Hist. Nat. Dipt., 1835 ; *Anthophilina*, Zetterstedt, Ins. Lapp., 1840.

1. *Anthomyza cinerea*, n. sp.   (Pl. XIV., fig. 170, head of ♂.)

♂, ♀. Front broad, narrowest opposite the insertion of the antennæ ; yellow, the vertical margin more or less cinereous ; with four rows of short bristles, reaching nearly to the root of the antennæ. Antennæ yellow, the third joint orbicular and more or less brownish ; arista nearly bare. Face and cheeks light yellow. Eyes small, oval. Occiput flattened, cinereous. Thorax black in ground-colour, but thickly covered with grey dust, that on the mesonotum somewhat yellowish ; hair of the mesonotum black. bristly, the true bristles, however, confined to the posterior part in the middle. Abdomen black, but more or less thickly whitish pollinose, and with recumbent white hair ; first two segments often in part reddish ; remaining segments with a more or less distinct yellowish or whitish hind border. Legs yellow, the moderately-thickened femora often infuscated distally ; terminal joints of the tarsi more or less brown ; bristles on the posterior inferior surface of the front femora not conspicuous. Wings cinereous or smoky hyaline ; third section of the costa only a little longer than the fourth ; second vein gently curved ; penultimate section of the fourth vein only a little longer than the last section of the fifth. Palpi slender, yellow. Length 2¼–2¾ mm.

Twelve specimens. " March. Common on the sandy sea-shore, alighting on the wet, wave-washed sand." The species seems to be allied to *A. gracilis*, Fallen.

2. *Anthomyza xanthopoda*, n. sp.

♂, ♀. Front narrower than in *A. cinerea*, narrowest below; red, the vertical margin brownish; on either side the vertical margin is white, and bears the outer row of short bristles. Antennæ yellow; arista bare. Face and cheeks light-yellow, the latter scarcely more than one-third as wide as the vertical diameter of the eyes. Thorax black in ground-colour, thickly ashy-grey pollinose, with a shade of yellowish on the mesonotum; hair of the mesonotum bristle-like. Abdomen black, greyish pruinose, opaque; rather slender in the male, the hypopygium protuberant; all the segments with a narrow yellowish or whitish hind border; hair short, wholly black. Legs yellow; last joint of all the tarsi brown; bristles of front femora not conspicuous. Proboscis and wings as in *A. cinerea*. Length 2–2½ mm.

Three specimens. The species is readily distinguishable from *A. cinerea* by the narrower front and cheeks, the less densely pollinose thorax, black hair of the abdomen, &c.

In addition to the foregoing species listed or described from the island of St. Vincent, there are, among the specimens submitted to me, about twenty others, the systematic positions of which are yet more or less doubtful. Several of them will probably require the erection of new genera for their reception. The descriptions will be given in a later paper, in connection with the report upon the Grenada Diptera now in my hands for study.

The present collection of Diptera is the first one of any extent that has been studied from the West Indian Islands. Isolated species, or small collections, chiefly of the larger forms, have been studied by various authors, but no collection has ever represented nearly so fully the microfauna as does the present one. The West Indian Diptera-fauna is essentially a common one, with a strong South American facies. Very few of the species, I believe, will be found restricted to any single island or group of islands. But comparatively few of the species will be found to occur in North America, and they for the most part are either species of wide-spread habitats, or else are confined to the southernmost portions of the United States, especially Florida, whose fauna seems to partake largely of the southern type.

It may, perhaps, occasion some surprise that so large a proportion of the foregoing species are determined as new. This is due to two facts. First, the larger portion of the species of the collection are small or very small, the majority not exceeding four millimetres in length and nearly a half requiring the use of a compound microscope for their study. Second, the small, obscure species are exceedingly difficult to recognize from the majority of the existing descriptions of South American forms. I cannot hope to have avoided all synonyms. That some of the species have been previously described from South and Central America will be a matter of comparative indifference if I have succeeded in so describing and figuring the present ones that the future observer of specimens from these regions will be able to determine them with tolerable certainty.

My thanks are due to Professor Aldrich for so kindly undertaking the study of the families Dolichopodidæ and Phoridæ, to which he has given so much attention in recent years.

EXPLANATION OF PLATES VIII., IX., X., XI., XII.,
XIII., & XIV.

PLATE VIII.—See explanation facing Plate VIII.
PLATE IX.   ,,   ,,   ,,   Plate IX.
PLATE X.   ,,   ,,   ,,   Plate X.
PLATE XI.   ,,   ,,   ,,   Plate XI.
PLATE XII.   ,,   ,,   ,,   Plate XII.
PLATE XIII.   ,,   ,,   ,,   Plate XIII.
PLATE XIV.   ,,   ,,   ,,   Plate XIV.

EXPLANATION OF PLATE VIII.

Fig. 1. *Diplosis* species, wing.
   2.   ,,   species, ,,
   3. *Winnertzia* species, wing.
   4. *Miastor* species, wing, 4*a* part of antenna.
   5. *Haplusia* species, wing.
   6. *Trichopteromyia modesta*, wing, 6*a* tarsus, 6*b* part of antenna.
   7. *Macrocera concinna*, wing.
   9. *Platyura ignobilis*, wing.
  10.   ,,   *pictipennis*, wing.
  11.   ,,   *fascicentris*, wing.
  12. *Ceroplatus longimanus*, wing.
  13. *Neoglaphyroptera nitens*, wing.
  14. *Manota defecta*.
  15. *Probolæus singularis*, wing, 15*a* head, 15*b* mouth parts, 15*c* hypopygium.
  16. *Neoëmpheria maculipennis*, wing.
  17. *Sciophila diluta*, wing.
  18. *Phthinia fraudulenta*, wing.
  19. *Mycetophila insipiens*, wing.
  20.   ,,   *nodulosa*, wing.
  21. *Sciara germana*, wing.
  22.   ,, *debilis*, wing.
  23.   ,, *zygoneura*, wing.
  24. *Zygoneura sciastica*, wing, 24*a* part of antenna.
  25. *Simulium tarsale*, wing, 25*a* ♂ front tarsus.
  26. *Scatopse pygmœa*, wing.
  27. *Paltostoma schineri*, wing, 27*a* hypopygium, 27*b* head of ♂.
  28. *Megarrhina portoricensis*, head of ♂, 28*a* wing.
  29. *Ædes pertinans*, antenna, 29*a* hypopygium.
  30.   ,, *perturbans*, ♀ head.

Explanation of Plate IX.

Fig. 31. *Hæmagogus splendens,* ♀ head, 31a palpus, 31b ♂ claw, 31c wing.

32. *Chironomus spilopterus,* wing.

33.   ,,   *longimanus,* wing.

34. *Orthocladius debilis,* wing.

35. *Tanypus indecisus,* wing.

36. *Ceratopogon maculithorax,* wing.

37.   ,,   *pygmæus,* wing.

38.   ,,   *venustulus,* wing, 38a front leg, 38b palpus.

39.   ,,   *punctipennis,* wing.

40.   ,,   *eriophorus,* tarsus, 40a antenna, 40b palpus.

41.   ,,   *propinquus,* tarsus, 41a wing.

42.   ,,   *flavus,* wing, 42a tarsus.

43.   ,,   *longicornis,* wing, 43a antenna.

44.   ,,   *thersites,* wing.

45.   ,,   *decor,* wing.

46.   ,,   *phlebotomus,* wing, 46a palpus.

47.   ,,   *lotus,* wing.

48.   ,,   *sequax,* wing.

49. *Psychoda alternata,* wing.

50.   ,,   *pallens,* hypopygium, 50a wing.

51.   ,,   *angustipennis,* wing.

52. *Pericoma albitarsis,* wing.

53. *Geranomyia pallida,* wing.

54. *Rhipidia bipectinata,* wing.

55.   ,,   *unipectinata,* antenna.

56.   ,,   *costalis,* antenna.

57.   ,,   *subpectinata,* wing.

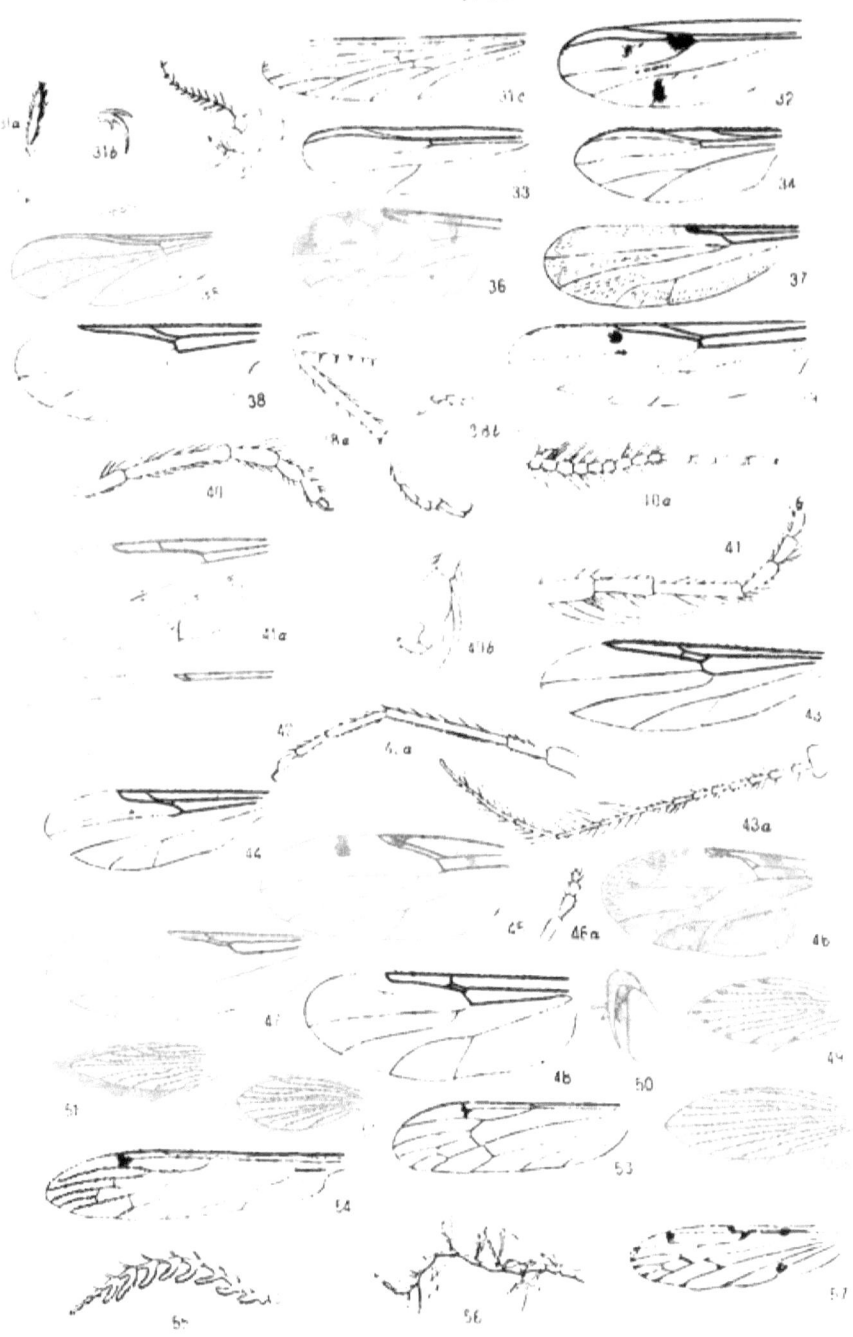

EXPLANATION OF PLATE X.

FIG. 57a. *Rhipidia subpectinata,* ♂ antenna.
   58. *Limnobia insularis,* wing.
   59. *Rhamphidia albitarsis,* wing, 59a hypopygium.
   60. *Atarba puella,* wing, 60a hypopygium.
   61.   ,, *pleuralis,* antennæ, 61a, 61b genitalia, 61c wing.
   62. *Teucholabis complexa,* wing.
   63.   ,, *annulata,* wing.
   64. *Elliptera* species, wing, 64a genitalia.
   65. *Diotrepha mirabilis,* wing, 65a hypopygium.
   66.   ,, *concinna,* wing.
   67. *Mongoma pallida,* wing.
   68. *Epiphragma suckeni,* wing.
   69. *Tipula subinfuscata,* wing.
   70. *Pachyrrhina elegantula,* wing.
   71. *Polymera albitarsis,* ♂ part of antenna, 71a ♀ antenna, 71b wing.
   72. Genus near *Rhipidia,* part of antenna, 72a hypopygium.
   73. *Dixa clarulus,* wing.
   74. *Rhyphus dolorosus,* wing.
   75. *Pelagomyia albitalus,* ♂ head.
   76. *Aochletus bistriatus,* antenna.
   77. *Tabanus alcis,* antenna.
   78.   ,, species, antenna.
78bis. *Chrysopila atra,* wing.
   79. *Erax rufitibia,* wing.

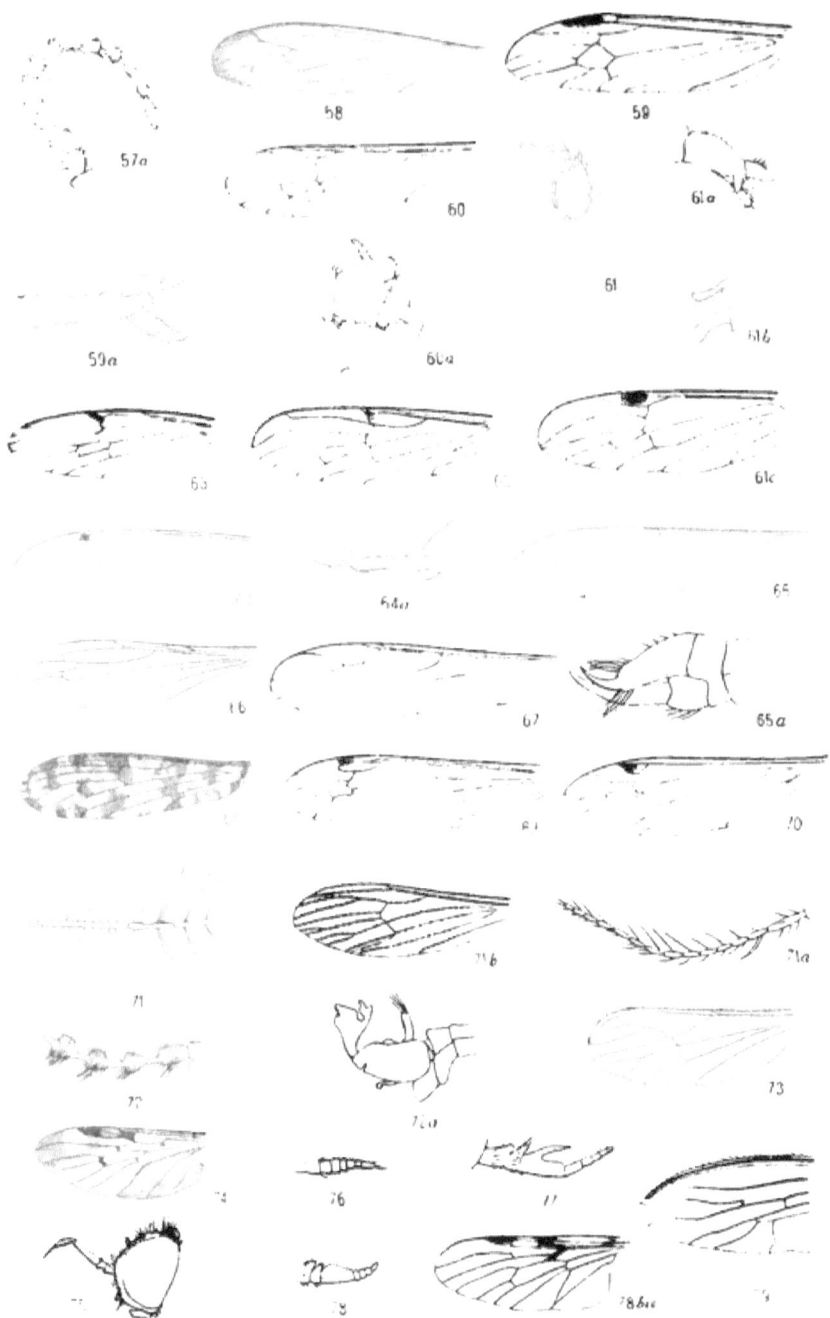

FIG. 80. *Leptogaster roederi*, wing.
 81. *Geron senilis*, antenna.
 82. *Psilocephala argentata*, antenna.
 83. *Hybos dimidiatus*, wing.
 84. *Syneches pusillus*, wing.
 85. *Drapetis xanthopodus*, antenna, 85*a* wing.
 86. „ *flavidus*, antenna, 86*a* wing.
 87. *Pipunculus aculeatus*, wing, 87*a* antenna.
 88. „ *politus*, wing.
 88*a*. *Jurinia* species, antenna.
 89. „ *apicifera*, antenna.
 90. *Gonia pallens*, ♂ antenna.
 91. *Phorocera puer*, ♂ head.
 92. *Exorista nobilis*, ♂ head.
 93. *Atrophopoda townsendii*, ♂ head and part of antenna.
   93*a* ♂ tarsus, 93*b* ♀ tarsus, 93*c* wing.
 94. „ *braueri*, ♂ head, 94*a* ♀ tarsus, 94*b* ♂ tarsus, 94*c* wing.
 95. *Didyma calyptrata*, ♂ head.
 96. *Degeeria nigriventris*, ♂ head.
 97. *Beskia cornuta*, ♂ head, 97*a* wing.
 98. *Rhynchodexia sororia*, ♂ head.
 99. *Elachipalpus macrocerus*, wing.
 100. *Trichopoda pennipes*, wing.
 101. *Pœcilobothrus unguiculatus*, ♂ last joint of front tarsus.
 102. *Paraclius filiferus*, tip of wing.
 103. *Polymedon superbus*, ♂ head.
 104. *Eutarsus sinuatus*, wing.
 105. *Cœloglutus concavus*, wing.
 106. *Xanthotricha cupulifera*, wing, 106*a* hypopygium.
 107. *Achalcus sordidus*, ♂ wing, 107*a* ♀ wing.

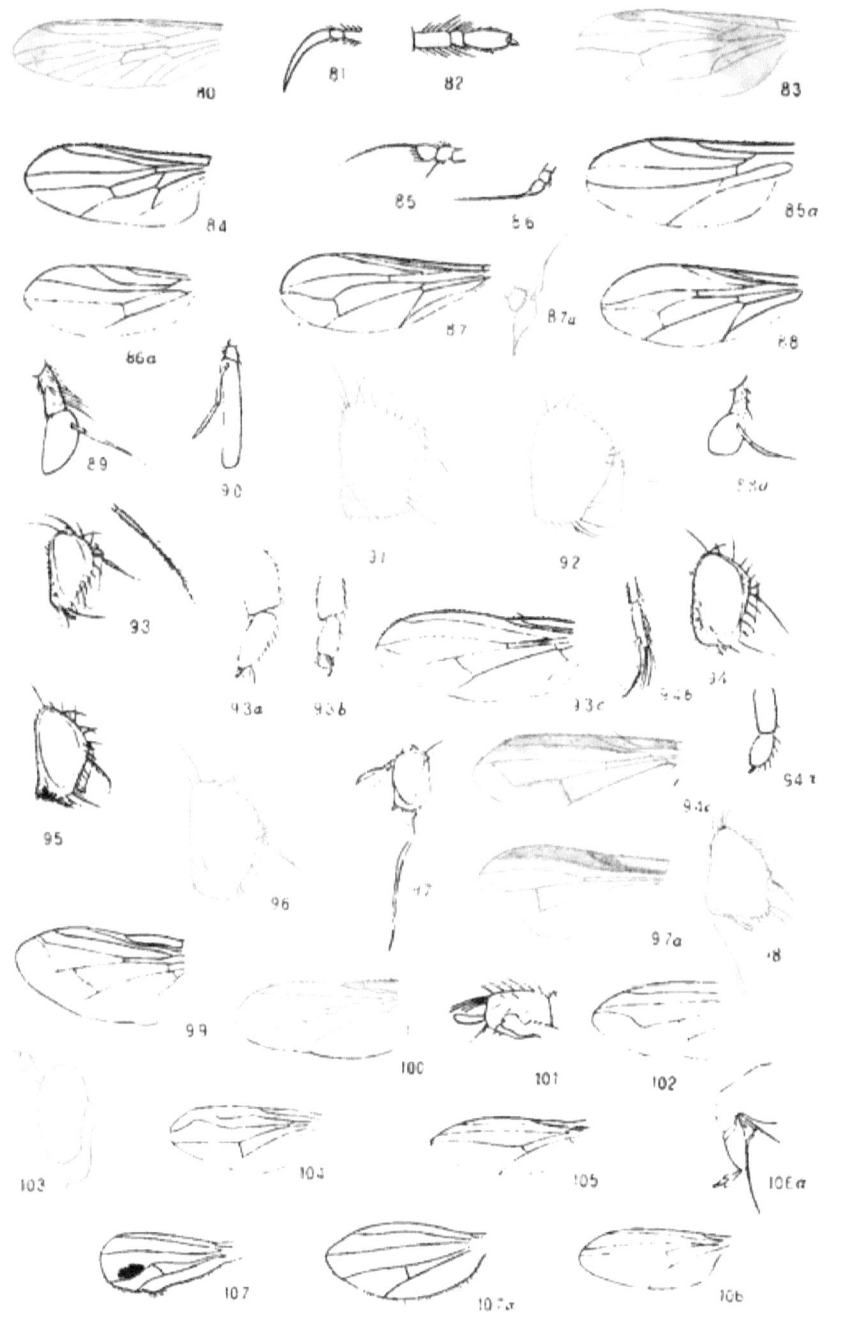

FIG. 108. *Leptorhethum angustatum,* ♂ wing.

109. *Gnamptopsilopus flacidus.* wing.

110. *Eutarsus sinuatus,* ♂ wing.

111. *Hercostomus latipes,* tip of wing.

112. *Leptocorypha pavo,* wing.

113. *Polymedon superbus,* wing.

114. *Asyndetus fratellus,* tip of wing.

115. *Eutarsus sinuatus,* ♀ wing.

116. *Pæcilobothrus unguiculatus,* tip of wing.

117. *Lyroneurus simplex,* ♂ wing.

118. *Polymedon superbus,* ♀ head.

119. „ „ ♂ head.

120. *Ophyra ænescens,* ♂ head, 120*a* wing.

120*bis.* *Sarcophilodes puella,* ♂ head.

121. *Cyrtoneura maculipennis,* ♂ head, 121*a* wing.

122. *Limnophora exul,* ♂ head, 122*a* wing.

123. *Cœnosia insularis,* ♂ head, 123*a* wing.

124. *Tanypeza claripennis,* ♂ head, 124*a* wing.

125. *Calobata mellea,* wing.

126. *Nerius bistriatus,* ♀ head, 126*a* wing.

127. *Euxesta stigmatias,* wing.

128. „ *apicalis,* wing.

129. *Trypeta (Tephritis) fucata,* wing.

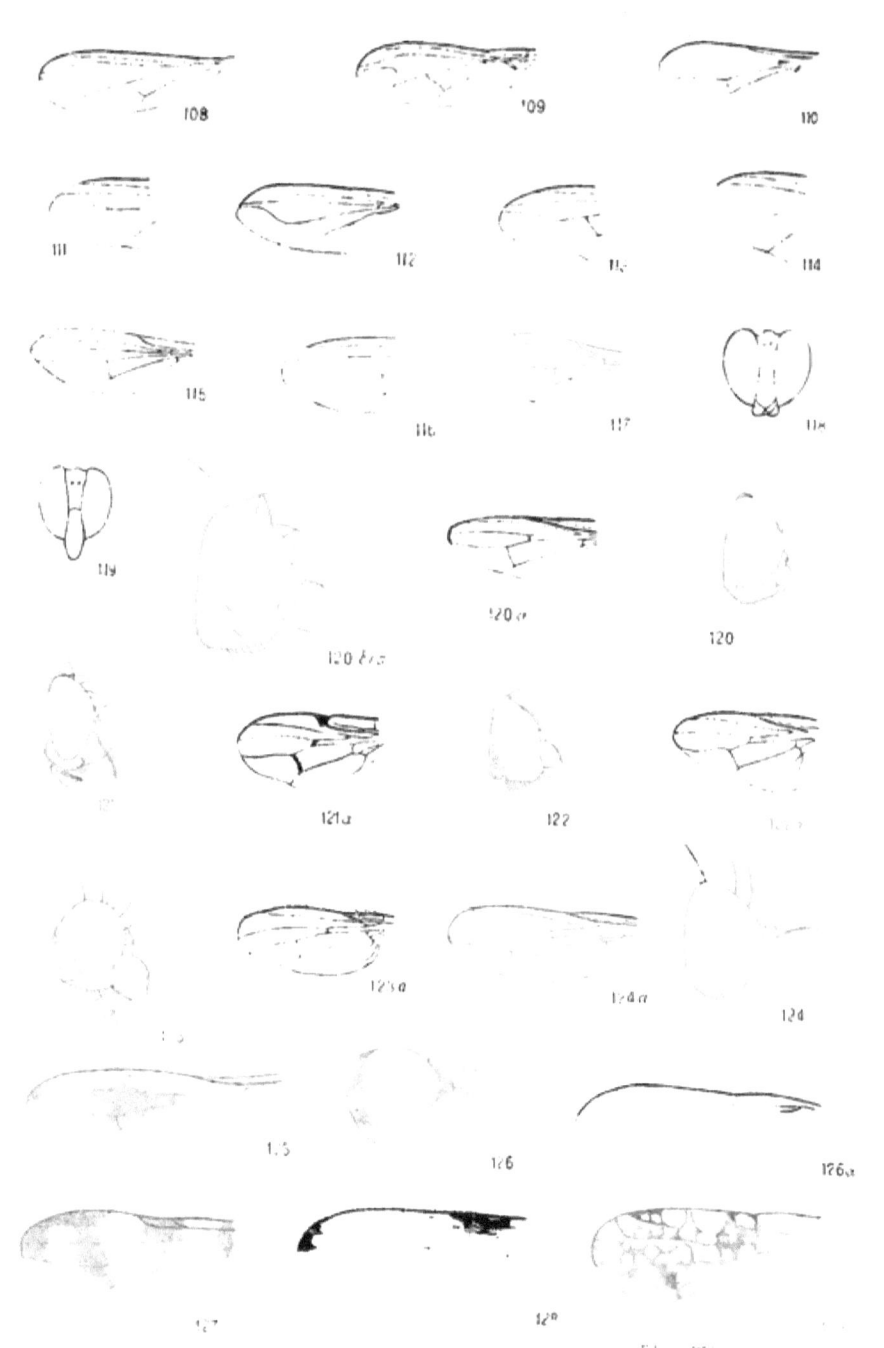

108

'09

110

111

112

115

114

115

116

117

118

119

120 a

120 b c

120 a

120

121 a

122

123 a

124 a

124

125

126

126 a

127

128

Edwin Wilson

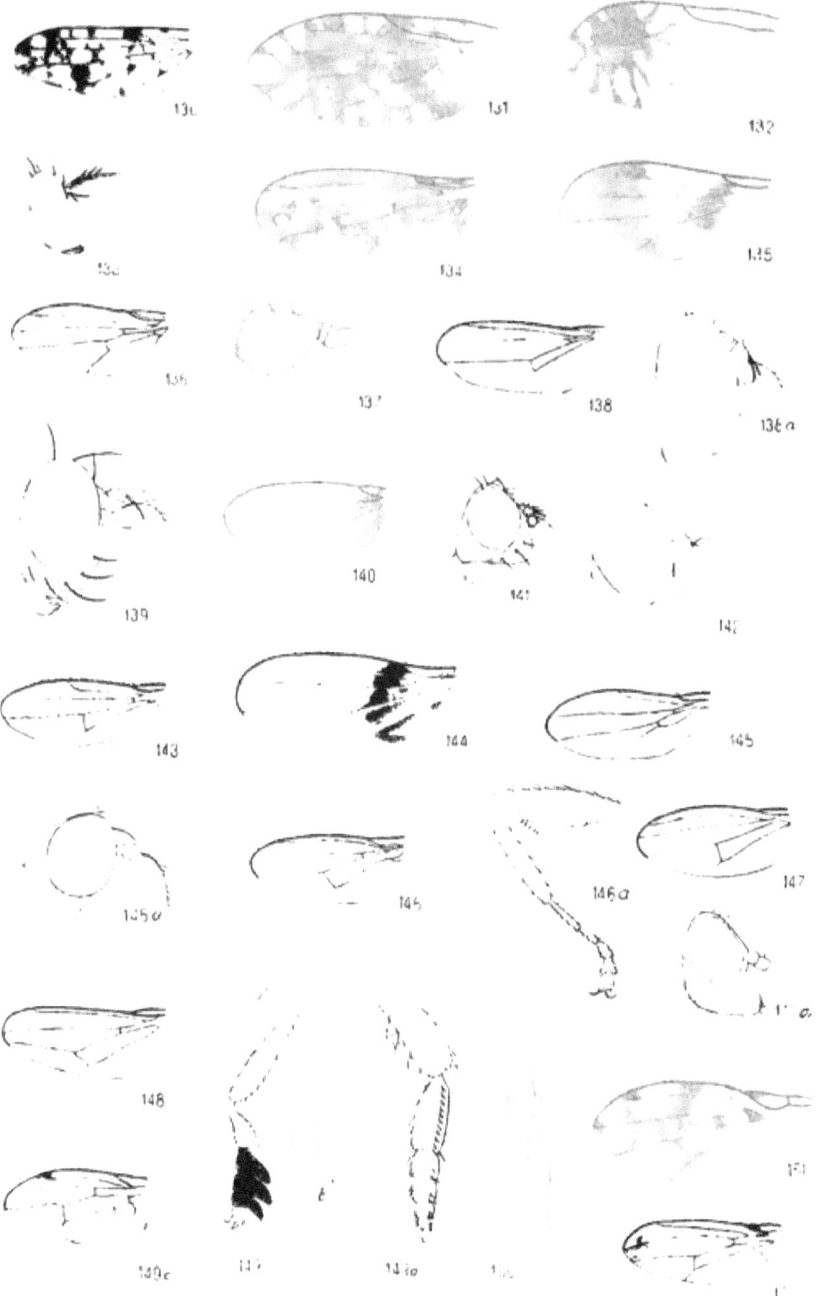

Explanation of Plate XIV.

Fig. 153. *Drosophila* species, wing.

  153a. *Oscinis triangularis*, wing.

  154. *Ophthalmomyia lacteipennis*, wing, 154a ♂ head.

  155. *Ceratomyza dorsalis*, wing, 155a head.

  156. *Agromyza lateralis*, head.

  157.   ,,   *xanthophora*, wing.

  158.   ,,   *innominata*, ♂ head.

  159. *Sepsis insularis*, wing, 159a ♂ front leg.

  160. *Limosina pumila*, wing.

  161.   ,,   *perparva*, wing, 161a antenna.

  162.   ,,   *lugubris*, wing.

  163. *Borborus renalicus*, wing.

  164.   ,,   *illotus*, wing.

  165. *Sphærocera bimaculata*, wing.

  166. *Hemeralvomia defessa*, wing.

  167. *Drapetis apicis*, wing, 167a antenna.

  168.   ,,   *minuta*, wing, 168a antenna.

  169. *Phyllomyza magnipalpis*, ♀ head.

  170. *Anthomyza cinerea*, ♂ head.